Axis of Evil

Book One

The Lone Star Series

by

Bobby Akart

Copyright Information

Other Works by Bestselling Author Bobby Akart

The Lone Star Series
Axis of Evil
Beyond Borders
Lines in the Sand
Texas Strong
Fifth Column
Suicide Six

The Pandemic Series
Beginnings
The Innocents
Level 6
Quietus

The Blackout Series
36 Hours
Zero Hour
Turning Point
Shiloh Ranch
Hornet's Nest
Devil's Homecoming

DEDICATIONS

To the love of my life, you saved me from madness and continue to do so daily. Thank you for loving me.

To the Princesses of the Palace, my little marauders in training, you have no idea how much happiness you bring to your mommy and me. Seeing your wiggly butts at the end of a long day behind the keyboard makes it all worthwhile.

Acknowledgements

Writing a book that is both informative and entertaining requires a tremendous team effort. Writing is the easy part. For their efforts in making Axis of Evil, book one in The Lone Star Series a reality, I would like to thank Hristo Argirov Kovatliev for his incredible cover art, Pauline Nolet for her editorial prowess, Stef Mcdaid for making this manuscript decipherable on so many formats, Sean Runnette and the folks at Audible Studios for producing the incredible narration, and the Team—whose advice, friendship and attention to detail is priceless.

A special thank you to Dr. Peter Vincent Pry, the Chief of Staff for the Congressional EMP Commission and the Executive Director to the Task Force on National and Homeland Security. His work with Congress began in the 1990s when he served on the staffs of the Vice Chairman of the House Armed Service Committee, the Vice Chairman of the House Homeland Security Committee, and the Chairman of the Terrorism Panel.

During his tenure, Dr. Pry played a key role in running Congressional hearings designed to raise awareness of the threats posed by terrorists and rogue nations using EMP weapons. He worked with Congressmen Roscoe Bartlett and Curt Weldon who held numerous hearings on the electromagnetic pulse (EMP) threat, culminating with the establishment of the EMP Commission in 2001 where he served on the staff from 2001 through 2008.

When the EMP Commission was disbanded, Dr. Pry's work to protect the nation's critical infrastructure did not end. He remained a tireless proponent of hardening our grid and raising awareness of the existential threat posed by a devastating EMP attack. These continued efforts earned him his position as the Executive Director of the newly re-established Congressional EMP Commission and the Task Force on National and Homeland Security.

Also, kudos to Kevin Baron and the team at *Defense One* for providing invaluable insight into the North Korean threat and how we'd defend against it. Also, thank you to Michaela Dodge, senior policy analyst at the *Heritage Foundation, Center for National Defense* for the extensive background material on missile defense, nuclear weapons modernization and arms control.

Thank you all!
Choose Freedom!

FOREWORD

by Dr. Peter Vincent Pry
Chief of Staff,
Congressional EMP Commission

Executive Director, Task Force
on National and Homeland Security

The recent escalating war of words and actions with rogue nations like North Korea and Iran has given rise to a new sense of urgency about threats we face—especially the existential threat that is nuclear electromagnetic pulse (EMP) attack. I am pleased to write this foreword for author Bobby Akart as he continues to inform his readers, through his works of fiction, about the EMP threat, both man-made and naturally occurring.

With the Lone Star Series, you will learn about the potential of nuclear-armed satellites flying over America daily in low-earth orbit, positioned to collapse our power grid, destroy our way of life, and possibly kill up to ninety percent of Americans.

The Congressional EMP Commission warns North Korea may already pose a worldwide threat, not only by ICBM, but by satellites, two of which presently orbit over the United States and every country on Earth.

A single satellite, if nuclear-armed, detonated at high-altitude would generate an EMP capable of blacking out power grids and life-sustaining critical infrastructure.

Yet, after massive intelligence failures grossly underestimating North Korea's nuclear capabilities, their biggest threat to the U.S. and the world remains unacknowledged — nuclear EMP attack.

The EMP threat continues to be low-priority and largely ignored, even though on September 2, 2017, North Korea confirmed the

EMP Commission's assessment by testing an H-Bomb that could make a devastating EMP attack.

Two days after their H-Bomb test, on September 4, Pyongyang also released a technical report "The EMP Might of Nuclear Weapons" accurately describing a "super-EMP" weapon generating 100,000 volts/meter.

North Korea's development of a Super-EMP weapon that generates 100,000 volts/meter is a technological watershed more threatening than development of an H-Bomb and ICBM because even the U.S. nuclear deterrent, the best protected U.S. military forces, are EMP hardened to survive only 50,000 volts/meter.

My colleague, EMP Commission Chairman William Robert Graham warned Congress in 2008 that Russia had developed Super-EMP weapons and most likely transferred that technology to North Korea allegedly *by accident*, according to Russian generals.

The results of this newly discovered relationship between Russia and North Korea was that the DPRK now has the technology to win a nuclear war. At the very least, a North Korean EMP attack could paralyze the U.S. nuclear deterrent and prevent U.S. retaliation, perhaps even by U.S. submarines at sea that cannot launch missiles without receiving an Emergency Action Message from the president.

However, the warning signs have gone largely ignored. Although North Korea, Russia, and China have all made nuclear threats against the United States recently, in the case of North Korea and Russia repeatedly, most analysts dismiss the war of words as *mere bluster* and *nuclear sabre rattling*, not to be taken seriously.

In the West, generations of leaders and citizens have been educated that use of nuclear weapons is unthinkable and the ultimate horror. Not so in Russia, China, and North Korea where their nuclear capabilities are publicly paraded — missile launches and exercises are televised as a show of strength, an important part of national pride.

Then, there is the issue of an EMP attack. An electromagnetic pulse attack would be perfect for implementing Russia's strategy of "de-escalation," where a conflict with the U.S. and its allies would be won by limited nuclear use. It's their version of "shock and awe" to cow the U.S. into submission. The same kind of attack is viewed as an acceptable option by China and North Korea as well.

An EMP attack would be the most militarily effective use of one or a few nuclear weapons, while also being the most acceptable nuclear option in world opinion, the option most likely to be construed in the U.S. and internationally as "restrained" and a "warning shot" without direct loss of life.

Because an electromagnetic pulse destroys electronics instead of blasting cities, even some analysts in Germany and Japan, among the most anti-nuclear nations, regard EMP attacks as an acceptable use of nuclear weapons. A high-altitude EMP ("HEMP") attack entails detonating a nuclear weapon at 30-400 kilometers altitude — above the atmosphere, in outer space, so high that no nuclear effects, not even the sound of the explosion, would be experienced on the ground, except the resulting EMP.

An EMP attack will kill far more people than nuclear blasting a city through indirect effects — by blacking out electric grids and destroying life-sustaining critical infrastructures like communications, transportation, food and water — in the long run. But the millions of fatalities likely to eventually result from EMP will take months to develop, as slow as starvation.

Thus, a nation hit with an EMP attack will have powerful incentives to cease hostilities, focus on repairing their critical infrastructures while there is still time and opportunity to recover, and avert national extinction.

Indeed, an EMP attack or demonstration made to "de-escalate" a crisis or conflict is very likely to raise a chorus of voices in the West against nuclear escalation and send Western leaders in a panicked search for the first "off ramp."

Axis of Evil, and the entire Lone Star Series, are books of fiction which are based upon historical fact. The geopolitical factors in this series leading up to a potentially catastrophic collapse of America's power grid are based upon real-world scenarios.

Author Bobby Akart has written several fiction and non-fiction books with the intent to raise awareness about the threats we face from an EMP, whether via a massive solar storm or delivered by a nuclear warhead. While many books have been written about the results of nuclear war and EMPs, few have tackled the subject of using satellites as a means of delivering the fatal blow, until now.

The Lone Star Series is written to be thought-provoking. It will be a reminder to us all that you never know when the day before is the day before. Prepare for tomorrow.

Dr. Peter Vincent Pry
Chief of Staff
Congressional EMP Commission
Executive Director
Task Force on National and Homeland Security

ABOUT DR. PETER VINCENT PRY

Dr. Peter Vincent Pry served as Chief of Staff of Congressional Electromagnetic Pulse (EMP) Commission (2001-2017), and is currently the Executive Director of the Task Force on National and Homeland Security, a Congressional Advisory Board dedicated to achieving protection of the United States from electromagnetic pulse (EMP), Cyber Warfare, mass destruction terrorism and other threats to civilian critical infrastructures, on an accelerated basis. Dr. Pry also is Director of the United States Nuclear Strategy Forum, an advisory board to Congress on policies to counter Weapons of Mass Destruction. Foreign governments, including the United Kingdom, Israel, Canada, and Kazakhstan consult with Dr. Pry on EMP, Cyber, and other strategic threats.

Dr. Pry served on the staffs of the Congressional Commission on the Strategic Posture of the United States (2008-2009); the Commission on the New Strategic Posture of the United States (2006-2008); and the Commission to Assess the Threat to the United States from Electromagnetic Pulse (EMP) Attack (2001-2008).

Dr. Pry served as Professional Staff on the House Armed Services Committee (HASC) of the U.S. Congress, with portfolios in nuclear strategy, WMD, Russia, China, NATO, the Middle East, Intelligence, and Terrorism (1995-2001). While serving on the HASC, Dr. Pry was chief advisor to the Vice Chairman of the House Armed Services Committee and the Vice Chairman of the House Homeland Security Committee, and to the Chairman of the Terrorism Panel. Dr. Pry played a key role: running hearings in Congress that warned terrorists and rogue states could pose EMP and Cyber threats, establishing the Congressional EMP Commission, helping the Commission develop plans to protect the United States from EMP and Cyber Warfare, and working closely with senior scientists and the nation's top experts on critical infrastructures, EMP and Cyber Warfare.

Dr. Pry was an Intelligence Officer with the Central Intelligence Agency responsible for analyzing Soviet and Russian nuclear strategy, operational plans, military doctrine, threat perceptions, and developing U.S. paradigms for strategic warning (1985-1995). He also served as a Verification Analyst at the U.S. Arms Control and Disarmament Agency responsible for assessing Soviet arms control treaty compliance (1984-1985).

Dr. Pry has written numerous books on national security issues, including:

Blackout Wars; Apocalypse Unknown: The Struggle To Protect America From An Electromagnetic Pulse Catastrophe; Electric Armageddon: Civil-Military Preparedness For An Electromagnetic Pulse Catastrophe; War Scare: Russia and America on the Nuclear Brink; Nuclear Wars: Exchanges and Outcomes; The Strategic Nuclear Balance: And Why It Matters; and Israel's Nuclear Arsenal.

You may view his canon of work by visiting his Amazon Author page.

Dr. Pry often appears on TV and radio as an expert on national security issues. The BBC made his book War Scare into a two-hour TV documentary Soviet War Scare 1983 and his book Electric Armageddon was the basis for another TV documentary Electronic Armageddon made by the National Geographic.

ABOUT THE AUTHOR

Bobby Akart

Bestselling author Bobby Akart has been ranked by Amazon as the #3 Bestselling Religion & Spirituality Author, the #5 Bestselling Science Fiction Author, and the #7 Bestselling Historical Author. He has written sixteen international bestsellers, in thirty-nine different fiction and nonfiction genres, including the critically acclaimed Boston Brahmin series, the bestselling Blackout series, his highly cited nonfiction Prepping for Tomorrow series and his latest project—The Pandemic Series, which has produced four #1 best sellers.

Bobby has provided his readers a diverse range of topics that are both informative and entertaining. His attention to detail and impeccable research has allowed him to capture the imaginations of his readers through his fictional works, and bring them valuable knowledge through his nonfiction books.

SIGN UP for email updates and receive free advance reading copies, updates on new releases, special offers, and bonus content. You can contact Bobby directly by email (BobbyAkart@gmail.com) or through his website:

BobbyAkart.com

Epigraph

The time to repair the roof is when the sun is shining.
~ President John f. Kennedy

*****

Success is where preparation and opportunity meet.
~ Bobby Unser, accomplished Indy Car driver

*****

On nuclear war, "the living will envy the dead."
~ Nikita Khruschchev

*****

I know not with what weapons World War III will be fought,
but World War IV will be fought with sticks and stones.
~ Albert Einstein

*****

Procrastination makes easy things hard, and hard things much harder.
~ Mason Cooley

*****

Because you never know when the day before,
is the day before. Prepare for tomorrow.

PART ONE

Two hundred years ago, there was written a story.

Henny Penny, also known as Chicken Little, was a folktale about a chicken who believed the world was coming to an end. As the fable goes, an acorn fell on Chicken Little's head, and he immediately yelled:

The sky is falling! The sky is falling!

But nobody listened.

What if Chicken Little was right?

CHAPTER 1

October 29, 2022
The North Star Classic
Valley City, North Dakota

Daddy taught us that we have three choices in life—give up, give in, or give it all you got. My older brothers followed a different path than I did. They were willing to get shot at in defense of our country, against enemies who wanted to end the American way of life. I chose the way of the American West. I chose to challenge a beast ten times my size. I chose to be a bull rider.

Minutes before Cooper Armstrong climbed into the chute, his adrenaline kicked in. The fans inside the two-thousand-seat arena in Valley City, North Dakota, a small town of sixty-five hundred in the southeast corner of the state, began to chant, "Coop, Coop, Coop."

Cooper couldn't explain how the human body worked, but he could certainly tell you what it didn't like. Riding a two-thousand-pound beast that was hell-bent on throwing its rider to the ground was not natural. Cooper once surmised the first bull rider probably was drunk and thought he'd give it a whirl, most likely paying a hefty price.

To him, the eight seconds was like anything a person would experience in their life. When you made a mistake, you paid the piper. The pain would be more than emotional. It was physical, and it could be deadly.

The eight-second span of riding a bull was an incredibly short period of time, yet everything slowed down, kinda like being in a car wreck. Your mind sensed the danger, saw it happening in real time, yet was incapable of stopping the impending doom.

For Cooper, his body and mind were uniquely suited for the sport. Somehow, he was able to produce the right amount of adrenaline to get on the beast and ride that bull for all its worth.

He closed his mind to the cheers and chants, then focused on his opponent. There are two stars in the arena—the rider and the bull. One Night Stand was a cross between a Brahma and a Plummer bull. The latter represented finesse. The former, power.

Today's bulls were the product of perfected bloodlines that had been designed to create the nastiest, strongest animals ever produced. Every bull Cooper rode was a superstar in its own right, and One Night Stand was no exception, but for different reasons.

You see, One Night Stand was a freak of nature. An unexpected result that neither breeder nor rider ever expected. He was a bull that woke up on the wrong side of the bed and grazed on the wrong type of feed. He wasn't the product of decades of genetic engineering. One Night Stand was simply a bad hombre that refused to be ridden for eight seconds. Cooper intended to break that streak.

I'm ready.

Cooper climbed over the dirt-covered fence rails and threw his leg over the brute. He had his rope on the one-ton behemoth and began to get his hand set. Then One Night Stand did something that puzzled Cooper. The bull dropped down and lay on his belly.

"What the—?" asked a confused Cooper, looking around to the cowboys who manned the chute and then to his brother Riley.

"Go on now, Coop," replied one of the men. "You get on him. He'll come back up when its time. You'll see."

Cooper glanced at his brother and shrugged. He got his head back into the ride. He wrapped the rope around his hand, back under again, and then back over again to get a good hold. Unconsciously, Cooper squeezed his legs to the sides of One Night Stand like he was riding a horse. He could feel the powerful bull's muscles tense up. One Night Stand was slowly rising out of his crouch.

"Here we go, boys! Here we go, boys!" Cooper shouted in a combination of exhilaration and fear.

The gate opened, and One Night Stand launched off the ground.

Both bull and rider were airborne. It was a photo-worthy moment that would have made the cover of *Pro Rodeo* magazine's December issue if circumstances had been different.

A bull basically moves in four directions, and it's incumbent upon the rider to get in sync with the constant up-down-left-right movements if they want to hold on. Get lazy—you get thrown. Anticipate incorrectly—you get thrown.

From the beginning, Cooper knew this ride was different from any other he'd experienced. It was not just the soaring launch, which was wholly unpredictable. It was looking into the fiery hatred of One Night Stand's eyes during that leap. His neck and head twisted in an ungodly contortion to stare into Cooper's eyes. It was impossible anatomically, yet it happened.

The twist caused Cooper to fall forward on the bull, dangerously close to the Brahma breed's deadly horns. He could see the prickly brown hairs on the top of the beast's head. Another inch forward, and their skulls would have collided, instantly knocking Cooper unconscious.

An inevitable collision was averted by One Night Stand's landing. When he hit the ground with his front legs, he turned sharply to the left, and Cooper deftly rolled over on the inside of the turn to counter the bull's maneuver. By the time One Night Stand made his second jump, Cooper was regaining some semblance of control.

Coop! Coop! Coop!

Bolstered by the screams of support, Cooper regained his balance as One Night Stand slid back under him and hoisted them into the air again. Cooper relied upon his strength and conditioning to stay in sync with each jump and spin. He stayed lightweight, giving One Night Stand less to throw as he ferociously fought off his rider.

When riding a bull, you can't think ahead because it's invariably too late. If you think about the bull's next move, it'll be a second behind and you'll hit the ground. Cooper didn't try to think about the time from start to finish, he just listened for the buzzer.

The bull had been jumping and spinning, bucking and twisting. It had become a choreographed dance between rider and bull. Cooper held on until the unpredictable One Night Stand surprised him.

It was on the last jump when One Night Stand, instead of twisting, planted all four feet on the ground. Cooper's weight had been forward, but the sudden change in momentum threw him to the rear, putting tremendous pressure on the end of his right arm. One Night Stand then kicked his rear legs high into the air, throwing Cooper forward, heels over head, so that he didn't have any weight on his feet.

I'm gonna fly off the front.

In that split second, Cooper knew he was in trouble. As he lurched forward, his feet rose into the air and cracked together. With all of his weight on his hand, it instinctively caused the rider to grip tighter—forcing it shut when it needed to open to get loose. Cooper knew he was gonna get hung in the rope.

It all happened so fast, too fast to react. The chants of Coop! turned to gasps of despair and groans of *oh my God!*

With his hand caught in the rope, Cooper landed on the ground and began to run alongside One Night Stand, who was still agitated. Using his body like a battering ram, the bull was forcing himself onto Cooper, trying to knock him down or hook him. One Night Stand ducked his head down and quickly lifted it up, trying to catch part of Cooper's body with his horns. The bull's goal was to toss the rider into the air—dealing the final blow by goring the rider's torso.

Cooper tried to avoid the horns while keeping his footing. He knew falling was the type of mistake riders didn't always recover from. He allowed One Night Stand to kick at his lower legs, hoping nursing beat-up shins would be the worst-case scenario.

He held his balance as he pulled his entangled hand away from the rope. He avoided the horns the best he could. His attempts to pull away lasted longer than the ride. The rodeo clowns closed around One Night Stand to help as Cooper continued to get beat up and stepped on. It was like being chained to a locomotive—an iron horse that never got tired.

One Night Stand didn't purposefully try to hurt his rider, for the most part. He just wanted him off his back, which was his natural instinct. But in that final split second, when Cooper pulled free of the rope, neither bull nor rider would be able to explain why that last vicious kick to the side of Cooper Armstrong's head was necessary to end the battle.

CHAPTER 2

October 29
The Armstrong Ranch
Borden County, Texas

Duncan Armstrong Sr. pulled on the reins and brought his horse to a stop in front of the barn. One of the hands emerged from the stalls and quickly led his horse inside as the retired lawman brushed off the dust from his ride. As a Texas Ranger, riding horses wasn't ordinarily part of his job, especially in the late years of his career when he was elevated to the rank of major of Company C, an honor that earned him his nickname.

Major, as he was now known by everyone, walked onto the gravel driveway and took a moment to watch the setting sun over the Armstrong Ranch. He reflected on what his family had accomplished since their arrival in Texas a hundred and fifty years ago.

He was a descendant of John Barclay Armstrong, a McMinnville, Tennessee, native and famous Texas Ranger from the 1800s. After the Armstrong family moved to Texas in 1971, John Armstrong joined the Texas Rangers under the command of Leander McNelly. As second in command, he earned the nickname McNelly's Bulldog for his heroics in capturing fugitives and battling rogue Mexican banditos.

After McNelly died, John Armstrong rose through the ranks and was instrumental in the pursuit of famed train robber Sam Bass. His career as a lawman led him to become one of the first U.S. Marshals in Texas and a subsequent life of retirement as a rancher.

Over the years, the Armstrong name became synonymous with Texas ranching. John B. Armstrong III, the grandson of the famous lawman, married into the King family and later became the CEO of King Ranch. His brother, Roscoe Armstrong, wanted to pursue both cattle and oil, ultimately settling in Borden County, halfway between Abilene to the east and Midland-Odessa to the west.

The Armstrong Ranch grew over the years into a sprawling ninety-six-hundred-acre tract containing beef cattle, crops, and nearly a hundred oil wells. It was not, however, the big corporate enterprise that the much larger ranches in Texas had become.

After his retirement as a Texas Ranger, Major Armstrong did not seek fame and fortune through signature Ford Trucks or fancy western wear. He wanted to provide for his family and leave a legacy for his heirs, just like his family had done for him.

A gust of cold, dry air came over his body as the sun set over the horizon. Winter was coming early this year, he thought to himself as he adjusted his hat and turned for the ranch house. With the setting sun came supper time, and he best not keep his wife waiting.

He knocked the dust off his boots with a thud against the porch posts and entered the foyer. The smell of home cookin' immediately struck his nostrils, and the sounds of the crackling fire promised warmth for his bones.

Major tried not to complain about the aches and pains he experienced each winter. Years of broken bones and gunshot wounds while he served in the Texas Rangers had taken its toll. He considered the scars badges of honor for achieving the success in the state's service while based in Lubbock. For thirty years, he'd upheld the laws of Texas in the Panhandle and was true to the Texas Ranger motto of *one riot, one ranger.*

It was a near fatal shot to Major's chest that forced his retirement four years prior. That and the death of their second son, Dallas. Dallas had followed in their eldest son's footsteps and joined the military. Major was proud of his son's accomplishments as a U.S. Army Ranger, and paused by the fire to view the Purple Heart awarded to Dallas posthumously. Their son's heroics in saving the lives of his fellow Rangers didn't soften the blow of his death. The loss left a hole in their heart for years.

Major closed his eyes momentarily until he felt his lovely wife's arms wrap around his waist. She whispered into his ear, "Hey, cowboy. This is the last night with the house to ourselves. Maybe we should turn on some George Strait, stoke the fire, and fan our flames. Whadya say?"

Major took her hands and pulled them tighter around his waist. "I'd say that you've forgotten how old this cowboy is. I'm afraid his flame-fannin' days are over."

"Listen to me, Duncan Armstrong, I happen to know better. Don't you sell yourself short."

Major turned around and kissed Lucy, giving her a tight, protracted hug in the process. He couldn't help hiding the gloom on his face.

She looked up into his sad eyes and touched his face. "Hey, are you okay?"

"Yeah, sorry. I was just thinking about Dallas. I don't think I'll ever get over losing him."

Lucy grimaced and hugged him again. "I won't either. Let's thank God for keeping Duncan safe and for convincing our rodeo kids to stay out of the military. The Armstrong family has already given one life in defense of our country. That's one too many."

Major smiled and kissed his wife on the cheek. He and Lucy had married when she was just eighteen. He'd joined the Texas Rangers that spring thirty years ago, and she'd caught his eye at the Midland County Fair. The two began dating despite their six-year age difference and the relatively long-distance relationship.

An eighty-mile drive, however, couldn't keep the two apart. Major would see Lucy when he was home at the ranch. After she graduated from high school, she started her first semester at Lubbock Christian University when Major was working out of the Company C offices in Lubbock.

The two were inseparable, in love, and destined to spend their lives together. A small wedding was held at the Armstrong Ranch, and Lucy moved in with the family. A year later, she gave birth to a son, Duncan Armstrong Jr., and three years after that, along came

Dallas. As their family grew to four boys and their youngest, a girl, Major was promoted up the ranks of Company C.

The family shared the sprawling ranch house with Major's widowed father, Roscoe *Pops* Armstrong III, who split his time playing with the grandkids and tending to the affairs of the ranch. His beloved wife had passed shortly after Major was born, which left him an only child.

"What's for supper?" Major asked, breaking their embrace to sit on the hearth and remove his boots.

"If I said meat and potatoes, would you believe me?"

"I wouldn't complain," he quipped as he pulled off the first boot. He wiggled his toes in his sweaty socks.

Lucy stepped back, put her fingers under her nose, and laughed. "Whoa. I have great news for us both. You've got time for a shower before we eat."

"What are you sayin'?"

"I'm sayin' no shower, no yummies, or dessert either, mister. Go on. Take your shower and I'll have supper on the table. I got a text message from Duncan I want to tell you about."

"Is he okay?" The first thought on any military parent's mind was whether their child was safe.

"Yeah, we're gonna FaceTime tomorrow. Go on now, please. Hurry. And take those smelly socks with you!"

CHAPTER 3

October 29
Mercy Health Trauma Center
Valley City, North Dakota

The ambulance, with the aid of a police escort, roared toward the entrance of the small Mercy Health Trauma Center in Valley City. Two paramedics and Dr. Madeline Luke, the town's only neurologist, who happened to be in attendance at the rodeo, tended to Cooper for the eight-minute ride from the venue. The moment she saw Cooper get kicked in the side of the head, she forced her way through the aghast crowd and jumped the rail into the arena. The rodeo clowns had been startled by her sudden appearance and were attempting to lead her away from the still-agitated One Night Stand when the paramedics on the scene recognized her.

Dr. Luke found Cooper to be alive, but his breathing was erratic. He'd lost consciousness and he was bleeding from one ear. Remarkably, he had no head lacerations other than some black-and-blue discoloration on the back of his head.

She had instructed the paramedics on what to do when the stretcher arrived. They held his head steady and placed him in a temporary neck brace. The bleeding from his ear was not substantial, and a few dabs of gauze brought it under control.

Cooper was not wearing a helmet, which was considered optional for bull riders. Concussions were the most pervasive injury in the sport. As a fan, she'd followed the reports from the Professional Bull Riders' medical advisors regarding the use of helmets. Despite their increased use, there had not been a precipitous drop in head injuries.

She recalled watching a YouTube video of a ride that ended badly.

Kasey Hayes had ridden a bull named Shaft for nearly four seconds before the bovine reared up on its hind legs and threw its rider to the ground. The bull stomped on Kasey's head, splitting the safety helmet in two. The concussion knocked him out for several minutes.

The ambulance backed into the entrance, and the trauma team was at the ready. After the doors swung open, the paramedics eased the stretcher out, and the wheels were about to be deployed when Dr. Luke stopped them.

"No! No wheels! He has a serious head trauma and cannot take the uneven surface. He needs to be carried into the ER."

"Dr. Luke?" asked one of the emergency room physicians.

"Yes. I witnessed the event. This young man took what appears to be a glancing blow to the left side of his head below the ear."

The emergency room physician nodded and confirmed the information. He opened Cooper's eyelids and flashed his mini-flashlight to observe the pupils.

"Equal size. Any signs of seizure?" he asked.

"No."

"Cessation of breathing?"

"Negative."

"Change in level of consciousness at all?"

"No."

The doors opened, and several medical staff members cleared the hallway for the team to rush Cooper into an emergency room marked Trauma Three.

"I'm Dr. Williams. We met when I first arrived at Mercy."

"Of course, Dr. Williams. I remember. You did your residency at UNLV."

"Yes, specialized in sports medicine. I've seen head injuries from mixed martial arts. This is my first bull-kick trauma."

"It's my first emergency situation of this nature as well," said Dr. Luke.

The male nurses on staff joined the paramedics in preparing to lift Cooper off the transport stretcher onto the emergency room bed.

Dr. Williams turned to Dr. Luke. "Would you like to assist?"

11

"Of course," she replied. "Let me position myself at the top of the gurney so I can support his head during the move. Is everybody ready?"

The medical personnel responded affirmative.

"Slow and steady. Okay, on three."

Everyone nodded and took their positions. She counted to three, and the group carefully placed the one-hundred-ninety-pound bull rider onto the bed.

The medical team went to work, immediately removing Cooper's clothing, and hooked him up to a variety of medical monitoring equipment—fluids, oxygen, blood pressure, etc.

"Has anyone notified the family?" asked Dr. Williams.

A male nurse responded, "Doctor, I have a brother and sister who've just arrived. They want to see the patient."

"Not just yet, nurse. Get all of the medical information you can and bring it to me. Tell them this young man is in good hands. What's his name?"

"Cooper Armstrong," replied Dr. Luke. "He's on the cusp of the top ten bull riders in the world. A very popular up-and-comer."

Dr. Williams addressed the staff. "Well, let's get a CT scan to check for intracranial hemorrhaging on the brain, swelling, or a possible skull fracture. For now, we'll allow him to regain consciousness on his own. A resting brain uses less oxygen, which will benefit him at the moment."

"I'm going to speak with the siblings," said Dr. Luke. "I'm a fan of the sport, and I think I can relate to them."

"I'll let you know the results of the tests," said Dr. Williams with a nod.

Dr. Luke approached twenty-three-year-old Riley Armstrong and his two-year-younger sister, Palmer, in the waiting room. Palmer was understandably distraught as she made eye contact with Dr. Luke. The doctor had seen the look before—hopeful, begging eyes.

Dr. Luke introduced herself and explained the situation in simple medical terms.

"Has your brother ever experienced a concussion before?"

"No," replied Riley. Palmer was still crying although she'd calmed down somewhat. "He's broken a lot of parts, you know, bones. But no head injuries other than a broken nose once."

"Okay, that's good," said Dr. Luke. "Listen to me. They're running tests now, and we'll know more soon. Would you like me to contact your parents for you? I'd be glad to give them a call and put their minds at ease."

Riley and Palmer looked at each other for a brief moment and then shook their heads in unison.

Riley continued to be the spokesman. "No, ma'am. I'll do it after Coop's had his tests run. Will it be much longer?"

As if on cue, a nurse entered the waiting area and whispered into Dr. Luke's ear. She smiled and reached out for the siblings' hands.

"They've finished the testing, and your brother has regained consciousness. He's asked for you both."

"That's good news, right?" asked a suddenly buoyant Palmer.

"I would say yes, absolutely. Let's go see how he's doing, but please, keep him calm. His attending physician and I will review the results of the CT scan. We'll be in shortly to discuss the results with you. Okay?"

"Okay! Lead the way!" Palmer's demeanor had changed considerably. She was now leading Riley toward Cooper's room.

Dr. Luke dropped them off at the entrance, where a nurse was just leaving. "Nurse, these are the younger brother and sister of our patient. I've told them to keep calm and not excite their brother. Dr. Williams and I will be along shortly."

The nurse nodded and exited. Riley and Palmer hesitated before entering the room. Cooper lay perfectly still on the bed with several multicolored wires coming out of his hospital gown. Various devices registered his vitals, but it was the smile that crossed his face when they appeared in front of him that said all they needed to know. *He's gonna be all right.*

Dr. Luke hovered just outside the door to eavesdrop on the conversation. The three kids seemed very close-knit and obviously part of a loving family. When she heard the conversation begin, it left her somewhat puzzled, making her wonder if she'd misjudged the family dynamic.

"Hey, Coop," said Riley. "I reckon nothin' can break that melon of yours."

"Dang straight," he replied. "Hey, sis."

"You scared us, Coop," Palmer responded. "You've never been kicked in the head before."

"See, now I'm good to go." He gestured toward the door. "Have they told y'all anything?"

Riley replied, "Nah, but they appear to be good doctors. I think you're fine."

"Do you want us to call Momma and Daddy?" asked Palmer.

Cooper raised his voice slightly. "No! The rule still stands. What happens on the road stays on the road. Agreed?"

"You got kicked in the head, Coop," Palmer insisted. "I mean, this is more serious than a busted-up shoulder or a broke arm."

"That's the rule, though." Riley answered Coop's question.

Reluctantly, Palmer confirmed it. "Okay, agreed. That's the rule."

CHAPTER 4

October 30
USS *Jack H. Lucas*
The Gulf of Oman

The men pushed forward, timing their steps and leaps in unison, lifting each foot at just the right second to avoid tripping. Captain Andrew E. Abbey led the way through the hatch coaming of the open door and ran onto the forecastle of the USS *Jack H. Lucas*, a recently commissioned Arleigh Burke-class destroyer patrolling the Gulf of Oman off the coast of Iran.

"Let's go, SEAL!" he shouted back at his companion as he continued to lead their run through the forward part of the ship.

His running companion, Duncan Armstrong Jr., was a former Navy SEAL who had been recruited by the Central Intelligence Agency to conduct rapid-response special operations. The two-man team of Duncan and Min Jun Park, an American of South Korean descent and a former Army Ranger, had joined the *Lucas* while she was in port at the U.S. Naval Forces Central Command in Bahrain. NAVCENT was home to the U.S. Navy's Fifth Fleet, which was responsible for patrolling the Red Sea, the Arabian Sea, parts of the Indian Ocean and the Persian Gulf, the traditional hotbed of activity in the never-ending wars involving the Middle East.

"I'm with ya," Duncan shouted back as he ran onto Abbey's heels. "You've got the home-field advantage."

Initially, Abbey had pushed back against the insertion of the CIA team onto his ship. He was not interested in being a staging ground for any black-ops crap, which would necessarily put his men at risk.

But over the last several weeks, he and Duncan had found they had a lot in common and became good friends.

"Twenty-two laps, three miles," huffed the sweat-soaked captain as he took the steel stairs two at a time and exited onto the port side of the *Lucas*. It was just before noon, but the sun was already strong enough to blur the visual horizon with evaporating water. The seas were calm, making their footing a little less treacherous.

Duncan, his short sandy-blond hair plastered to his forehead from sweat, darted past Abbey to take the lead. His U.S. Naval Academy tee shirt stuck to his skin, causing the large gold *N*, the logo of the Navy Midshipmen, to blend with his tan skin.

USS JACK H. LUCAS (DDG 125)

The two men continued side by side, cutting a path between the forward-located missile launcher of the *Lucas* and the five-inch gun mount. The large gun mount stood out as a distinctive feature on the deck of the *Lucas*. Its odd, boxy shape looked like the top of a *Star Wars* four-legged armored transport and was far different from other Arleigh-class variants. The long steel barrel pointed across the bow, making no mistake as to its purpose.

The missile launchers were not as pronounced. A series of hatches were set flush into the deck, reinforced with Kevlar steel, and shrouded vertical missile silos that contained the real destructive capability of the ship.

"Aren't you scheduled to link up with your family today?" asked Abbey as he turned their run back toward the ship's superstructure.

"Yeah, at seventeen hundred. They're early risers, like all ranchers. They pull on their boots, get in the saddle, and plan everything around feeding time."

Abbey glanced at Duncan and managed a laugh. "Do I detect a little sarcasm in that statement? Since you're here, I take it ranching wasn't your thing."

The men took a turn into the starboard-side blast doors and entered the ship once again. Abbey enjoyed the breath of cool air before ducking under a door opening and toward the aft deck.

"No, don't get me wrong," said Duncan. "I'm proud of what my parents and the Armstrong family have accomplished over the last hundred fifty years. I just never got into it, ya know. Neither did my brother Dallas, who died in Kandahar. It wasn't really a rebellion thing."

Abbey, who could've easily been mistaken for a boxer due to his toned body, reached the amidship's break and a narrow section of open deck before they hit the aft deck. Several sailors stood flush against the superstructure to allow the tandem runners to pass.

"Parents never get over it, do they?" asked Abbey.

"Nope. None of my family did, especially my brother Cooper. He and my other brother and sister were still in their teens at the time. My parents were concerned they might follow my lead and join the military too. It was kinda weird, though. Dallas and I had the wandering genes in the family. We were the ones looking for a life outside of Borden County, Texas, population all of six hundred forty-two. Those three, that my parents call the rodeo kids, stayed close to home."

"Livin' the life, obviously," interjected Abbey with a laugh.

"Oh, yeah. Bulls and blood, dust and mud. You know, just like Garth said."

The men passed an exhaust vent and took in a quick burst of fresh, cool air as they circled the aft deck. Two imposing obstacles greeted them in the form of the fifty-caliber guns mounted on each corner, both port and starboard. Working their way around the aft missile launcher marked the halfway point of their lap, a routine the two men shared daily when their duties permitted. Thus far, the last few weeks aboard the *Lucas* had been uneventful, until now.

CHAPTER 5

October 30
USS *Jack H. Lucas*
Off the Coast of Muscat, the Gulf of Oman

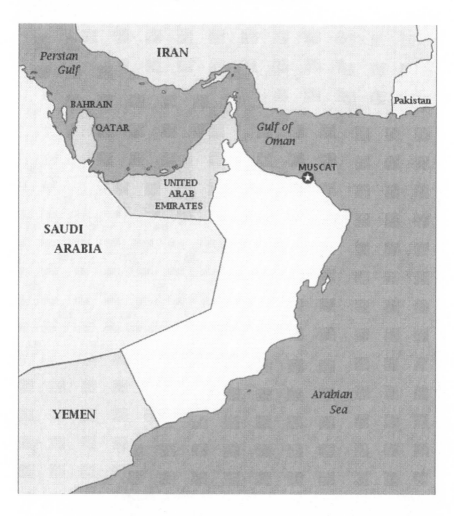

The men increased their stride as an oil tanker passed on their port side along the coast of Oman, destined for the Strait of Hormuz. Part of the duties of the *Lucas* was to police the perilous waters stretching from the Persian Gulf to the west, through the Strait of Hormuz and Gulf of Oman. The *Lucas*, positioned slightly closer to the shores of Iran, was less than one hundred miles from either coastline. The heat of the day obscured their visibility somewhat, but the enormous three-hundred-thousand-ton vessel could be seen easily from their vantage point as it passed.

The supertanker was nearly a mile away and would provide the *Lucas* a wide berth. With each subsequent lap, the vessel's position would change until soon it was fading into the haze created by the heat.

The men reached the boat deck and ducked under the ship's rigid hull inflatable boats known as RHIBs. They had just reached the foredeck when an alarm sounded.

Duncan's first thought was to look toward the passing supertanker. He wondered if the ship had been some kind of ruse. The alarm sounded again, a loud electronic wail that pounded his eardrums and echoed off the steel of the destroyer built by the now Boston-based Huntington Ingalls Industries.

Abbey didn't hesitate, and the casual run instantly turned into a sprint. Duncan scrambled to keep up with the smaller, more athletic captain of the USS *Lucas*.

Abbey had ducked through the starboard break when the piercing alarm was replaced with the booming baritone voice of the officer of the deck, or OOD.

"General quarters, general quarters. All hands! All hands man your battle stations. Material condition ZEBRA. Repeat. Material condition ZEBRA."

When Duncan and Park arrived on the *Lucas*, Abbey had insisted they be given an extensive orientation of the ship, especially as to what events resulted in certain conditions of readiness. Duncan learned there were three conditions of readiness—XRAY, YOKE, and ZEBRA.

XRAY provided the least watertight integrity and allowed for the greatest ease of travel through the ship. Condition XRAY was typically used when the *Lucas* was at port with no danger of attack.

YOKE provided a moderate degree of watertight security. While in the Persian Gulf region, U.S. naval vessels operated at YOKE conditions, which required certain openings to remain closed at all times.

Condition ZEBRA, which had been called for by the OOD, required the greatest degree of security and state of readiness for the ship's crew. Duncan had learned that ZEBRA was set anytime general quarters was sounded. The crew immediately prepared the ship for imminent attack and undertook steps to maximize the ship's watertight security.

The alarm sounded again, followed by an announcement on the speaker system.

"General quarters. General quarters. CO, your presence is requested on the bridge."

Duncan hesitated momentarily, unsure what to do. During their orientation, he and Park were not assigned battle stations because technically they weren't even there. He assumed he should report to his quarters until further instruction. The captain of the ship provided him his answer.

Abbey briefly turned to shout back to Duncan, "Come on. This is not a drill."

"Aye-aye, Captain. I'm with ya."

Duncan raced to catch up as the two men ascended the first of four steep ladders that led to the bridge. Sailors were scurrying in all directions, heading for their battle stations.

Abbey reached his at-sea cabin, which was near the bridge. He had just opened the door and reached for his coveralls when the OOD made another announcement over the ship's communications system.

"Tac-sit one. Repeat. Tac-sit one. This is not a drill. SCAT away. Repeat. Away the small craft action team."

SCAT was an on-call unit whose members were trained to use a variety of weapons to defend the *Lucas* when there was a limited distance to respond. The concept came from the terrorist attack on the USS *Cole* off the coast of Yemen in 2000. Seventeen sailors died, and another thirty-nine were injured.

The attack forced Washington to modify its rules of engagement with respect to approaching small boats. Following the attack, in June of 2001, an al-Qaeda recruitment video was released featuring Osama bin Laden boasting about the attack's success and encouraging more like it. The Bush Administration responded by allowing U.S. Navy captains approval to fire upon the small vessels in order to protect the crew and the ships. A decade later, this approval was rescinded, leaving the U.S. Navy captains in a precarious position of having to choose between their crew and a political firestorm in Washington.

The OOD's announcement jarred Abbey, who dropped his coveralls and opted to enter the bridge in his running clothes. Duncan followed and closed the door behind him.

The bridge of the USS *Lucas* was markedly different from past designs of the Arleigh Burke-class destroyers. Instead of the walk-around-style pilothouse that stretched from port to starboard, the new design offered a more compact module that protruded from the leading edge of the ship's superstructure like a cantilevered sunroom on a beach house. The new design increased the view from the bridge substantially, allowing a clear field of vision of two hundred seventy degrees.

The electronics of the bridge were a marvel of technology. Resembling the cockpit of the largest commercial jet in operation— the double-deck, wide-body Airbus A380—the newly commissioned *Lucas* was state of the art.

Two contoured chairs surrounded by instruments packed into curved consoles were positioned in the center of the floor space. The forward chair was occupied by the helmsman, a junior petty officer who responded to the OOD's orders on which way to steer the ship and commands regarding engine speeds.

The chair behind the helmsman belonged to the officer of the deck. This console was raised to provide the OOD unrestricted views through all the windows of the bridge. All other personnel, including the commanding officer and his second in command, the executive officer, stood at their stations.

Duncan, through conversations with Abbey, learned that the captain was a wanderer. On his bridge, subordinates were expected to man their stations and stay out of his way. He preferred to have the freedom of movement to assess any threat. Duncan had never seen Abbey take the OOD's chair.

"Captain's on the bridge!"

Everyone stood to attention except the OOD and the helmsman.

"Talk to me, John," said Abbey in a take-charge tone. Lieutenant John Doherty was a five-year veteran and had been continuously assigned to the *Lucas* since it was commissioned.

Lieutenant Doherty provided Abbey binoculars and pointed out the starboard windows toward a pair of dark shapes bouncing across the water at a high rate of speed. They were headed in formation directly for the *Lucas*.

Duncan surveyed the instrumentation and the displays inside the bridge. One screen revealed two red diamond shapes blinking as they approached a symbol marked DDG-125, the designation for the *Lucas*.

Lieutenant Doherty replied, "Cigarette boats, two of them, sir. They're now two thousand yards out and approaching at just under eighty knots, sir. We first noticed them coming from the general direction of Kereti on the coast of Iran. Their approach seemed to be timed with the passing of the oil supertanker."

"And they're taking advantage of the haze," muttered Abbey as he studied the fast boats, which had now closed the gap to fifteen hundred yards.

"Sir, this is their second approach," added Lieutenant Doherty. "They've made a run at us already, suddenly veering off to return towards shore, only to now make a second approach."

"Are they armed?" asked Abbey.

"The helmsman thought he saw RPGs on each of the boats, sir."

"I did, sir," interjected the helmsman. "I also saw a laser pass across our bow."

Abbey turned to the other members of the crew on the bridge. "Anyone else? Did anyone else see a targeting laser?"

The crew shook their heads, leaving only the helmsman to have identified a potential weapons threat.

"Sir," the helmsman insisted, "I know what I saw."

"Understood, Helmsman, carry on." Abbey turned to glance at Duncan, who shrugged slightly.

The speakers on the bridge hissed to life. "Captain, this is the TAO." The tactical action officer was responsible for weapons release, sensors, and overall defense of the ship. His crew was on the ready in the event of an imminent attack.

Abbey pressed the comms button and responded, "Go ahead, Lieutenant."

"We've got two sledgehammers rapidly approaching. Have you got them on the MMS? Shall we engage, sir?"

Sledgehammers was NAVSpeak for rapidly approaching, armed suicide boats.

The OOD immediately brought up video images of the approaching boats. Although the live stream was black-and-white, the picture contrast was excellent. Duncan could count the heads in each boat and clearly see that one man in each vessel was holding a tubelike device on his shoulder.

"There!" shouted the helmsman as others on the bridge saw the images. He rose from his seat slightly and pointed at the monitors. "Right there, sir. One RPG visible per boat. Sledgehammers."

"They're almost in range for most RPG variants, sir. Shall we engage?" asked an excited Lieutenant Doherty, who continued to maintain his duties as OOD despite the captain being on the bridge.

"Negative. Give me a still shot of the interior of the boat."

As Abbey issued his instructions, the cigarette boats made an abrupt turn and sped off in opposite directions.

"They're turning again, just like before," announced a member of the crew from the starboard side of the bridge. "Last time, they made a wide arc, bouncing across the water, and then moved side by side for another run."

"At what distance did they make their turn?" asked Abbey.

"Roughly five hundred yards, sir," responded Lieutenant Doherty.

Duncan knew what Abbey was thinking. Washington had always made the mistake of publicly announcing its rules of engagement to the entire world. Their enemies knew how to push their buttons. The Iranians were notorious for attempting to create a situation in which a Navy captain fired upon a so-called defenseless vessel with the hope of creating an international incident.

He leaned into Abbey's ear and asked, "What's your ROE?"

Abbey nodded as he responded, "Five hundred yards."

"They're trying you," said Duncan.

Abbey nodded and then asked the TAO to provide still images of each of the attack boats at five hundred yards.

"Back in formation," announced the helmsman. "Two thousand yards and closing at a high rate of speed. Sixty-five knots. Seventy knots. Seventy-five knots. They're near their max, sir."

The monitors changed, and still images appeared on the screen. Abbey walked closer to get a better look.

"Could be RPG-7s," he mumbled.

"Fifteen hundred yards, sir."

Another image appeared on the screen, which was generated by the TAO. He had magnified the image to show a grainy detail of one of the boats' occupants. He was holding onto the windshield, his clothing being whipped by the wind. A cylindrical object was resting on his right shoulder.

Abbey pressed the comms button and said, "Got it, Lieutenant."

The screens all changed to live feeds again as the helmsman announced, "One thousand yards."

The TAO's voice returned to the speaker system. "Sir, we believe that to be a missile launcher. At one thousand yards, they are well in range. Those boats are depicting classic sledgehammer attack profiles. If we let them get to the ROE line, our defensive measures won't be effective. Sir, we've got to take them out before they get a shot off at us."

Duncan studied the situation from an outsider's perspective. Something didn't feel right. *If the cigarette boats were in fact attacking the Lucas, why were they waiting? Why would they telegraph their intentions when it meant possible failure and their certain death?*

Abbey continued to hesitate and assess.

"Seven hundred yards, sir!" announced the helmsman.

Abbey watched the boats through the binoculars even though the monitors provided a very clear live stream of their approach.

"Six hundred yards, sir!"

The TAO was shouting through the comms. "Sledgehammers are inbound. Say again, attack imminent. Request permission to engage, sir!"

A flicker of red light bounced through the windows onto the bridge. They were being targeted.

Duncan wasn't in charge of the USS *Lucas*, but a chill ran down his spine nonetheless. It had nothing to do with the sweaty tee shirt he was wearing and the cold air being pumped into the bridge. It was anxiety, excitement, the feeling every soldier experiences when a split-second decision was upon them. Abbey faced a no-win situation. There was not a good choice. Both action and inaction would most likely lead to an international incident.

Abbey gripped the rail next to the OOD and began to give the order when, suddenly, one of the boats swerved to avoid debris in the water. The passenger lost his balance and fell to the deck, allowing the cylindrical object on his shoulder to fall against his seat. Duncan instinctively moved forward toward the screen to get a better look.

"That's a PVC drainpipe," said Duncan.

"Stand down! Stand down!" shouted Abbey.

"They're turning, Captain," announced the TAO.

Unlike their previously orchestrated maneuvers, the two fast boats peeled off and scattered in different directions, quickly becoming specks on the Gulf of Oman.

"They're aborting, sir," the OOD announced excitedly. The young lieutenant appeared pale as beads of sweat covered his forehead.

Abbey followed the attackers with his binoculars and then nodded to himself, an imperceptible pat on the back for a job well done. He turned to the OOD. "Stand us down from general quarters. Take the conn, John."

"Yes, sir!"

The OOD issued his orders, and Abbey turned to Duncan, who was smiling in awe of his friend's steely nerves.

"How about a beer, Captain? I think you've earned it."

"Can't disagree with that. Another lesson learned, right?"

Duncan opened the door for Abbey and said, "There can be no regrets in life, just lessons learned."

"Roger that."

CHAPTER 6

October 31
The Oval Office
The White House
Washington, DC

The Oval Office had been the sanctuary of seventeen U.S. presidents since it was constructed in 1909. The current occupant had dreamed of becoming the first female president of the United States, but she certainly didn't expect it to happen under unusual circumstances.

President Alani Harman had assumed the office after the unexpected death of the newly elected president just a year prior. At seventy-eight, President Joe Billings had been the oldest person elected to the presidency. During the campaign, his age was an issue, although his opponent was also in his mid-seventies.

Health-wise, President Billings had been given high marks although it was later revealed that he'd had a history of heart palpitations, which had not been disclosed during the election campaign. His sudden heart attack stunned the nation but quietly pleased many activists, as President Harman was the first female president as well as the first occupant of the Oval Office of Jamaican and Indian descent.

When she entered the Oval Office for the first time, she knew it was by fate although she'd hoped to earn her spot behind the executive desk on her own. Her entire life—from the early years as an activist in Berkeley, California, through the period in Canada after her parents divorced—had steered her in the direction of the Oval Office.

After law school, she took a position as a deputy district attorney and advanced through the ranks until she became the San Francisco district attorney. Her sudden thrust into the limelight caught the attention of many Californians, who encouraged her to run for the United States Senate, which she'd won handily in 2016.

Her charisma and political positions were a perfect fit for President Billings, and she was tapped as the vice-presidential choice after only three years in the Senate. Now she was president and facing multiple international crises, which she had little experience in handling.

The late President Billings, known as a consensus builder, had stocked his cabinet with loyalists, many of whom were moderates, and a few from the opposite side of the aisle. In the media, this was hailed as a positive approach for the country, which had been through decades of political rancor and open hostilities toward one another.

The cabinet choices didn't necessarily mesh with President Harman's political views, but she was happy to be a part of the administration and immediately set her sights upon a likely run of her own in 2024.

Her ascension to the presidency was welcomed by many, except some within the cabinet, especially on the defense and homeland security side. Her predecessor, whose sons served in the military, was strong on national defense and placed war hawks in position of authority in the Defense Department and the Department of Homeland Security.

President Harman frequently clashed with these members of her cabinet, but she elected to stay the course due to her perceived inexperience in matters of national affairs. Besides, as she frequently told her chief of staff, I can always push back against the warmongers and say *no*.

Her chief of staff entered the room and greeted her with a Microsoft tablet containing the day's agenda. After some small talk, President Harman got down to business.

"Charles, before we attend the cabinet meeting, let's talk about this bill that passed the Senate regarding the power grid."

Her chief of staff, Charles Acton, was a long-time congressman and ally of President Billings. After the former president's death, Acton immediately offered his advice and counsel on matters in Congress. President Harman saw the advantage a seasoned veteran of Capitol Hill would provide her and asked him to come on board as chief of staff. He readily accepted the offer and the two made a good fit.

"Well, Madame President, the bill that was passed in the House has now cleared any Senate committee hurdles. I expect a floor vote before Thanksgiving but after the midterm elections on November eighth."

"Did the Senate materially alter the House bill?" she asked.

"No, not really, other than the name."

"They changed the name?"

"Yes, very petty if you ask me. The house version was called the Enhancing State Energy Security Planning and Emergency Preparedness Act of 2022."

President Harman laughed. "Good grief, that's a mouthful."

"Yes, Madame President. The Senate agreed and changed the name to the Protect Our Power Act of 2022. POP, for short."

"Congress always has to put their mark on things, but the name is better," added the president.

"Much better. There were some grumblings and hurt feelings in the House, but they were pleased to see the bill clear committee without alterations."

"I read in the *Washington Post* this bill is rare in that it is truly single subject. Is that correct?" asked President Harman.

"It is. As you know, the prior administration pushed Congress to adopt the single-subject rule on federal legislation, which limits the content of bills introduced in Congress to a single issue. Like a lot of the prior president's suggestions, the proposals fell on deaf ears in the chambers of Capitol Hill."

"Indeed. They paid a hefty price in the election two years ago, which is why you and I are sitting in the Oval."

President Harman checked her watch and went to her desk to

retrieve a bottle of water.

"The problem with the bill is that it isn't revenue neutral. The Congressional Budget Office released its analysis, which reveals it blows a hole in the deficit. The House aims to pay for the required upgrades to our infrastructure by cutting several domestic programs, which would be a blow to our constituency. They're trying to keep their plans under wraps until after the upcoming midterms."

"Should we get it in the media?" she asked.

"Our team is working on options," replied Chief of Staff Acton. "After it passes, we'll consider a veto based upon the deficit issue."

President Harman raised her wrist for Acton to see the time. She was anxious to address her cabinet and dress down a certain retired general who'd been a pain in her ass from the day he joined the new administration's transition team.

"I'll say this. I think part of this whole thing might be a little overblown. As it relates to a solar flare, or whatever, I'm told we'd have at least *36 Hours* to warn the public. I have confidence in our emergency responders to do what's necessary. I'm certainly not willing to add to the deficit. Also, there's no way I'm gonna take food out of the mouths of single mothers and their babies for this."

Acton stood and gathered his notes as the two made their way to the Roosevelt Room. "Well, worst case is we force them to retool the bill and punt it to the new Congress. We will have some new faces to help see it our way."

"I agree," she added. "We need to focus on the threats that are real, like North Korea's nuclear proliferation. I'm tired of a bull's-eye being on the backs of my friends in California."

CHAPTER 7

October 31
The Roosevelt Room
The White House
Washington, DC

Defense Secretary Montgomery Gregg was the first to arrive at the cabinet meeting that morning along with his closest aide-de-camp, former Assistant Secretary of Defense Jackson Waller. The two men had served together at Fort Hood in Texas and were trusted allies. Secretary Gregg never met with the president or her chief of staff without Waller being present. He was a strong believer in accountability, and he'd learned in the world of politics that every conversation required a witness.

Secretary Gregg did not consider himself a political animal like the others who inhabited the Washington swamp. He was born a soldier. The son of a military family stationed at Fort Hood, the largest military installation in the world encompassing more than two hundred fifteen thousand acres, Secretary Gregg was destined to be one of the nation's great military leaders.

Every aspect of his childhood, from his education at military-based schools through his daily life, which involved basic-training activities, led him to his dream position within the United States Army—commanding general, III Corps and over Fort Hood. Commissioned as an armor officer following graduation from Texas A & M, he rose up the ranks and commanded troops at Armored Divisions based in Germany, Fort Riley, and ultimately, III Corps at Fort Hood.

He first met now-deceased President Billings during his testimony following the deadly Fort Hood shooting in 2009 by a U.S. Army major and psychiatrist turned terrorist, resulting in the death of thirteen people on base. Under questioning by then-Senator Billings, Secretary Gregg refused to waver on his opinion that the shooter was a terrorist, despite the White House's insistence the incident be labeled *workplace violence.*

When President Billings took office, he didn't hesitate in tapping Lieutenant General Montgomery Gregg to be his Secretary of Defense. The nomination and approval process was not an easy one. In order to serve in the cabinet, General Gregg was required to resign his post at Fort Hood, retire from the military, and gain a waiver from Congress of the five-year hiatus rule prohibiting former military personnel from taking a cabinet-level position like Secretary of Defense.

During the transition, many in President Billings's party, including then-Vice President Harman, publicly grumbled about the choice and the manipulation of the process. This did not go unnoticed by General Gregg, and despite the fact his nomination was approved, he refused to let bygones be bygones, as they say. Instead, he began to compile a political enemies list.

In the first two years of the Billings-Harman administration, Secretary Gregg became a rising star in Washington. His straight talk about the threats the nation faced and the matter-of-fact solutions he proposed might have been at odds with the administration's official position, but they were wildly popular across the heartland and with like-minded people in government.

After the death of President Billings, Secretary Gregg's name was bantered about as a VP choice for newly sworn President Harman. The suggestions came from more than a positive endorsement of Secretary Gregg's capabilities. The media roundly criticized President Harman's lack of foreign policy experience and dovish approach to the nation's defense. Many suggested her presidency would be doomed to failure without someone of Secretary Gregg's mettle at her side.

None of this sat well with loyalists to the president, and it most certainly doomed Secretary Gregg's opportunity to advance to the VP slot. What it did, however, was further entrench the former general's feet into the concrete of Washington. He was now considered by all to be indispensable, which made him a powerful player within the deep state.

Today, Secretary Gregg wore a suit to do battle with the President of the United States, but he could feel the Distinguished Service Medal, the Legion of Merit bronze oak leaf clusters, and the Bronze Star on his chest as if they were on full display.

As the other cabinet members arrived and the press got their photo ops, Secretary Gregg sat aloof at the end of the table. The seating arrangements for cabinet meetings were designated by the chief of staff, and Secretary Gregg was certain he had been positioned as far away from the president as possible for a reason. Not that it mattered. His booming voice from years of addressing soldiers commanded attention in any room, including this one.

President Harman covered her typical mundane matters regarding domestic programs and spending. She rarely led a cabinet meeting with matters of international importance. Like so many presidents before her, she made every attempt to kick the can down the road when it came to tough decisions. But as years passed, America's adversaries that remained unchecked got stronger and more dangerous.

The Democratic People's Republic of Korea, the DPRK, as North Korea was commonly referred to, was a perfect example. Secretary Gregg, like most within the military, saw the conflict escalating to a point where war was inevitable. The U.S. had now lost its military advantage as the war of words between the two countries had allowed the Hermit Kingdom time to develop a full nuclear arsenal. Today, in front of the cameras, Secretary Gregg intended to bring the matter to a head.

CHAPTER 8

October 31
The Roosevelt Room
The White House
Washington, DC

"Madame President, war with North Korea is inevitable," said Secretary Gregg, a man not known for mincing words. He'd made his position known more than once when testifying in front of Congress and in a much maligned interview with *60 Minutes* in which he clearly stated President Harman's inaction was detrimental to America's national security.

"Look, we've been through this before, Secretary Gregg," started the president. "We've reached the highest level of sanctions that our ambassador to the United Nations can achieve. I have been extremely vocal in making our position clear without unnecessarily provoking Kim Jong-un. Now we let the sanctions and geopolitical pressure do its job to force Pyongyang into a peaceful resolution."

"Madame President, if I may continue," gruffed the former general. "In July, I outlined the Defense Department's reasoning for its war recommendation. Over the last three decades, North Korea has advanced toward developing a nuclear-tipped intercontinental ballistic missile. Each administration took the same approach as the current one—condemnation, political pressure, and UN sanctions."

"Mr. Secretary," said Chief of Staff Acton, attempting to stave off a potential verbal conflict in a room full of media, "this topic has been addressed repeatedly and, I might add, behind closed doors."

Secretary Gregg scowled at Acton and continued as if he hadn't spoken a word. "We have now entered a realm of bad choices. Kim Jong-un has proven the pundits right. He has shown that our threats of military action on the Korean Peninsula was nothing more than bluster. While we've engaged in a war of words, he's not only developed ICBMs capable of striking all corners of the United States, but his arsenal has now surpassed that of India and Pakistan. He's capable of attacking us on multiple fronts while launching against our allies Japan and South Korea at the same time. The time for talk and empty measures is over. We simply must act now before the DPRK brings the war to our shores."

The president leaned forward in her chair and stared down the table at her defense secretary. "Secretary Gregg, while there is still hope of a diplomatic breakthrough that can change the DPRK's path, we must energetically and exhaustively pursue those breakthroughs. If or when those efforts fail, then we'll explore the options you so anxiously seek to employ."

"May I add something?" asked Jane Tompkins, the Secretary of State.

"Please," said the president, gesturing to Secretary Tompkins to take the floor. "There are many options available to us short of a military conflict in the region. While this is not popular with some in this room, the United States could accept North Korea's development of the ICBMs for the sole purpose of achieving a stable deterrence relationship with us."

"Hrrrmph," grunted Secretary Gregg. He stared at Secretary Tompkins and shook his head in disbelief. He whispered under his breath, "Naïve."

"Monty, let me finish, please," continued Secretary Tompkins, who noticed his reaction. "By choosing not to act militarily, as has been the U.S. position for decades, North Korea has peacefully continued its program, which included a long-range atmospheric nuclear test over the Pacific Ocean. Their recent successes have, quite frankly, provided a very real deterrent from our intervention. As their arsenal expands and diversifies, the State Department believes Pyongyang will be more likely to stand down in order to protect its newfound status on the world stage."

"You are absolutely ignoring the warlike history of the Hermit Kingdom and the consequences of standing down while their weapons proliferate," Secretary Gregg snapped back. "Now that the DPRK has achieved a survivable second-strike capability and a supposed nuclear deterrence relationship with our country, Kim Jong-un is completely unrestrained with respect to their goal of reunification of the Korea Peninsula under the Kim dynasty's rule and their longstanding feud with Japan. What would be our response if the DPRK launched conventional missiles into Seoul or Tokyo, killing scores of civilians? Will this administration authorize a robust military response to defend our allies? Would we caution South Korea and Japan against escalating the conflict in fear that a weakened or threatened North Korea might retaliate with nuclear warheads launched against our homeland?"

"These are all hypotheticals," interrupted Secretary Tomkins.

"You call them hypotheticals, but at the Pentagon, we call these realistic scenarios in our planning to defend this great nation. And let me add this. For those seeking a peaceful, political resolution, consider how this makes America look in the eyes of its allies in the region and around the world. We'll be humiliated as nothing more than a paper tiger—a boisterous, threatening menace that is ineffectual and unable to withstand the challenge of a rogue nation like North Korea. Consider what that means for our posturing in the Middle East against the Iranians. More importantly, NATO's credibility would be destroyed, and Putin might pounce upon our weakness."

"With all due respect, Monty, we are aware of your position," argued Secretary Tompkins. "At the *State Department*, we are advancing the policies of the president. She has made it abundantly clear to me to continue our diplomatic efforts until the first bomb drops."

Secretary Gregg shook his head in disgust. "Madame Secretary, whose heads are you willing to sacrifice for that *first bomb* you so casually refer to, hmmm?"

The Roosevelt Room became uncomfortably quiet. Secretary Gregg had lots more to say on the subject, but the reaction of the other members of the cabinet, the media in attendance, and the president's nervous, fidgety hands said it all. This meeting was over.

CHAPTER 9

November 1
The Armstrong Ranch
Borden County, Texas

"Mornin', Preacher," Major greeted his longtime friend and the man he entrusted with the deployment of his ranch hands every day. Caleb O'Malley was no longer a preacher, having removed himself from the pulpit at the Mount Zion Baptist Church in nearby Big Springs decades ago. Major's friend, who went by the nickname Preacher, had never disclosed the nature of what caused him to fall from grace. All Major knew was that Preacher Caleb O'Malley could no longer preach to his congregation, but it didn't turn him away from God.

"Mornin', Major. Ain't nothin' much goin' on out of the ordinary. I've got some of the boys separatin' the herd to get ready for the auction tomorrow morning in Abilene."

"How many head you gonna run?" asked Major.

"I'm thinkin' the large-frame feeder steers this go around. I reckon we've got seventy or eighty in the six- to eight-hundred-pound range."

"Are you savin' the heifers?" asked Major.

"I think I will," replied Preacher. "I was lookin' at Randy's report online and saw a lot of ranchers are dumping feeder heifers right now. It'll drive the price down. Nobody's brought any cow-calf pairs, and we've got half a dozen of 'em. They'll bring top dollar, maybe even fifteen hundred."

"Well, you've got this, as always, Preacher. Ya got anything that needs tendin' to?"

Preacher removed his wool felt cowboy hat, worn from years of wear and aged to a dark brown. He ran his fingers through his thinning hair and stared out across the grasslands.

"If you could pick up the feedin' and check on them boys on the south fence, I can focus on getting the herd ready for transport. We'll pull out pretty dang early tomorrow mornin', and it would be nice to turn in early tonight."

"You got it," Major responded. "I could use a full day in the saddle. Got lots to think about."

"No problems, I hope," Preacher said as he pulled his horse out of its stall.

Major laughed. "You know, it's stuff I shouldn't worry about and probably wouldn't give it a second thought except I watch too much news."

"You talkin' about Governor Burnett's re-election? I thought she was way ahead in the polls."

"Yeah, she is," replied Major. "As a matter of fact, I'm gonna see her in Lubbock in a few days when she comes out our way for a last-minute campaign stop. She's a good friend to have, you know."

"Yes, sirree. Especially if Texas secedes from the Union."

Major slapped his friend on the back and then stood back in amazement as a cloud of dirt floated off his leather coat. He wondered how the man could get so dirty before the sun rose in the east for the day.

"Come on, Preacher. You know that's all talk to keep her voters stirred up into a frenzy. That'll never happen, and Washington would never allow it. They're stuck with us, and unfortunately, we're stuck with them."

Preacher pulled his wiry six-foot frame on top of his horse and adjusted his seat in the saddle. "I wouldn't be too sure, Major. This country is in a heckuva mess. People don't go to church. They don't dress up for work. Their kids are runnin' all over without supervision, and lord knows what they're bein' taught in school."

"Texas has all the same problems as the other states, don't you think?" Major asked.

"Yeah, it's because the federal guvment is forcing their morals and values on good God-fearin' Texans," Preacher replied.

Major rubbed the nose of Preacher's horse. He agreed in many respects with his Christian conservative friend, but he didn't want to get involved in a long political discussion first thing in the morning.

"I should never have given you that iPhone where you could listen to Glenn Beck on the radio," quipped Major. "Go on now, round 'em up and cash 'em in tomorrow. I'll tend to everything while you're gone."

Preacher encouraged his horse with pressure from his heels and began to leave in a slow trot, but not before he got in the last word. "You know I'm right."

Major laughed and waved his arm, indicating Preacher should go on. Then he mumbled as he stood alone next to the barn. "Yeah, you're right, but I'm afraid we're heading for bigger problems than the loss of morality and social values."

CHAPTER 10

November 1
The Armstrong Ranch
Borden County, Texas

Lucy Armstrong considered herself to be the last of a dying breed—an American housewife. She grew up in a religious, conservative family in Midland along with three brothers and a younger sister. Her teenage days were spent in suburbia, hanging out with her girlfriends and the occasional date with guys her own age. Her family stayed heavily involved in her academics and after-school activities, yet she never felt smothered. Lucy never felt that teenage urge to rebel and bolt from the nest. In fact, she'd enjoyed their life and envisioned it for herself.

To be sure, by modern standards in the early nineties, marrying at age nineteen was young. That was not necessarily the case in Texas. Today, the average age for women to get married in the state was twenty-five. In the early nineties, it was twenty-one. Over time, fewer couples respected the sanctity of marriage, as indicated by rapidly ascending divorce rates and children born out of wedlock.

As a teen, Lucy Cooper was determined to be different. She intended to marry the man of her dreams, be a devoted wife and mother, and end her days by his side on those matchin' white rockin' chairs that resided on the front porch. She wasn't interested in being *empowered* or demanding equal pay or wearing pink hats or fighting for the rights of others.

She was only interested in loving and protecting her family. She truly didn't understand why some might consider her choice as subservient or weak. Maybe, Lucy often thought, if more strong women chose the path of family instead of self-interest, our country might be in a better place.

Lucy was excited to join the Armstrong family after she and Major married. Because Major's mother had passed away years prior, she was suddenly thrust into the role of the matriarch of the family at nineteen. Major's dad, whom everyone called Pops, instantly took to Lucy. They became best friends during the early years.

Pops continued to look after the ranch while Major became a rising star within the Texas Rangers. Lucy managed the household and learned the ways of ranch life in a desolate part of the state. She'd reflected on those days many times and how it molded her outlook on life. She loved her husband and was anxious to have more babies, but she also had this innate desire to protect everyone within her charge.

This led her into homesteading. Lucy's family had taught her self-reliance. Her mother told her that it didn't matter whether your home was big or small, rural or urban, you could still manage to apply common-sense homesteading principles to your daily life.

Their home in Midland had a small garden in the backyard, which was Lucy's domain. When she arrived at the Armstrong Ranch, she'd gazed in wonder at the crops that were growing just outside the white fence surrounding the ranch house. Because the Armstrong property included parts of the Texas version of the Colorado River as it opened up into Natural Dam Lake, also known as the J.B. Thomas reservoir, irrigation for their fields was not a problem. The Colorado River in Texas originates just south of Lubbock and meanders to the Gulf of Mexico. It was not connected to the more well-known Colorado River system that flows from the Rockies through Nevada and Arizona.

Unlike the arid grasslands that were predominant in this part of the Texas Panhandle, the area surrounding the Armstrong homestead was a bright green oasis of fertile land and pristine farmland, thanks to an extensive irrigation system put into place by Pops and his father decades ago.

Initially, Lucy had considered herself a traditional homesteader.

She began to create a scrapbook of notes, articles, recipes, and checklists to keep herself organized. Soon, it was burgeoning with information, so she created a homesteading library, which included multiple three-ring binders.

One included recipes, canning techniques, and food storage tips. Another was devoted to gardening, especially as it related to crops that could be grown in their location. Major hired the wives of two ranch hands, and they helped Lucy manage the garden, which grew enough vegetables to feed the family every year.

One of her helpers, a Mexican woman who had come to Texas after her husband was naturalized, encouraged Lucy to include herbs and wildcrafting, the process of gathering plants from their natural growth habitat. Their interest in foraging led the two to set up a specially designated garden for home remedies and natural herbal supplements.

Over the years, as the kids entered high school, Lucy encouraged all of them to be active in the Texas FFA—the Future Farmers of America. She reminded Pops and her husband that there could be more to ranching than raising cattle. The result was the expansion of the Armstrong Ranch farther up the Colorado River for the addition of pigs, goats, chickens, and even honeybees.

Throughout the nineties, Lucy and the Armstrong family evolved into cattle ranchers and top-notch homesteaders. Everyone from Pops down to their youngest, Palmer, became actively involved in the day-to-day homesteading activities. It wasn't a chore, it was a way of life and something the family enjoyed.

Then it got real.

Most Americans remembered where they were on September 11, 2001, the day terrorists attacked their homeland. Major was working a case in Odessa, and Pops was out on the ranch. At that point, Duncan and Dallas were in school, and Lucy, eight months pregnant with Palmer, was home canning with the television playing in the background.

The first reports of the planes flying into the World Trade Center shocked her, and America, to her core. When the news reporters announced the second plane had crashed into the building, she knew it was not an accident. She gathered up Riley and Cooper to move them out of the room. She ran outside and found one of the hands, who was quickly dispatched to fetch Pops. If this was the start of something bigger—an unprecedented attack on America—she needed her family close by.

For many, 9/11 became a life-changing event. For Lucy Armstrong, it gave her the final nudge needed to elevate herself from a homesteader into a prepper. In that seminal moment, Lucy began to prepare for the worst threats that mankind could inflict upon one another—for the protection of her family.

*****

"Trick or treat," shouted Palmer as she burst through the front door. It was late that afternoon when Lucy's rodeo kids arrived home from their trip to North Dakota. "Momma, we're home!"

"I hear ya," Lucy replied dryly. "You're a day late for Halloween, but I figured y'all would show up in time for supper today. Come here and give me a hug."

Lucy wiped her hands off on her apron and greeted her daughter in the family room. She gave her youngest a hug and a peck on the cheek.

As part of the family's routine when the three of them returned from a rodeo, Palmer pulled away and, like a young child, spun around in front of her mother. "Ready for inspection, Momma. No broken bones."

"Good, but you're not the one I worry about. Where are your brothers?"

"Here I am, Momma," responded Riley as he hauled two armfuls of duffle bags and gear through the front door. "I ain't got any broken bones either. Hey! What's cookin'?"

"Preacher killed a wild hog that was tryin' to poke our pigs," responded Lucy. "We butchered it so we can have pork sliders with peanut slaw and redskin potato salad."

"Oh yeah, there's no place like home," said Riley with a laugh. He approached his mom and leaned in to get his welcome-home kiss.

"All right, you look like you're in one piece," started Lucy. "Where's Coop hidin'?"

"I think he was gonna wait on Daddy, who was walkin' over from the barn," replied Palmer.

Lucy wandered toward the front door and shielded her eyes from the bright sun as it set beyond the ranch. She saw the silhouette of Major and Cooper standing against the sunset, with her husband, the taller of the two, holding his outstretched hand on Cooper's shoulder. She resisted the urge to holler at them to come in for supper. They appeared to be discussing something serious she would quiz Major about later.

She returned to the family room and threw another log on the fire. The house was filled with warmth and family once again, except for Duncan and Dallas, of course.

CHAPTER 11

November 2
The Armstrong Ranch
Borden County, Texas

The next morning, Major finished with the feedin' and returned to the ranch house to gather up Cooper. He'd promised his son a little extra sleep this morning after their long trip home. It didn't take Major, who had become an expert at reading people during his tenure as a Texas Ranger, but a few seconds to discern that something serious had happened to Cooper during his ride. Cooper didn't even attempt to lie about the battle with One Night Stand and the kick to the back of the head. He did, however, beg his father not to tell his momma. He didn't want her to worry, especially since the concussion was relatively minor.

Father and son reached a compromise. Major said he'd stick to the story concocted by the kids on the way home, that Cooper had slipped off a wooden railing and struck his head on a fence post. In return, Cooper agreed to go into Lubbock with Major in a couple of days to see a neurologist and meet with the governor after the campaign rally.

The other condition was Cooper was to ride the ranch with Major this morning, as there were several things to discuss. Cooper readily agreed to all the conditions because, as Major had calculated on his own, he'd need to ride again to qualify for the Pro Rodeo World Finals in Las Vegas next month. Major, however, was firm in his admonishment to his son. *Without medical clearance, you don't ride. No exceptions.*

Cooper saddled up and joined his father near the round pen, a

47

large enclosure used for horse training. Armstrong Ranch was going to increase its horse population in the next couple of weeks with two dozen new quarter horses from Governor Burnett's ranch.

"Mornin', Daddy," started Cooper. "Two dozen new horses comin'? Are we gonna put together our own posse?"

Major laughed and patted his horse's neck. "Son, I'd love to see it. You know, the newly minted Texas Rangers wouldn't know how to mount a horse, much less ride one. Now, don't get me wrong, they can do things with computers and I can barely turn the dang things on."

Major pulled the reins on his horse and urged him into a trot as Cooper rushed to catch up. When he pulled alongside his father, he asked, "Where we headed?"

"Just checkin' on things. Preacher and a lot of the boys headed over to Abilene Auction early this morning. I'm gonna pick up the slack while they're gone. I thought we'd head up to the river first and check on Miss Lucy's barnyard critters."

Barnyard critters was Major's term for Lucy's homestead animals. When they'd acquired the additional land along the Colorado River years ago, Pops thought the concept of raising chickens and pigs might be a passing fad for Lucy. Instead, it became an operation in and of itself within the ranch that provided a constant source of food for the Armstrongs.

"Two dozen horses are a lot, Daddy. We're gonna need more stalls. Heck, even a new barn."

"That's right, son. Construction starts tomorrow as soon as Preacher returns. I'm gonna need you and Riley to pitch in too."

Cooper sat a little taller in the saddle and slowly turned his head away from the bruise on his neck. He was constantly testing the injury to see if it had somehow miraculously healed itself since the last test. At least the headaches were gone, thanks to the industrial-strength, eight-hundred-milligram ibuprofen prescribed by the doctor in Valley City.

"Riley loves construction," said Cooper. "Daddy, I'll help all I can, you know."

"I understand, son. Just put on a good show when your mother is around. I'm not a hundred percent sure she's buying your story."

"Couldn't you sell it?" asked Cooper.

"I tried after we turned the lights out last night," Major replied. "If she could've looked into my eyes, it wouldn't have worked. Still not sure it did. Let's get you looked at in Lubbock and take it from there."

Major picked up the pace. The Armstrong Ranch was over nine thousand acres, the equivalent of fifteen square miles. On most days, a complete circuit around the ranch would involve a ride in Major's Ford Super Duty F-450. Lately, he'd opted for horseback, as a melancholy nostalgia was overtaking him that he couldn't quite put his finger on. Major hoped this conversation with Cooper would help him identify why this feeling of gloom had come over him.

"Coop, it took Pops years to groom me for running this operation. While we're nowhere near the top ten biggest ranches in Texas, it's a sizable operation nonetheless."

"Daddy, do you ever regret not trying to take it to the next level, you know, like Grandpa's brother did at King Ranch?"

Major slowed down their trot as the wind picked up, just like it always did when the sun rose in the morning. As they got closer to the river, they crossed through a shady dry creek bed that eventually found its way to the water's edge.

"We were never destined to be big commercial ranchers like them boys down near Corpus. They're nearly a million acres now, but their operation is more glitzy self-promotion than it is ranching. For the King Ranch, the cattle business became less profitable over time to the point that the original descendants of the Kings ended up being fired. That's not what we're about."

"Daddy, I never pry into your finances because you've never shown that we were in any kind of trouble. But—"

Major cut him off. "No, son. Don't get me wrong. Financially, we're set. Here's what we've got going for us that's different from the other ranches across the state—we don't owe money to anybody. Pops made sure of that."

"That's good," added Cooper.

"I was down in Big Springs the other day, talkin' to the mayor, who has a sizable ranch of his own, as you know. A couple of out-of-towners robbed the Prosperity Bank last week. You know what he said to me?"

"What?"

"The mayor said most people didn't care that it happened. As he put it, Prosperity Bank had been robbin' all of the local ranchers for years, and they had it comin'."

Cooper laughed. "The mayor said that?"

"Yes, sir," replied Major with a chuckle. "Here's my point. The Armstrong Ranch, while a big operation in the eyes of many, is still just a family-owned operation that benefits only the family. Miss Lucy doesn't grow crops to sell in a farmers' market somewhere or at Albertson's. We're not raising beef cattle to line the pockets of the Koch Brothers like so many others around us. Everything we produce here—whether cattle, chicken eggs, or vegetables—is for the benefit of this family and our ranch hand's families."

Cooper rode alongside his father in silence for a moment as they reached the edge of the Colorado River. It began to widen at this point as the river slowly emptied into the lake.

"I understand, Daddy. I think the whole family is proud of what you and Pops have accomplished."

"Good, because, Coop, I'm gonna need your commitment to run things around here someday."

"Of course, I'm always here to help, but it's not like you got a foot in the grave. Heck, look at Pops. He didn't pass until he was eighty-five. His horseback ridin' days were over, but he certainly ran things pretty well until you retired."

"I know that, son, but life deals some nasty cards sometimes, and as you know, your older brother ain't cut out for ranchin'. Riley is a good kid, but his maturity is many years behind yours. I don't know when that boy is gonna be done sowin' his oats. And your sister ..."

Major's voice trailed off as he contemplated his next words. They rode on for a moment in silence, Cooper choosing to listen to his father pour out his inner thoughts rather than interrupt.

Major continued. "Coop, your sister is, you know, different. I mean, do you know what I mean?"

Cooper couldn't contain himself and began laughing. "Daddy, are you asking me if Palmer's gay?"

"Well, I mean," Major began to stammer, completely uncomfortable with the conversation. "She's never really shown an interest in boys other than wrestlin' with them. Half the young men she's dated, she's ended up whoopin' for some reason."

"Daddy, maybe that's because they did something they shouldn't have done, like not keeping their hands to themselves."

"Coop, your sister is pretty, but that young gal is as wild as the West Texas wind. I don't see any man marryin' her. She's too awnry."

Cooper began laughing hysterically. He subconsciously massaged his neck as he spoke. "Daddy, because you did me this favor, I'm not gonna tell Palmer what you said. I'm pretty sure she's not gay, although we haven't really talked about it. And I know you and Momma well enough to know y'all wouldn't care if she was. She's dated a few guys, but she hasn't found the right one yet. Besides, if you think she's rough on potential boyfriends, how do you think Riley and I are when they come sniffin' around. She's lucky a boy even talks to her!"

Major began to chuckle, somewhat out of relief, but mainly because he had relaxed while talking with Cooper.

"Okay, Palmer can do what she pleases," said Major. "Things are different than the days Miss Lucy and I dated. Now they call it *hookups*, or somethin' like that."

"Daddy, that's it, or I'm goin' back to the house. Palmer ain't hookin' up with guys. As far as I know, she never has, which is a miracle nowadays."

Major reached into his saddlebag and pulled out his binoculars. He studied the river where it narrowed and then handed them to Cooper.

"Look over there, Coop," said Major, pointing toward a wooded stretch of the river. "See the beavers. Is that amazing?"

Cooper took the glasses and studied the activity. "They've got a great start on a dam. As big as it is, we may have to blow it up before it diverts the dang Colorado River."

"Yeah, I'll tell Preacher tomorrow. But this is the type of thing I'm talkin' about. I rely heavily on Preacher and the hands to watch over things, but only family will take pride to check on every aspect of the ranch. That beaver dam has been under construction for a week or more. Somebody should've caught it."

"Daddy, are you sayin' all this 'cause you want me to quit the rodeo? I've just about qualified for the PBR World Finals. I've been working towards it all my life."

"No, son, not at all. If you agree to take over when I can't continue for some reason, I'd like to start teaching you now. It's too much to learn on the fly. Do you understand?"

Cooper handed the binoculars back to his father. "Daddy, I'm okay with it and hoped you'd ask me at some point, but I didn't want to step on Duncan's toes. He is the oldest."

"Duncan's a military man, not a rancher. He'll be happy for you, but I know there's one thing he'd like from you more than anything else. Forgiveness."

"Daddy, do we need to go there today?" asked Cooper, who shifted uncomfortably in his saddle.

This was going to be a difficult subject for Major, but he was gonna ask for Cooper's help while the two were having this father-son talk.

"Coop, I'm asking for Duncan, your momma, and for me. Please don't hold your brother responsible for Dallas's death. He never encouraged Dallas to join the Army."

Cooper shook his head and looked down to the ground. "Daddy, he didn't discourage it either. Maybe if Duncan had been a little more forceful, Dallas would never have joined the Army and got himself killed in Afghanistan. And for what? Why were we over there, beyond our own borders, fighting someone else's battles? It was stupid."

"Coop, it wasn't your brother's fault. If you should blame

anybody, blame me. I could've put my foot down. But like most military parents, you feared for the life of your child, but you never thought it would happen."

Cooper wiped a few tears from his face. He and Dallas had been close growing up, far more than he and Duncan. He looked up to Dallas as a role model, and when news came of his death, Cooper took it hard and immediately looked to assign blame. Duncan was a logical target for Cooper's anger because he'd broken the family mold and joined the Navy to become a SEAL.

"Daddy, I understand. Honestly, this has been weighing on my mind 'cause I see the sadness in Momma's eyes when I avoid the ranch on those rare occasions Duncan comes home."

Cooper stretched his hand out, offering it to his father to shake. Major grasped his boy's hand and shook it heartily.

"Do you mean it, son? It would make your momma happier than anything on earth other than a grandbaby."

Cooper laughed through the tears. "Daddy, well, I can't do anything about giving y'all a grandbaby just yet, but I can make peace with my brother when he comes home. I promise."

"Thank you, son. God bless you. Now let's go see about Miss Lucy's barnyard critters."

CHAPTER 12

November 3
USS *Jack H. Lucas*
Near Chabahar, Iran
The Gulf of Oman

Duncan and his partner, Min Jun Park, stood on the starboard side of the USS *Lucas* and stared toward the coast of Iran, which was only a few miles to their north. The men had just received a communique from Langley advising them to insert themselves into a VBSS Team to be used by Captain Abbey within the hour. VBSS was an acronym used by agencies engaged in maritime boarding actions and tactics. Visit, board, search, and seizure was one of the primary functions of the U.S. Navy as it searched the Persian Gulf.

Duncan and Park had been recruited into the Special Operations Group, an element of the Special Activities Division of the National Clandestine Service. Part of SAD/SOG, they were involved in high-threat covert operations that could not be associated with the United States government. Members of the paramilitary arm of SOG did not carry any objects or clothing that would associate them with the military. If they were compromised during a mission, the government would most likely deny any knowledge of their activities.

Following the Benghazi debacle, dozens of two-man teams were created to act as rapid-response forces capable of entering a hostile situation. Their jobs could be rescue related, or it could be to take advantage of a weakness in an enemy nation's defenses, allowing a tactical advantage in a covert political action.

Duncan and Park had engaged in a variety of missions from

assassinations to munitions work. Park, who spoke fluent Persian and Korean, was an invaluable asset to Duncan. On most operations, Duncan took the lead because of his training, but Park was the member of the team who could talk them out of trouble in foreign countries.

"Do you find it odd that a VBSS action has been ordered for an inbound ship into Iran?" asked Park, Duncan's right arm for two years.

Duncan shrugged and then responded, "According to the intel, the ship is bound for Chabahar, a port city on the extreme southeastern tip of Iran. It's a free-trade zone, so I imagine it gets a lot of activity."

Park added, "I don't think the ship has entered their view yet. That's why I wanted to come out here and watch for it."

Suddenly, the low rumble of an approaching ship could be heard. The larger tankers and merchant ships had their own distinctive sound—lazy, methodical, and heavy. The merchant ship, which Langley had identified as a cargo vessel called *FooChow*, was over five hundred feet long. It was trudging along several hundred yards to their east at about ten knots.

"C'mon," said Duncan as the ship came into view. "Let's get up to the bridge so we can volunteer for duty."

"What if Abbey says no?" asked Park.

"Then I'll have to tell him he doesn't have a choice."

They hustled up the stairwells and arrived at the bridge just as Captain Abbey was assessing the situation with his crew.

"By their lack of reaction or course adjustment," started the helmsman, "they haven't noticed us at all. Personally, I think any captain worth his salt would notice a hundred-ton destroyer off his port beam and give us plenty of space."

"I agree," said Abbey. He turned to acknowledge Duncan and Park, who stood respectfully to the side. "OOD, position the *Lucas* on the *FooChow*'s port beam. I don't want to approach her from the aft. The possibility of her captain making an abrupt turn into Iranian waters might draw the attention of a couple of Iranian missile boats.

Let's not provoke an international incident or a missile attack. Whadya think?"

"Can't argue with those orders, sir," the OOD replied, reflecting the casual attitude Abbey enjoyed on his bridge.

The OOD gave the commands, and the *Lucas* eased closer to a parallel position with the *FooChow*, which was maintaining a steady twelve-knot speed.

Abbey turned to update Duncan and Park on the situation. "When we first picked up the *FooChow* on radar, she was well north of established shipping lanes and hugged the territorial waters of Iran approaching Chabahar. We've seen this before, and according to our tactical memos from command, that's a tactic favored by smugglers who are trying to skirt Iran territorial waters but also use them as protection in case we attempt to board them. They can dart into Iranian waters if they think they'll be intercepted."

Duncan took this opportunity to insert himself and Park into any search mission. "As I understand it, Iran has no particular interest in harboring smugglers, but are naturally fiercely protective of their borders. Park and I have been on several VBSS operations in the past. If you don't care, we'd like to join your teams as they go on board. Park is gettin' fat and a little rusty. I need to give him something to do."

"Hey!" protested Park as Abbey laughed.

"I noticed he doesn't join our run," said Abbey.

"I didn't want to interrupt your special quality time together," said Park with a chuckle. Then he leaned in to whisper, "You know, everyone is beginning to talk."

Abbey began to laugh, but Duncan moved swiftly to place Park in a playful chokehold. He gently applied pressure to Park's throat until he held his arms up.

"Okay, okay. I take it back," begged Park. "Seriously, Captain, I'm going stir-crazy. Can we join the team for this one?"

Abbey turned to his OOD. "Lieutenant, what's the status of your VBSS teams?"

"Sir, all equipment and comms checks have been performed. The boats are ready and at the rail. VBSS teams Red and Black are manned and ready to deploy on your orders."

"Okay," Abbey responded. "Advise the team leaders that they'll have two more joining them. Ensign, take these gentlemen to get suited up and issue their weapons of choice. Get them comms as well."

"Yes, sir!"

"Thanks, Captain," Duncan and Park said in unison.

"You're welcome, gentlemen," said Abbey as he picked up a headset. "You've got time to get ready, and the teams can stand easy for a few minutes. I have to establish comms with the captain of the *FooChow* and give him the good news."

*****

Prior to Duncan and Park's arrival on the bridge, the communications officer on deck had tried to raise the captain of the *FooChow*. They'd failed to respond to several requests, and Abbey had grown weary of the game playing. With his VBSS teams in place, plus two, it was time to get serious.

Abbey was ready to break the stalemate. He pulled the radio headset over his ears and positioned the microphone in front of his mouth. He began his customary wandering of the bridge, an indication to his crew it was time to get rolling.

"Gentlemen, it appears the *FooChow* is experiencing radio difficulties. Perhaps we should provide them a little technical assistance in making the necessary repairs. TAO, this is the captain. Over."

A second later, the tactical action officer's voice came back in his ear. "Captain, this is the TAO. I read you Lima Charlie. Standing by for your orders, sir."

"TAO, I need you to lay a five-inch round across the bow of the *FooChow*."

"Roger that, Captain."

Abbey patted his OOD on the shoulder and laughed.

"Gentlemen, I suggest you put in your hearing protection."

The crew scrambled through their coveralls and pulled out the standard-issue orange rubber earplugs that were an essential part of their at-sea uniform.

A few seconds later, the five-inch gun mount affixed to the deck below them spun ninety degrees toward the bow of the *FooChow*. The electronics weapons system of the *Lucas* locked the large-bore cannon on the bow of the Singapore-flagged vessel and tracked it with an eerie, stalking precision.

As the two ships pitched and rolled along the Gulf of Oman, the cannon continuously made adjustments to compensate for the change in positioning of the target. Without warning, the ninety-four-pound round exploded out of the five-inch barrel with a flash and thunderous retort.

The shell propelled itself toward the bow of the *FooChow*, easily breaking the sound barrier. It splashed into the water a second later only fifty yards off the vessel's bow, throwing up a plume of water that hovered in the air long enough for the ship to sail into it.

The sea spray was still evident on the horizon when the bridge's comms came to life. It was the chief communications officer.

"Captain, I have one rattled sea captain chattering his head off in Arabic. He's on channel eight, sir."

"Thank you, Lieutenant. Apparently the *FooChow* captain has found a way to fix his batteries. Please put our interpreter on bridge-to-bridge channel eight. Have him respectfully request the *FooChow* to heave to and drop anchor. Over."

"Comms, aye-aye."

"OOD, let's provide some cover for our VBSS teams. All hands on deck. Helmsman, keep a safe distance but close enough to allow our gunners to engage if necessary."

Captain Abbey took the binoculars and studied the ship from bow to stern. *Now, let's see what the* FooChow *is carrying.*

CHAPTER 13

November 3
Aboard the *FooChow*
Near Chabahar, Iran
The Gulf of Oman

An hour later, Lieutenant Frank Wilson, the Red Team leader, stood on the starboard of the *FooChow* and looked across the three hundred yards of choppy water that separated the two vessels. He keyed the mic that was built into his headset.

"*Lucas*, Red Team leader. Over."

"Red Team Leader, this is *Lucas*. Go ahead. Over."

Wilson turned to look towards the bridge of the freighter. Two of his men were holding the crew of the *FooChow* with their guns held at low ready. Thus far, they'd received no resistance other than some discrepancies in the ship's manifest.

"Red Team has secured the bridge and below-deck engineering compartments. We have divided the vessel's crew between the bridge and the remainder who are assembled on her fantail. Black Team has watch on the stern. Over."

"Red Team Leader, do you have a head count? Over."

"Nineteen, sir. That is one-nine including captain and crew. Over."

Wilson listened for a response and waited nearly a minute before keying his mic once again. The sun was beginning to set over the Strait of Hormuz and he didn't like being outnumbered on a strange vessel, in the dark, off the coast of Iran.

"*Lucas*, Red Team Leader. Copy that? Over."

"We did, Red Team Leader. Be advised, vessel's filed manifest provides for captain and twenty crew members. Repeat. Twenty-one, including the captain. Over."

"Roger that, *Lucas*. The ship's captain was calm until questioned about his crew. Black Team has conducted its initial sweeps of all spaces except the cargo holds. In progress now, but comms are spotty due to ship's superstructure. Over."

Suddenly, another voice entered the conversation. "*Lucas*, this is Black Team Leader. Request permission to set ROE to security level two. Over."

Under United Nations guidelines and maritime law, when conducting a board and search mission, the U.S. Navy's VBSS teams were not allowed to conduct body searches of the vessel's crew unless they exhibited acts of physical aggression. Lack of cooperation and hostile attitudes did not warrant a physical search. As a result, the VBSS teams had to be aware each of the *FooChow*'s crew could be carrying concealed weapons.

Captain Abbey responded with a sense of urgency in his voice. "Black Team Leader, do you have an emergency or hostile situation? Over."

"Negative, sir. As darkness sets in, it's difficult to see in the cargo hold, and we have no comms. Over."

"Be advised, Black Team Leader, manifest indicates two missing crew members. Repeat. Two unaccounted for. Over."

Again, silence overtook the comms. Both lieutenants in charge of the VBSS teams would be justifiably nervous as the skies grew darker. After several moments, Abbey returned with his orders.

"Team Leaders, this is *Lucas*. You have authorization to increase to security level three. Level three is authorized."

Level three involved noncompliance after an official request to inspect a ship in sovereign waters. The vessel's lack of initial responsiveness, the uncooperative nature of the captain, and now the unaccountability of two crew members warranted Abbey's escalation. Operating with their weapons drawn and pointed at the crew members was inherently more threatening than levels one and two.

Circumstances above deck were guaranteed to become tense, but nothing compared to the uncertainty below.

*****

Two decks below, deep in the cargo hold, Duncan and Park were not privy to the orders issued by Captain Abbey because their communication devices were not working. Nor were they aware of two missing members of the *FooChow* crew.

They moved in tandem through the darkened space, illuminated only by widely spaced fluorescent lights, which flickered constantly. They had just passed through the forward cargo hold and cleared several crew quarters when they reached a series of compartments that rose two levels toward the deck.

The space was dark and cramped due to the large numbers of shipping containers that provided a maze of narrow walkways created by high walls of corrugated steel.

"What are we looking for?" asked Park.

"Something other than these Conex containers," replied Duncan. "We'll leave the opening and tagging of the containers for Black Team."

With their weapons leading the way, having disregarded the assigned threat level from the moment they went below deck, the two operators methodically walked along the bottom of the cargo hold, looking down every passageway and up towards the deck, which was obscured by a series of large steel doors. Both men had holstered their sidearms and were carrying Mossberg 590A1 Mariner shotguns with short, fourteen-inch barrels. In close-quarters situations like this one, they didn't need the firepower of an M4, opting instead for the versatility and broad spray pattern of a shotgun.

A loud clank was heard by both men, causing them to stop and lower themselves into a crouch.

"Was that ahead of us?" asked Park.

"Yeah," Duncan responded as his head swiveled back and forth to get his bearings. "Black Team is still working in the forward cargo area. This is something different."

A scraping sound caused Duncan to stop talking. Both men shut off their flashlights.

"I wish we had our NVGs," whispered Park, referring to the night-vision goggles they carried in their gear.

After a moment, their eyes adjusted. They were not completely in the dark, as some ambient light found its way into the massive cargo hold.

The sound of a man grunting ahead of them told them they were not alone.

"Come on," said Duncan. "We can't clear this using our usual right-left methods. We gotta go high-low, but quickly. There's somebody trying to get away."

"Moving," said Park as he led the way. He was shorter than Duncan and was adept at running in a low crouch. This would enable Duncan to see over his head as they moved through the narrow passages.

In perfect unison, Park pushed toward the source of the sound, moving his weapon from side to side in rapid, but precise, arcs. Duncan followed behind, constantly surveying the containers above them, his eyes and weapon scanning the openings between the large metal boxes.

The clanking sound of metal on metal could be heard thirty feet in front of them. Park began to race toward the sound, causing Duncan to pick up his pace. The men reached an opening that was wider than what they'd seen thus far.

Duncan took the lead as he moved toward their left. He whispered to Park, "This way. Something's different."

They raced to the end of a Conex container, and a void appeared in the middle of the stacked boxes. A faint light could be seen through the cracks of a container door. In front of it, two chairs and a table sat to the side, completely out of place in these cramped surroundings.

Muffled voices could be heard, but neither Park nor Duncan could make out the words. Duncan used hand signals to instruct Park to approach from the left while he would move toward the door from the right.

As they got closer, the whispers intensified, and even a country boy from the Texas Panhandle could identify it as Asian or, more specifically, Korean. Then the lights went out, and they were in complete darkness.

CHAPTER 14

November 3
Aboard the *FooChow*
Near Chabahar, Iran
The Gulf of Oman

Duncan felt his way along the container walls, making his way toward the entrance of the container. Although he couldn't see Park, he sensed his presence as the two men arrived near the table and chairs simultaneously.

"Are they hiding, or planning an ambush?" asked Park in a barely audible whisper.

"If they're hiding, they're not doing a very good job of it," replied Duncan. "They forgot their furniture."

"Either way, we gotta decide if we're gonna bust in there weapons hot," said Park.

"We could wait on Black Team," said Duncan. "Whoever's in that box is stuck now."

Park nudged his partner's arm with his fist. "I have a better idea. Let's give them the universal signal for the jig is up. Nothing says *hello, how are you* like racking a round into a Mossberg. There's no other sound in the world like that metal on metal."

"Agreed. Let's rack one, pound the sides, and then you holler at them in Korean."

"Yeah, we'll give them a chance," said Park as he inched closer to the doorway.

Park slid into position as the two men flanked the entrance to the container. After they pulled the slide on their shotguns, they immediately began to pound the side of the container. The racket they caused could've raised the dead. In between the pounding, sounds of screaming and pleas of mercy emanated from the container. Duncan presumed it was Korean because Park began to engage the occupants in conversation.

Between the shouting and the noise created by the duo, the Black Team was alerted, evidenced by the sound of running feet and shouts of instructions that could be heard from the other side of the cargo hold.

The lights turned on inside the container, and the doors slowly opened. Two elderly Korean men stepped out with their hands in the air. They were shaking, and one was shedding tears.

With the doors open, Duncan could see that the two were not a threat, but he had Park order them to the floor nonetheless. Within minutes, three members of Black Team arrived with their weapons drawn and joined Park in holding the stowaways on the floor at gunpoint.

Duncan entered the forty-foot-long sea container, moving his shotgun from side to side in case he was surprised by a gunman. The container didn't contain any more stowaways, but it was far from empty.

"Whoa," exclaimed Park as he joined Duncan's side. "What do we have here?"

Duncan walked through the container and studied the wooden crates holding various parts of a machine or vehicle. Each container was marked in Korean.

"Park, what does it say?" asked Duncan.

Park shouldered his weapon and began to walk through the container. At first, he mumbled the words, but the more he read, the louder and more excited he became.

"Communications antenna. Grapple module. Attitude control. Antenna boom. Solar panels. Ground-link antenna. Internal computer."

"C'mon, man. Are you gonna tell me what it says?" insisted Duncan.

"Dude, I think it's some kind of spacecraft. Maybe a satellite."

Duncan walked through the maze of crates and boxes before marching out of the container. He grabbed one of the Koreans and pulled him to his feet.

The man held his arms up, pleading for mercy in his native language. Duncan was being intentionally rough with the older man, shoving him forward toward the first container.

"What is this for?" he screamed at the old man.

He responded in Korean, again appearing to plead for mercy.

"Park, ask him!" shouted Duncan.

Park and the man began to rapidly converse in Korean. Throughout the brief conversation, the man would look in the direction of Duncan, who provided a death stare in return. The man began to sob and then fell to his knees.

"What's his problem?" Duncan asked brusquely.

"He's afraid you'll return him to North Korea," replied Park.

"The DPRK?"

"Yeah. These men are scientists, and this, my friend, is a satellite destined for Tehran. The Iranians are apparently in the satellite business with Pyongyang, and if this guy is telling the truth, they have been for years."

CHAPTER 15

November 4
Silent Wings Museum
Lubbock, Texas

Major stood toward the rear of the Silent Wings Museum in Lubbock, a facility built in 2002 to honor the former pilots of the U.S. Army and Air Force's Glider Program utilized in World War II. Their first goal had been to restore the WACO CG-4A glider and display it inside the museum. The facility became an instant local attraction for visitors.

Major understood politics enough to know that Governor Marion Burnett was about to speak to some of her staunchest supporters. As politics go, Texas was a deep red state, and the Texas Panhandle was the reddest of the red. In a statewide race, Governor Burnett would focus most of her attention on the parts of the state where so-called independents were abundant, like the counties surrounding large metropolitan areas in Dallas/Fort Worth, Houston, and Austin.

This trip to Lubbock was about getting out the votes in the final days of the campaign and pocketing a few campaign donations for her trouble. Major had his check in his pocket and looked forward to talking with his old friend.

"My family has been in Texas for generations," said Governor Burnett as she started into her stump speech. "At the Four Sixes ranch, we started a legacy of cattle, horses, and oil, which continues to this day. Over time, we've grown to nearly three hundred thousand acres here in the Texas Panhandle, and as I look out into the crowd of friendly and familiar faces, I couldn't be prouder to say I'm a Texan!"

Major applauded along with the rest of the crowd. He too recognized a lot of the faces who were here to pay their respects to the governor looking for a second term. Governor Burnett had done a fine job, in his opinion, and was deserving of re-election. Personally, he thought her rhetoric regarding secession was a little over the top, but he understood politicians felt the need to toss red meat to their loyal base.

"As your Texas land commissioner, I was part of this new generation of Texas leadership that fought against the overbearing federal government through their illegal land grabs by the Bureau of Land Management. When those lefty environmentalists entered our state with their high-powered lawyers from California, I stood up to their radical agendas and the trial lawyers' abuse of the Endangered Species Act. And when social justice warriors tried to tear down our historic symbols in the name of political correctness, I said *no, not on my watch!*"

The room burst into a higher level of excitement as the governor continued. She turned to point to a large banner behind her, which was a replica of the Texas state flag. The words *Texas Strong! Texas Free!* were emblazoned across the front of the banner. The room took her cue and began shouting.

"Texas strong! Texas free!"

"Texas strong! Texas free!"

Major didn't join in the chants, but he did study the crowd. He marveled at how high passions ran on both sides of issues. He was sure that somewhere in the south of Texas, Governor Burnett's opponent had whipped his constituents into a similar frenzy screaming *La Raza*, which was Spanish for *the race*. It had become the battle cry of those promoting open borders and unfettered immigration into the United States.

"As governor, I've pushed back against Washington. While our friends in the federal government refuse to even consider adopting policies of self-reliance, Texas continues to maintain its own power grid completely separate from the rest of the country. While this administration refuses to prepare for the threats we face from countries around the world who don't like us very much, Texas has adopted policies that will protect all Texans, including those who oppose me, in the event a catastrophic event tears down the nation's power grid. While Washington sticks its head in the sand like an ostrich, Texans can go to sleep at night knowing that this governor has done her part in protecting the lifeblood of any modern society— the electric grid!"

More raucous applause came from the crowd, and Major even clapped a little louder. Throughout its history, Texas had been fiercely independent. As he and Lucy had adopted a preparedness lifestyle, one that was devoted to the concept of self-reliance under all contingencies, he began to appreciate the work done by Governor Burnett and past Texas governors regarding power grid protection and reliability.

Cooper entered through the front door and craned his neck to look for his father. Major had dropped him off at the neurologist's office a short distance away to see if he could get an appointment on short notice. Major waved his son over as the governor continued.

"Wow, Daddy, it's loud in here," said Cooper as he slid past a group to join his father.

"Yeah, Marion is doing what she does best, whippin' 'em into a frenzy. Did you get to see the doctor?"

"Not yet, but we can stop by in an hour. Will we be done here?"

"Yeah, she's winding it up now."

Governor Burnett continued. "Unlike other states, Texas has broken away from Washington's control. Other states have become dependent on DC dollars to meet their budget shortfalls. Not in Texas, no, sirree! We balance our budgets on our own. If we can't afford to spend on something, we wait until we can.

"You see, Washington has imposed its will on the states of this great nation as they govern with a carrot and a stick. You know. Do it our way, and we'll give you a carrot. But if you push back or refuse to follow their demands, they'll give you the stick."

The crowd began to boo, and Cooper chuckled as he looked up to his father. Major managed a smile and shook his head at the spectacle of politics.

"Well, Washington, I've got a message for you. You can keep your carrot, and guess what? Our stick's bigger than your stick! And why's that, my friends?"

Governor Burnett held one hand up to her ear and leaned into the crowd, which immediately answered her question.

They crowed at the top of their lungs. "Because everything's bigger in Texas!"

"You're dang straight!" the governor shouted in return. "God bless you, my fellow Texans. Together, we will make Texas stronger than ever!"

The chants began again as Governor Burnett entered the crowd to shake hands.

"Texas strong! Texas free!"

"Texas strong! Texas free!"

CHAPTER 16

November 4
Lubbock Neurology Clinic
Lubbock, Texas

As they approached the Lubbock Neurology Clinic, Major asked his son, "So, whadya think of the governor?"

"She's really nice. Y'all have known each other since before she got into politics?"

"Quite a long time, actually," replied Major. "As you know, the Four Sixes ranch is located just east of here in Guthrie on the road to Wichita Falls. Our families have helped one another for decades."

"Was she like this before she became land commissioner and then governor?" asked Cooper.

"Marion was always strong-willed. Since she entered politics, she's become hard-nosed. In some respects, almost coldhearted."

"Whadya mean?" asked Cooper.

"She's very tough on illegal immigration, Coop. Don't get me wrong. I know those ranchers along the border had their hands full before the border wall was completed. Trust me, it would break my heart to see the dead bodies of those poor souls who made it all this way only to die of dehydration or at the hands of the traffickers."

"Once the wall was built, she stopped the illegal immigration. They could, however, still apply for citizenship, right? How's that coldhearted?"

"It wasn't that. It was her deportation methods. Listen, let's not get into all of this today. Why trouble ourselves with things we can't control, right?"

71

Cooper pointed his father into the parking lot, and Major wheeled the big truck into two vacant parking spaces far away from the entrance. "I'm guessin' politics is not in your future."

"No way, Daddy. What I saw was no different than an evangelical preacher under a tent handlin' snakes. She had those folks so worked up that if she shouted march to Washington and shoot all the politicians, they would've done it!"

"Coop, I wonder sometimes," muttered his father.

Cooper led the way into the Lubbock Neurology Clinic, which was nationally known for its state-of-the-art diagnostic equipment and neurotrauma care.

After Cooper signed in, he and his father sat alone in the waiting area like a couple of old men waiting for the next available barber. After several minutes of silence, Cooper spoke up.

"Daddy, you and I have made a lot of secret deals the last few days."

"That we have, son."

"Listen, you can't let Riley or Palmer know that you've come with me today. We, um, have this secret deal of our own."

Major began to laugh. "Doesn't appear this family is very good at keeping secrets."

Cooper continued. "Well, it's not a big one, but we kinda have a kids' pact that what happens on the road stays on the road. You know, like the folks in Vegas are always saying."

"Okay, so what are you sayin'?" asked Major.

"Well, when they took me to the hospital, after I woke up, I made them both swear to live up to our pact. And they did. So I can't have you tellin' them you know about what happened. Okay?"

Major busted out laughing so loud that the receptionists rose out of their chairs to see what the uproar was. Major surmised it wasn't likely that many neurology patients had much to laugh about. He held his hands up to indicate to them everything was okay.

"What?" asked Cooper.

"Son, your sister spilled the beans to Miss Lucy the next day. Let's just say a mother's intuition is most often right, and no child can withstand your momma's interrogation techniques."

Cooper shook his head. "Are you referring to *the look*?"

"That's the one. She's used *the look* on me for as long as we've known one another, which is why I had to fib to her after the lights were turned out the night y'all came home. I reckon she didn't buy it for one second."

"Great," said Cooper with a laugh. "Palmer broke the code."

"Actually, son, you did first, remember?"

Cooper threw himself back in the seat and laughed. "I reckon I did."

A nurse entered the waiting room. "Mr. Armstrong?"

Father and son responded in unison, "Yes?"

The nurse studied them both and said, "I need the Mr. Armstrong with the busted noggin'."

Cooper and Major pointed at one another. "That's him."

The nurse grinned, rolled her eyes, and motioned for the guys to join her. Major thought to himself, *No sense of humor around here.*

*****

"Cooper, you're a grown man and I can only caution you on what's best based upon your injury," started the doctor. "There is no way that I can sign off on a rodeo event for you in a week. Granted, your injury was minor compared to others; we still need to follow a post-concussive protocol."

"Doc, we went through the list of symptoms," Cooper protested. "You said the neck pain was the only thing of concern. That's getting better every day."

"That's good, and your recovery is remarkable considering you were kicked by a pissed-off bull. When dealing with post-concussion syndrome, those initial weeks are critical. Some people may have the telltale signs such as headaches, dizziness, or vision problems right away. For others, the symptoms don't manifest themselves for weeks."

"Okay, I understand." Cooper was clearly dejected. If he couldn't ride at the next rodeo, that gave him only one more chance at the Calgary Stampede on Thanksgiving weekend. There would be no margin for error.

"Cooper, you have to be very careful over the next several weeks," the doctor continued. "Experiencing a second concussion in this time frame, what we call second impact syndrome, before the signs and symptoms of your first trauma have been resolved, could result in rapid and sometimes fatal brain swelling. A concussion, even a minor one like yours, changes the levels of brain chemicals. It usually takes a week for these levels to stabilize again, but recovery time varies. From my examination of you, I believe you're on the road to recovery, just don't exacerbate your injury."

Cooper shut down, so Major addressed the neurologist.

"Doctor, I can speak for my son and assure you he will heal fully before he gets anywhere near a bull or I'll knock him upside the head myself."

The doctor laughed, and even Cooper managed a smile. During his quiet moment, he was calculating.

Let's see. I got kicked on October twenty-ninth. Today's November fourth. That's seven days. If I skip the next ride, that takes me all the way to Thanksgiving, which is the twenty-fourth. That's twenty more days, for a total of twenty-seven. That's pert near a month. I'll be good to go!

The doctor and his father were still making small talk as a wide grin crossed Cooper Armstrong's face.

CHAPTER 17

November 5
Home of Secretary of Defense Montgomery Gregg
Georgetown
Washington, DC

Secretary Gregg asked his wife to turn in without him. She'd learned over their thirty years of marriage not to question her husband when he became this serious. The Secretary was loyal to all who returned the favor, and Mrs. Gregg never once wondered if he had strayed. Since their arrival, the late evening visits from mysterious men had become commonplace. She didn't question him, and he never volunteered to tell her the subject matter.

A steady rap at the door indicated his guests had arrived. Secretary Gregg lifted himself out of the leather chair, which flanked the large stone fireplace in his study. He allowed the cigar to burn, the smoke easily finding its way to a heat source and up the chimney. Secretary Gregg was not a drinker, but he allowed himself a quality cigar from time to time, when the mood warranted.

He opened the heavy oak door and welcomed in his guests—the most frequent visitors to the Gregg home in Georgetown. He nodded to his security team and closed the doors behind the two men, who quickly moved into the foyer and began to remove their overcoats. Washington had experienced a cooling trend as November arrived.

"Monty, thank you for seeing us on short notice," said Carl Braun, the director of the Special Activities Division of the National Clandestine Service, who was arguably the nation's top spy. Braun had spent his entire career in government service within the FBI,

CIA and now as head of the Special Activities Division of the NCS.

"Of course," said Secretary Gregg. He extended his hand to shake Braun's. Then he addressed Braun's companion, Billy Yancey, a fellow Texan and head of the Political Action Group, or PAG, within the NCS. PAG was responsible for covert activities related to political regime change, economic warfare, and psychological operations. Secretary Gregg was surprised at the unannounced attendance of his old friend.

"Billy, didn't expect to see you tonight."

"Hello, Monty," said Yancey. "There's been a game-changer, and it requires a conversation between all of us."

"Us?" asked Secretary Gregg as he led the men into his study. He reached for his cigar box and opened the lid, offering one to his guests. They both passed.

"Monty, based upon this conversation, we may have to go to others whose departments are directly impacted by our decision."

"Sounds serious. Take a seat, gentlemen, and tell me what's happened."

To most Americans, the government was run by a large, wholly encompassing federal government whose tentacles controlled most aspects of our daily lives. What didn't fall under the purview of Washington was delegated to the fifty states.

Very little happened in an individual's daily activities that wasn't controlled by, or supplemented with, government actions. What most Americans suspect, but can't necessarily prove, was that there was a cabal, of sorts, deeply rooted in the administrative apparatus of Washington, that operated independently of the elected officials who run the government.

These long-term, career public servants achieved a position of power by sheer longevity in their positions, or through the careful exploitation of the system, which allowed for the acquisition of power. Political scientists and foreign policy experts have referred to these individuals as being part of the *deep state*, a term used to describe those who exercise power independent of, and oftentimes in contravention of, elected political leaders.

Secretary Gregg, Undersecretary Yancey, and Director Braun were not only part of the deep state, they were three of a dozen who acted as final decision makers. When Braun called the meeting, Secretary Gregg knew it was important. When Billy Yancey showed up at the front door, it meant the subject matter most likely meant one thing— North Korea.

"I'll get right to it, Monty," started Braun. "Two of our field operatives were on post in the Gulf of Oman and participated in a VBSS of a Singapore-flagged freighter we've had the NSA monitoring. There was a container and two passengers under South Korean passports added to the ship's manifest at the eleventh hour, which caught the eye of a CIA analyst."

"What did they find?" asked Secretary Gregg.

"In addition to the two North Korean scientists, the container held parts for a medium-sized, low-earth orbiting satellite," replied Braun.

"Destination?"

"We believe they were headed for Iran," Braun replied. "During the initial interrogation, the scientists admitted that Pyongyang has been working with Tehran for years on their satellite program. Once we got them under the microscope in one of our dark facilities, they told us about a technology-sharing arrangement between the DPRK and Iran."

"That explains how North Korea's nuclear program advanced so rapidly during the period from 2010 through 2016," added Secretary Gregg. "We always suspected as much, but Iran was hands-off during those years, if you remember."

"As a result," added Yancey, "we have a nuclear Iran and North Korea, both of which are now increasing their nuclear weapons stockpiles in complete defiance of those idiots in the United Nations."

Secretary Gregg put out his cigar and tossed it into the fireplace. "Okay, so how is the satellite a game-changer? I mean, both countries have been launching satellites for years."

"It confirms that the nations are trading technology and actively working together," replied Braun.

"And, I might add, it provides a potential weapon for both countries to be used against the West—an EMP," said Yancey.

"Do you think they have the technology to strap a nuclear warhead to a satellite?" asked Secretary Gregg.

Braun nodded. "According to our singing scientists, they've already done it. But let me say this. Towards the end of our enhanced interrogation techniques, those two might have admitted to being space aliens. That said, all the pieces of the puzzle seem to fit."

Secretary Gregg rolled his head around his shoulders and stood to stare out onto Thirty-Fifth Street. With his back to his guests, he asked, "Why hasn't *little un* pulled the trigger. He's been blustering for years."

"We think he's waiting until his nuclear arsenal is sufficient to back us down in case we threaten to retaliate," replied Braun. "Taking down a nation's power grid is one thing, nukin' the hell out of 'em is another."

"Ironic, isn't it?" asked Secretary Gregg rhetorically. "He takes the same position as our president. Those two should get together."

Braun reached into his coat pocket and removed a sterling silver flask. He took a swig of the brandy and offered it to Yancey, who declined.

Braun continued. "The theory is that an electromagnetic pulse attack is a nonlethal use of a nuclear weapon. It doesn't result in direct loss of life."

"So naïve," muttered Secretary Gregg, who finally turned around and returned to his seat. He looked to his friend from Texas. "Billy, you haven't had much to say thus far. I take it you're not along for the ride."

"That's right, Monty. I have a proposal."

Secretary Gregg spread his arms out in front of him. "Let's hear it."

"We take him out," Yancey replied.

Secretary Gregg shrugged and then chuckled. "A first strike? The president wouldn't even consider it."

"No, Monty. We'll send in a team to assassinate Kim Jong-un."

"Come on, guys," said Secretary Gregg. "With all due respect, the DMZ is full of the graves of commandos who've tried to kill the Great Leader, or Dear Leader, or any other members of the Kim dynasty for decades."

"Hear me out, Monty," said Yancey. "We've got an angle."

"It better be a good one."

"We've got a mole, an accomplice, if you will. High up and close to Kim Jong-un."

Secretary Gregg laughed again. "Who? One of his wives? A concubine? They know nothing of his activities."

"Nope, better than that," replied Yancey. "His most trusted advisor, friend, and family member. Someone who wants the reins but who is interested in another path for the Hermit Kingdom."

Secretary Gregg suddenly got very serious. He sat forward in his chair and looked both men in the eye.

"Are you kidding me? You turned little sis, Kim Yo-jong. No way!"

"We have," replied Yancey. "She will work with us to eliminate her brother from power so that she can lead the country. There are conditions, namely related to autonomy and protection from the south and China. But we can make it happen."

"Why doesn't she just do it herself?" asked Secretary Gregg.

"It has to be from the outside; otherwise her transition would be doomed from the beginning," replied Braun.

"When?"

"With your approval, we'll set the plan in motion for immediate implementation," replied Braun.

Secretary Gregg reached for another cigar, cut off the end and lit it, allowing a cloud of smoke to float into the air, reminiscent of a nuclear explosion.

"Let's put a plan together!"

PART TWO

CHAPTER 18

November 6
The Armstrong Ranch
Borden County, Texas

Roscoe Pops Armstrong, a lifelong teetotaler, had a saying—*there are only two liquids in my life, water and oil. My body is made up of one, and usually I'm held hostage by the other.* Tens of thousands of wells dotted the Texas landscape, some drilled in areas the Spaniards once declared to be *desplobado*, or no-man's land. These parts of Texas were so dry nothing could survive because they lacked one crucial element of life—water.

Borden County, Texas, nearly a third of which was made up of the Armstrong Ranch, was part of the Southern High Plains, an area encompassing eastern New Mexico and into the Western Panhandles of Oklahoma and Texas.

In most years, the geographic region receives about twenty-four inches of rain. The vast majority of the precipitation on the Southern High Plains never reaches the ground, having been lost to evaporation in the upper atmosphere. The water-challenged plains are dominated by tall prairie grasses, creosote bushes and mesquite plants. It was the visionary rancher who bought up land along the meandering rivers and lakes of the Panhandle to irrigate their fields and provide ground water to their wells.

When Pops purchased this part of the Armstrong Ranch in the late fifties at a bank foreclosure, the water levels of the river were much higher. A single windmill stood on the tract and was restored by Pops in the sixties.

Only sixty feet from the river, the well had been drilled to seventy feet, which was great news for Armstrong Ranch. With the ground water at such a shallow depth, they would be able to expand their oil production as well as provide enough water to expand the grazing areas of their steers. He was able to triple the size of this herd.

Major insisted on keeping the windmill and the well operable despite the fact it pumped a meager five gallons per minute into the water trough that fed Miss Lucy's barnyard critters. He considered the windmill and its riverside location to be a sacred spot, one that symbolized the waters necessary to sustain the lives within his charge.

Over the years, the river began to recede as more landowners upriver toward Lubbock began to divide up the resource and depleted it for their own ranching operations and oil wells. This issue began to create friction between the ranchers. Ranchers who had mineral rights were able to sell that precious water for a dollar a barrel to an oil company for use in drilling. Each well could use as much as two million gallons of water, the state's rarest of assets.

Soon the state established laws and guidelines to prevent the unlawful overuse of the precious resource. The Armstrong family, through Pops, stood at the forefront of the effort and used their influence on the Texas land commissioner to marshal this precious asset in Borden County.

As a result, they became stewards of the Colorado River in the county, and the state granted them an additional fourteen hundred acres, which encompassed nearly half of Natural Dam Lake. In exchange, the Armstrongs agreed to keep the river flowing into the lake free of obstructions and debris.

Major and Cooper stood next to one another under the branches of a cottonwood, marveling at the workmanship of the beaver colony. The water had backed up, creating a half-acre lake that caused the water levels to rise near the windmill.

"It's a shame we have to do this," started Cooper. "I wish we could harness the energy of these little guys. They get more work done in a day than half a dozen of Preacher's boys."

"C'mon now, lay off the ranch hands, unless you wanna do their work for 'em," said Major, who had always been appreciative of the Armstrong employees. He prided himself in creating loyal, long-term ranch hands, rare in this day of low unemployment across Texas.

Labor had never been a problem for him as a result. For many ranches operating on thin margins, there was the temptation to hire illegals and pay them cash. Major didn't want to embarrass himself and the family by going against the governor. She'd provided his family too many accommodations in the past, such as the land grant for half of the lake, to insult her over saving a few bucks on labor.

"What's the plan, Daddy?" asked Riley, who had just arrived in the farm truck, a beat-up Chevy that was used to drop hay bales around the ranch in remote locations. "Are we gonna blast 'em?"

"What?" asked Major. "Do you wanna blast the beavers or the dam?"

Riley kicked at some rocks in the dust near his feet, clearly feeling the brunt of his father's admonishing tone. "Nah, Daddy. It's just that I was reading up about explosives on the internet last night. Did y'all know that you can purchase everything you need to make a bomb on Amazon?"

"Come on, Riley," said Cooper with a laugh.

"It's true, Coop. There are certain ingredients that are innocent on their own, but when combined together, they produce explosives. You can buy the ingredients to make black powder, thermite, steel ball bearings for shrapnel, igniters, and even remote detonators."

"Son, we have plenty of explosives around here to deal with prairie dogs and tree stumps."

Cooper added, "Momma hates us blowin' up the prairie dogs, but I swear the little devils are born pregnant. It's amazing how fast they breed."

"Well, not to mention they carry diseases like the plague," said Major. "That's the last thing we need around here."

"No kiddin'," said Cooper, turning his attention back to the beaver dam. "That ammonium nitrate does the trick. Why don't we just use it on the beaver dam?"

Major looked behind him and around the gently sloped landscape that rose up from the river. "Because Miss Lucy threatened me within an inch of my life this morning that we better not take out any beavers in the process. It wouldn't surprise me if she was out here somewhere, watching."

"I'm tellin' y'all, we could blow up the dam with those ingredients from Amazon and not have to use the big stuff like what we keep in the shed," interjected Riley.

Major put his arm around Riley's shoulders. "Son, I'm no expert on using the internet like you and your momma. Google is my friend when I want to research something. I have my favorite websites I visit to get the news from different perspectives, knowing full well you can't believe everything you read on the internet."

"I know that, Daddy."

"Here's something I hope you've learned," Major continued. "There's something on these websites called *cookies*. Do you know what that means?"

"Yes, sir. It's when you visit a site, the internet sites kind of follow you around, suggesting similar websites or advertisers. Why do you ask?"

Major stifled a laugh. "Well, son, are you desirous of importing yourself a Korean bride? I mean, ain't we got enough pretty Texas girls to choose from?"

Cooper crashed against the side of the truck, laughing hysterically. He could barely spit out the words. "Korean. Brides. Really?"

"No, well, it's not like that, y'all," protested Riley. "Once, I accidentally clicked on a picture of this girl. I mean, dang it, Coop, shut up!"

Cooper was still laughing so hard he had to wipe the tears away from his face.

Riley took off his cowboy hat and slapped his leg with it. His face was beet red with embarrassment.

"Now, listen up, boys," Major began as he tried to diffuse the situation before Riley got mad at his brother. "Miss Lucy has lived with a family of boys since the day I married her. And that includes your sister, who's pert near a boy herself. She's seen plenty from all of us, and she decided early on that being surrounded by cowboys was the life she wanted. But do me a favor, stay off the Korean bride websites, and know this, the first half-naked woman that shows up on Miss Lucy's iPad will result in a row none of us wanna be a part of, am I clear?"

"Yes, sir," replied Riley sheepishly. He always took criticism hard.

"Coop, that applies to you as well, son."

"Loud and clear, Daddy." Cooper gave his brother a playful shove. "Let's get to work. How do you wanna do this?"

The rumble of heavy machinery could be heard coming over the hill. Years ago, Major had gone to an equipment auction and invested in a backhoe as well as a Bobcat. These became indispensable tools on the ranch for fencing, spreading manure in the garden, and now, beaver dam modification.

"Boys, we're gonna leave the dam in place," started Major, who quickly continued when he saw the puzzled looks on the boys' faces. "My agreement with the state is to keep the water flowing in the lake. It isn't to blow up beaver dams. Do you see how much water has accumulated upriver in a short period of time?"

The water had risen several feet, causing a newly formed lake of nearly an acre. As the water rose, the beavers built the structure higher.

"I know, it's amazing," said Riley.

Preacher and the ranch hands pulled alongside the farm truck and began to unload ten-foot sections of PVC pipe.

"I'm always thinking ahead, boys," said Major. "You never know when circumstances might dictate that we control the flow of water for our own benefit. Governments change their minds, and you can find yourself at their mercy. I think it would be wise to take advantage of what our beaver friends have done, and prepare for unforeseen events."

Cooper turned to watch the guys unload. "What's all that stuff for?"

"Today, we're gonna install what's called a beaver pipe. They're usually used to prevent beavers from damming up the water. We'll install it for that purpose, except with a slight modification. If the time comes that we need to shut off the downriver flow, we'll be able to cap the pipe and allow the water to accumulate here, for the benefit of our ranch."

"How's it work?" asked Riley.

"We'll use the backhoe to cut a notch in the beaver dam near the bank. This will work to drain the water levels into the lake. Then, we'll insert the pipes into the notch and secure them with steel fence posts to create a gradual drop from the higher ground toward the lake. On the river side, we'll cap the pipe at a level that allows for the water to back up and create our lake."

"Won't the beavers try to repair the breach?" asked Cooper.

"I'm countin' on it. Once it's installed, we'll stand out of the way and let the beavers do the rest. As the water begins to flow through the notch, the beavers will quickly move to stop the flow over and around the pipes, sealing them under the dam. The water level will rise once again, and when it reaches our pipe, it will begin to flow down toward the lake. We will have built a new lake, yet allowed the free flow of water to be in compliance with the state mandate."

Cooper shook his head in disbelief. "This is brilliant, and just in time for the winter snows, which fill the river anyway."

"Here's the thing, boys," started Major. "Your momma and I have adopted a mindset. A way of thinking that goes beyond living our day-to-day lives. It involves planning, preparation, and in a way, prognostication."

"Like a crystal ball?" asked Riley.

"I guess you could say that," replied his dad. "It's like adopting a certain mentality, I guess. Like most aspects of your life, it comes down to making choices. Years ago, we committed to a self-sustainable, preparedness lifestyle. We took the best of Lucy's homesteading techniques, coupled it with preparedness tips I'd picked up over the years, and combined it into a well-organized plan designed to keep us safe if something bad happens around us."

"Bad, like catastrophic?" asked Cooper.

"That's right, Coop. Listen, I've always allowed you boys to give me a hard time about watching the news and keeping up with world events. But the fact of the matter is we live in dangerous times. Our nation faces many threats, both man-made from countries who hate us and natural disasters. Miss Lucy and I recognized years ago, especially after 9/11, that our personal lives are subject to unexpected setbacks and our world is fraught with danger. We decided then to protect our family against all possible threats. We love you boys, as well as Duncan and Palmer. If the crap hits the fan, we'll be ready. Make sense?"

Cooper and Riley looked at one another and nodded. The boys began to understand where their father was coming from.

"Here's the thing, guys. The day before catastrophic events occurred—from Pearl Harbor, to 9/11, to that massive tsunami in Japan—folks were going about their daily lives, not giving a second thought to what might turn their world upside down. All I'm saying is that when it comes to catastrophic events, we never know when the day before is the day before. So we prepare for tomorrow."

CHAPTER 19

November 6
Texas Gubernatorial Debate
KERA-TV Studios
Dallas, Texas

After a long day of swiping away pesky beavers and sloshing through the muddy bottom of the Colorado River, the beaver pipe was installed, and the guys found their way back to the house. It was eight o'clock by the time they'd cleaned up and finished dinner. Miss Lucy entered the family room with mugs of coffee and hot chocolate for everyone, as the temperatures that night dipped down into the mid-forties.

Major had tuned the DirecTV to the local Lubbock station to settle in for the final debate between Governor Burnett and her opponent. Governor Burnett, as the incumbent enjoyed a comfortable lead in the polls and barring an unforced error, would easily win on election day.

The debate had been uneventful and lacked a game-changing moment. The narrators, all Dallas television news hosts, had been relatively fair in their questioning. The next issue to discuss, Texas power grid independence, was intended to show the divide between the two candidates on the future of ERCOT, the Electric Reliability Council of Texas.

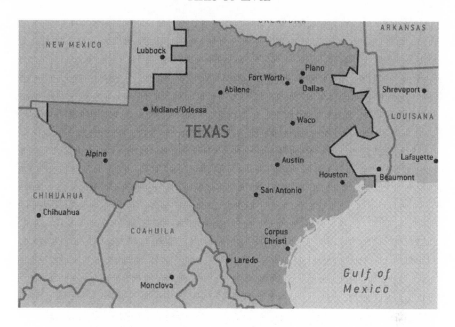

"Governor Burnett, this question is for you," said the moderator.

Governor Burnett smiled and readied herself by taking a drink of water.

"ERCOT manages the flow of electricity to twenty-eight million Texans, or ninety percent of the state. This independent system manages forty-six thousand miles of transmission lines and nearly six hundred generation units. Many experts have claimed that ERCOT's ability to produce cost-effective energy with a low environmental impact is admirable, but that the state, and you in particular, should be chastised for not sharing with others, namely the western and eastern interconnected grid, which serves much of the continental United States. How do you respond, Governor?"

"Well, it's no secret that Texas has a bit of an independent streak," started Governor Burnett to the chuckle of the small audience packed into the newly built auditorium at KERA-TV just for this purpose. "I have to give credit to prior administrations for following this path of independence in creating a power grid that was not beholden to the federal government. When President Roosevelt signed the revised Federal Power Act in 1935, yet another in a long line of socialist power grabs, pardon the pun, in response to the

Great Depression, Texas utilities came together and avoided crossing state lines. Throughout our history as a state, we've believed that freedom from federal regulation was a cherished goal. Our state has been built upon a mindset of self-reliance, and the energy companies in those early days relied upon our abundance of coal, natural gas, and petroleum resources to fuel our power plants."

"Governor, may I interrupt you there," said the moderator.

"It appears you just did," Governor Burnett bristled. She had little use for the media, whether friend or foe.

"Governor, there have been occasions where Texas was forced to call upon other, adjacent utilities for power when ERCOT customers were underserved."

"That is true, and it has happened on rare occasion, which is why we maintain a working relationship with our partners in El Paso, Lubbock, and Beaumont to pick up the slack. Despite those isolated regions being outside of the ERCOT power network, we do help one another at times."

"What about Mexico?" asked the moderator.

"What about Mexico?" Governor Burnett fired back. She took another drink of water and glanced over at her opponent, addressing him directly. "Am I debating you or these people?"

The debate moderator continued. "Governor, there have been occasions where ERCOT has received power from Mexico, correct?"

"Sure, once, so let's not overexaggerate, shall we? In 2011, a decade or more ago, the state experienced rolling blackouts and imported some power from Mexico. At the time, ERCOT had three ties to the grid in Mexico, and the governor elected to tap into that resource for a short-term fix. That has not happened since, and ERCOT has taken measures to prevent it from happening again."

"Governor, are you opposed to the Southern Cross project, which has been endorsed by your opponent?" asked the moderator. The Southern Cross project was a proposed transmission line capable of transferring enough electricity for hundreds of thousands of homes between East Texas and Mississippi. The project was to be financed by private investors and carried a two-billion-dollar price tag.

Southern Cross had been proposed by the Department of Energy to help Mississippi and Louisiana recover from hurricanes.

The governor responded without hesitation. "I've been clearly against it. Listen, I'm sorry for the problems our neighboring states might have following a storm. We've had our share, and Texans always pull together to help one another. From the first time I announced my run for the governor's office, I let Texans know who I was and what I stood for. I stand for Texas and Texans. What happens beyond our borders is not my concern. You can call me isolationist, selfish, a horrible person, I don't really care what names or labels you throw at me. Blowing out someone else's candles won't make yours shine any brighter."

Governor Burnett leaned forward into the camera, revealed her toothy, signature smile, and paused before finishing her statement. "A strong, self-reliant Texas is a free Texas. Texans who agree with me will vote their conscience on Tuesday, you can take that to the bank."

CHAPTER 20

November 7
Oval Office
The White House
Washington, DC

President Harman studied the faces of her chief of staff, Charles Acton, and her chief political strategist, Jackie Jennings, a longtime political operative who had worked for campaigns on both sides of the aisle and was known for candid, apolitical analysis of any issue that an administration faced.

Her closest confidants had arrived prior to the President's Daily Brief in order to inform her of an early morning vote at the United Nations General Assembly. As the verbal battle escalated between the United States and North Korea, news surfaced that Kim Jong-un had ordered another intercontinental ballistic missile test.

After the president had been sworn in, she immediately labeled the North Korean hostilities the biggest threat to America's sovereignty in modern times. At the time, she drew the proverbial line in the sand, stating that further ICBM testing by Kim would be met with military force in the form of U.S. missile defense systems shooting down their rockets.

Since that statement, the North Koreans had tested their ICBM missiles twice, and the president stood down. Now they were readying a third launch in seven months, and the president ordered the ambassador to the United Nations to take action.

The UN ambassador lobbied the Association of Southeast Asian Nations, or ASEAN, to stand with the United States in approving new sanctions against the Pyongyang government. The proposed resolution would ban North Korean imports of coal, iron, lead, iron ore, and seafood products that were worth over a billion dollars a year to the North Korean economy.

This embargo on a third of the nation's gross domestic product represented the single largest set of sanctions ever leveled against the dictator. The U.S. ambassador argued to the Southeast Asian countries that the threat of a rogue nation like North Korea would impact all of them if war broke out in the region. She also encouraged them to discourage any joint venture agreements with North Korean companies.

Harman stood in front of her desk and waited for her advisors to take seats opposite one another on the sofas. Neither spoke up, so she started the conversation.

"Well? Out with it. What happened?" she demanded.

Chief of Staff Acton spoke first. "Not good, Madame President. The entire assembly turned against us. The measure was soundly defeated."

"You've got to be kidding," said President Harman, both confused and angry. "We had the support of ASEAN, the countries in the region who stand the most to lose if war breaks out."

"The vote was one-ninety-one to two. Only Israel stood with us."

President Harman shook her head in disbelief and fell into a wing chair between the two sofas. Her slumped posture was indicative of her mood.

"It actually gets worse, Madame President," started Jennings. "The Secretary General issued a stunning rebuke of our request. He urged us to stop taking advantage of the international community's goodwill with continued provocations of the North. He said that we've, quote, *engaged in harmful verbal discourse against North Korea*, and that none of our fears have materialized."

Jennings stopped and gestured to Acton to elaborate.

"Our belief is the Chinese have flexed their muscle in favor of their ally. They've been actively working behind the scenes with their Southeast Asia neighbors, both politically and economically. At this point, only the Philippines, South Korea, and Japan stand with us."

"With the Philippines and South Korea gradually distancing themselves from our hard-line policy," interjected Jennings, "the fact of the matter is we've complained for decades about the North Korean nuclear program, and nothing has come to fruition. I believe we've screamed fire in the movie theater once too often."

President Harman stood up and retrieved a bottled water from her desk. She stared out the windows of the Oval Office onto the South Lawn, where the leaves had changed color and begun to fall.

"The world has turned against us," she surmised. "Just that quickly."

Acton continued with his analysis. "Madame President, this would have been the eighth round of sanctions imposed upon the DPRK, none of which have deterred their nuclear goals. We have taken every step imaginable to stem the advance of their ICBM and nuclear program, to no avail."

"Jackie, how is this playing in the polling and focus groups?" asked the president, who was always aware of the political ramifications of every decision she made.

"First, with respect to today's vote, it won't impact your favorables at all and will have no impact on the midterms tomorrow," responded Jennings. "This issue is more a long-term one."

President Harman addressed her advisors. "I'm getting pressure from the Pentagon. My whole national security team is urging us to take action to stop the proliferation. And based upon this morning's UN lack of action, we apparently are on an island here, all alone with our loyal and faithful friends in Jerusalem. I've got to make a decision here."

"Do you?" asked Jennings.

The president tilted her head slightly, trying to discern the meaning of the question.

Jennings continued. "I mean, really? Do you need to make a decision? For nearly four decades, presidents have made the same moves you have with respect to North Korea—public statements, back-channel negotiations, and UN sanctions. Nothing has worked, yet nothing has happened either. Why not continue to play this charade with Kim Jong-un?"

"Madame President," interrupted Acton, "I think Jackie may have a point. We're in a catch-22 when it comes to North Korea, and the world knows it. If we undertake a first strike, world opinion may come down on us hard, or worse. China may stand up for their ally and retaliate on their behalf. North Korea will go after the South and Japan. Iran may use our weakened condition and decide to take on Israel and the Saudis. Who knows what the Russians might do?"

"I get it, a first strike may bring matters to a head, but we may not be pleased with the results," said the president. "Secretary Gregg and his staff will have the floor during today's PDB to outline our first-strike options and our defensive positioning. Let's see what he has to say, and then we'll make a decision that's based upon military options and additional diplomatic approaches."

CHAPTER 21

November 7
Roosevelt Room
The White House
Washington, DC

Only students of history and military strategists fully understood North Korea's attitude toward the rest of the world. Most don't realize the tiny nation's moniker as the *Hermit Kingdom* applied long before it's modern isolationist policies of the last seventy years.

For centuries, Korea had been under siege by the Mongols, who slaughtered two hundred thousand men, women and children as they embarked upon their East Asian scorched-earth conquests. Then the Manchu invasions from China in the sixteen hundreds replaced repeated Japanese wars that plagued the Korean peninsula.

This was a nation that knew nothing but war. But it wasn't until the last great power clash after World War II when Soviet and American political leaders agreed to divide the Korean peninsula along the thirty-eighth parallel in the name of peace that North Korea truly pulled within itself and gave rise to the Kim dynasties for decades to come.

Beginning with Kim Il Sung's repeated provocative actions against South Korea, through the rhetoric of the Kim Jong-un regime, the DPRK dictators had shown little regard for global political opinion and even less for the lives of the North Korean people. The regimes had adopted a communist-style division system, which had failed miserably. Kim Jong-un's only means upon which to hold power was to isolate his people from outside influences and continue to blame others, namely the United States, for the people's poor living conditions. By casting blame everywhere else and instilling fear of military attacks upon their country, Pyongyang rallied its people against a common enemy for the hope of a better life someday.

In 1951, during the Korean War, when General Douglas MacArthur was unceremoniously dumped by President Harry Truman for insubordination—he dared to disagree with the president publicly on the progress of the war—he was very vocal in stating the United States should drive the communists from the North to create a stable, unified Korean Peninsula. President Truman disagreed, instead adopting a limited-war approach, which did not include regime change, but strictly focused on driving the North Korean Army back across the 38th parallel. MacArthur disagreed, maintaining a divided Korea would necessarily result in instability in the region.

The general, who famously said *old soldiers never die, they just fade away*, knew seventy years ago what the rest of the world had come to accept. The North Korean problem was not going to fade away.

"Madame President," started Secretary of State Jane Tompkins, "before I turn the floor over to Secretary of State Gregg, I can confirm through our conversations with the Chinese ambassador that North Korea is readying another nuclear test at their facility at Kusong. Their primary test site, especially for nuclear weapons, has collapsed."

"What do you mean by *collapsed?*" asked Chief of Staff Acton.

"Their missile-testing site adjacent to Mount Mantap in the northern part of the country has been experiencing what's known as *tired mountain syndrome*," continued Secretary Tompkins. "Recent USGS reports have indicated their underground nuclear testing and detonations have taken its toll on the surrounding rock mass and along the tectonic faults. Several temblors have been recorded, and then late last night, a strong 6.6 magnitude earthquake was reported."

A representative of the NSA interrupted and began to hand out some photographs. "Madame President, one of our birds flew over this morning and have provided the following imagery. As you can see, the image on split screen left is the original testing site. On the right, you can see a chasm has opened up and the missile launchpad was swallowed by the earth."

"This development hasn't slowed them down, has it?" asked Chief of Staff Acton.

"No, sir, it hasn't," replied Secretary Gregg. "We suspect the North Korean geologists anticipated this, which is why they relocated their next ICBM missile test to Kusong, hundreds of miles away."

"Do we have an estimated date for this new test?" asked President Harman.

"We do, Madame President, based upon our past observations," replied a representative from the CIA. "Once site preparations begin, the launch takes place within two to three weeks, pending weather."

"Okay, keep me posted, naturally," said the president. "Today, as you know, we suffered a stunning defeat in the United Nations General Assembly. I want to make one thing perfectly clear. This does not mean we are going to abandon our diplomatic efforts or any other types of overt political pressure at our disposal. With that said, I've asked Secretary Gregg to brief us on our defense options and then what our first-strike strategy looks like. Every time Kim Jong-un readies another ICBM missile launch, we have to work under the assumption it's meant for us or our allies. General."

General Gregg stood and instructed his aide to bring up a series of graphics on the large monitor installed on the end wall of the Roosevelt Room opposite the portrait of President Teddy Roosevelt as a Rough Rider.

"Thank you, Madame President," Secretary Gregg began. "I want to address our defensive posturing in generalities first, and then look at our specific deployments. First screen, please."

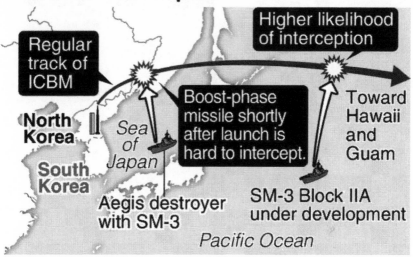

How intercontinental ballistic missiles could be intercepted

Regular track of ICBM

Higher likelihood of interception

North Korea

Sea of Japan

Boost-phase missile shortly after launch is hard to intercept.

Toward Hawaii and Guam

South Korea

Aegis destroyer with SM-3

SM-3 Block IIA under development

Pacific Ocean

"Currently, we have thirty-six interceptors. Thirty-two at Fort Greely in Alaska and four at Vandenberg Air Force Base in California. Our mobile interceptors consist of Aegis Destroyers equipped with ship-based missile systems deploying Ratheon Standard Missile 3 short- and intermediate-range ballistic missiles. The SM-3 has advanced avionics, which can track and destroy an ICBM mid-flight.

"As you can see from the graphic, however, the reaction time and the margin of error associated with destroying an ICBM based upon our Aegis positions is not optimal. During the boost phase, minutes after launch, the ICBM will be difficult to intercept. Let me add, however, that the change of locale from Mount Mantap to Kusong allows our destroyers a few additional, vital seconds to accomplish this task."

The president got out of her chair and walked toward the monitor. "You show the Block IIA as under development. I understood during last year's budget battle that continuation of this project was necessary because it was near completion. Was that incorrect?"

"No, Madame President," replied Secretary Gregg. "The SM-3 Block IIA, a joint effort between Raytheon and Mitsubishi, is fully operational and ready for deployment to the Japanese Navy. It hasn't been tested yet by our Navy, so the Pentagon hasn't provided its final stamp of approval for deployment on our vessels."

"Has Japan tested the new technology?" asked the president.

"Yes, with limited success," replied Secretary Gregg. "But I'm not willing to pass judgment on its effectiveness until our people have conducted a controlled test."

"Let me ask this, hypothetically," began the president. "Could we deploy this SM-3 and test it on the DPRK's upcoming ICBM launch?"

"We could, Madame President, but that could have serious repercussions," answered the Secretary of State before Secretary Gregg could answer. "This could be seen as a provocation and an act of war."

"We're already at war," said Secretary Gregg with a snarky tone. "Let me remind everyone, the Korean War never ended with the Korean Armistice Agreement. They just hit the pause button. Make no mistake, Kim Jong-un looks at our relationship that way."

"Point taken, Mr. Secretary," said Acton. "Yet we've managed to avoid shooting at one another for nearly seventy years. Why start now?"

"Okay, perhaps it was a bad idea," said the president as she found her way back to her chair.

Secretary Gregg resumed his presentation. "Madame President, to answer your question," he started, providing the Secretary of State a dirty look. "The bigger problem with your hypothetical is if the new Block IIA technology fails to bring down their ICBM, the ramifications of a failed intercept could be much greater than a successful one."

"Understood," said the president.

Secretary Gregg nodded to his aide. "Next slide, please."

"This graphic illustrates our existing missile defense program, and it allows me to point out the various defense weaponry at our disposal. From the Sea of Japan to the coast of California, we've deployed a variety of defenses to bring down a North Korean, Russian, or Chinese nuke. For years, many in Congress have questioned the Defense Department's expenditures on the THAAD system and the Aegis Ashore deployments as overkill.

"There's something I need to make perfectly clear to everyone. Shooting down an ICBM in mid-flight is not as simple as sitting behind a computer console like you're playing a video game. And it's never been done under live-fire conditions such as a North Korean launch. In twenty years, we've only conducted eighteen tests, and individually, these systems only took down ten rockets. That's less than sixty percent per target in less-than-realistic conditions."

The attendees in the Roosevelt Room began to mumble among themselves. The president whispered to her chief of staff, who began to scribble some notes on a pad. Secretary Gregg allowed this number to sink in for a moment and then continued.

"Now, that's not to say we can't successfully bring an ICBM down. Based upon the Pentagon's computer models, with most likely assumptions, we believe it would take four to five of our interceptors to give us a ninety-seven percent success probability."

"Mr. Secretary, what you're saying is we would have to expend five of our available interceptors to knock out one of their ICBMs?"

"That's correct, Madame President," he replied.

"With simple math, if they fired seven at us in any manner of succession, we would have exhausted our defenses against future missiles from North Korea or any other source, correct?"

"In theory, yes, Madame President," replied Secretary Gregg. "The deduction you've reached is why the Defense Department has been ringing the clarion bell for decades about North Korea's nuclear proliferation. With every successful test, and with the continued passage of time, this rogue state can build up an arsenal that can overwhelm our existing defense levels, leaving us no choice but to react with our own offensive capabilities."

"You mean a nuclear war?" asked President Harman.

Secretary Gregg stood a little taller and pulled his jacket a little tighter in the front. "In this case, pardon the colloquialism, the best defense would have to necessarily include a much better offense."

CHAPTER 22

November 7
The Roosevelt Room
The White House
Washington, DC

The room began to settle down after the realities of Secretary Gregg's revelations struck them. He believed in the axiom that fear was a great motivator. Sometimes, in order to move someone to act, it took blunt, straight talk with a tinge of embellishment to achieve the desired result. Although the means might be questioned, the end result—a better-prepared, safer America—was worthy.

"Secretary Gregg, I think we all fully understand what our defensive capabilities are, and clearly, there is no margin of error," started the president. "Before we move on to part two of our briefing, could you tell me what kind of time frames we'd be working under in the event of an attack?"

Secretary Gregg nodded and leaned over to his aide, who efficiently produced another graphic. "Madame President, I think you'll find this slide self-explanatory. It's based upon our understanding of the DPRK's technological capabilities."

He continued. "As you can see, at just twenty minutes' flight time, Hawaii would be most vulnerable, but our opinion is that it's not a primary target for the North Koreans. Most likely they'd seek out large population centers on the U.S. mainland—Los Angeles, Chicago, New York, and of course, Washington."

"When would our interceptors deploy, and where would they engage the ICBMs?" asked the president.

Secretary Gregg responded, "Under our current state of readiness, Madame President, Greeley and Vandenberg would react immediately. Most likely they would intercept the ICBMs over the middle of the Pacific Ocean, approximately halfway through their projected flight time to the continental U.S. of roughly thirty-six minutes."

"If they miss, would we get a second chance?"

"Possibly, but it would be with marginal success," replied Secretary Gregg. "Once the ICBMs re-enter the Earth's atmosphere during the terminal phase, they continue until impact or detonation. This stage takes less than a minute for a strategic warhead, which can be traveling at speeds greater than two thousand miles per hour."

"What are our capabilities?" asked Acton. "The THAAD system?"

THAAD was an acronym for *terminal high-altitude area defense*, which was designed as the ultimate hit-to-kill interceptor for short- and medium-range ballistic missiles. The systems had been successfully deployed in Europe along Russia's borders and into South Korea as a defense against North Korean missile attacks.

"The THAAD system does engage ballistic missiles during the terminal stage, but the reentry speed of a long-range ICBM would make its success rate very low," replied Secretary Gregg. "Our only defense is the GMD, ground-based interceptors, we've already discussed. Frankly, that's why we've always suggested utilizing our first-strike options to keep the war on their side of the Pacific."

Secretary Gregg leaned over to his aide and advised him to leave the graphic up on the screen for now. He wanted the short time frames for the destruction of Los Angeles and other major cities to sink in to the president's psyche.

"Okay, let's shift gears," said President Harman. "I'm not going to get into the geopolitical ramifications of a first strike upon North Korea. I want to focus strictly on the mechanics. Unfortunately, we're up against an adversary who seems to have adopted a survival-at-all costs approach in dealing with the rest of the world. I won't go so far as to say he welcomes a military conflict, but he sure doesn't appear to be willing to back down from one."

"Madame President, that is a correct assessment," added Secretary Gregg. "I'm a believer in studying the history of warfare when planning. All military engagements provide us something to consider when making decisions about future conflicts. I'd like to say something about the 2003 Invasion of Iraq, which we all know as the Iraq War. I know that many in this room, in hindsight, argued against our reasoning and stated rationale for entering Iraq. I don't wish to relitigate that now. What I will point out is that we chose to take the fight to the enemy on their soil, not ours. Granted, Iraq was in no position to invade America, although terrorists obviously were not afraid to do so. The end result, after many years, was a free and democratic Iraq, a weakened Iran, and the death of the radical Islamists who fought for ISIS."

President Harman leaned back in her chair and clasped her fingers in her lap. "Secretary Gregg, are you suggesting we need to strike North Korea first because they might invade the United States?

Surely Kim Jong-un is not that stupid."

"On the contrary, Madame President, I think this dictator is quite cunning and, just as important, fearless," said Secretary Gregg. "A war on U.S. soil could, by definition, include a nuclear attack, as well as a subsequent ground war. The Pentagon suggests a preemptive strike against the North Koreans to back them down by showing them who's the boss."

"Please explain," said the president.

"We have at the ready, Madame President, awaiting your orders, a squadron of B-1 Lancer heavy bombers located at Andersen Air Force Base in Guam. The B-1 has the largest internal payload of any bird in our arsenal. We suggest sending three pairs of B-1 bombers simultaneously to pre-identified locations across North Korea. Each plane has a max payload of one hundred sixty-eight five-hundred-pound bombs. Our stealth attack would have a devastating impact on North Korea and would effectively shut down their nuclear program and quite possibly eliminate Kim Jong-un himself if we can confirm his whereabouts."

Secretary of State Tompkins spoke up. "In recent years, his exact location has only been based upon speculation. Only the members of his tight inner circle know for sure."

"Let me add this, regarding the political aspect and the world's reaction to our proposal," Secretary Gregg said. "We've specifically suggested the B-1 Lancers because they are not capable of carrying nuclear weapons, and the other major powers, including North Korea, know that. We would be sending a signal to our nations that our goal is not to obliterate the North Korean people or make a bad situation worse. Our goal continues to be, and always has been, arresting their nuclear proliferation."

Chief of Staff Acton spoke up. "The sheer numbers of bombs you suggest dropping, over a thousand by my count, would necessarily kill many thousands of innocent Koreans and likely destroy their critical infrastructure. Wouldn't this compel Kim Jong-un to respond with his nukes?"

"Not if they're destroyed by our birds," replied Secretary Gregg, who had always labeled Acton as a dove on military matters. "Madame President, within thirty minutes of entering North Korean airspace, we could wipe them out. We've already been sending B-1s near their airspace as a show of force. Under our strategy, Pyongyang would think it's more bluster on our part, until it was too late."

"What about loss of life on our side? Could our pilots be shot down?" asked the president.

"Madame President, my boys are ready to do their duty in defense of their country," replied Secretary Gregg. "When called upon, they will act with precision and honor."

"*Our boys*, Secretary Gregg," said the president.

The room grew silent as the president and her defense secretary studied one another. Neither was prepared to continue. For Secretary Gregg, this was the president's last chance to sign off on the military's preemptive-strike option. If she didn't, the deep state's covert plan would move forward. All he knew was that the time to act had passed long ago. It might be too late.

"Ladies and gentlemen," started President Harman, "do I have military options? Of course I do. As Commander-in-Chief, that's my responsibility to consider both military and diplomatic approaches to solving an international crisis. We always want to use diplomacy as our first choice because it doesn't involve killing innocent people on their side or the loss of life in our military. Overall, I consider our defenses to the North Korean nuclear threat to be robust. I believe we have the capability to shoot down an ICBM directed at America. And once we do, then we'll evaluate whether a nuclear retaliation is necessary, or perhaps we'll go the route of the B-1 bombers. Until then, we'll stay the course. Thank you, Secretary Gregg, for your comprehensive presentation."

The president stood and immediately left the room, her chief of staff and political strategist in tow. Secretary Gregg tried to compose himself before he screamed out loud what he was thinking.

Comprehensive presentation? This was not a PowerPoint dog-and-pony show for a bunch of suits in a boardroom! I'm trying to avoid an all-out nuclear war. I'm done!

CHAPTER 23

November 7
Home of Secretary of Defense Montgomery Gregg
Georgetown
Washington, DC

Another late-night meeting was called at the Georgetown home of Secretary Gregg. Once again, the attendees included Carl Braun, director of the Special Activities Division, and Billy Yancey, head of the Political Action Group. For purposes of the shadowy relationship these men shared, titles and positions didn't matter other than the access they afforded the men. There was no hierarchy, although Secretary Gregg, as a member of the president's cabinet, was given considerable respect in the decision-making process. By their very nature, the activities engaged in by men such as these was long-lasting and much bigger than the individuals meeting on this particular evening. Over the years, new recruits would be brought in under the veil of secrecy as men like Gregg, Braun, and Yancy retired to their ranches, mountain homes, and Caribbean retreats.

"Gentlemen, I've tried my best to sway the president to do the right thing without outright lying to her," started Secretary Gregg. "Of course, Acton and that political hack Jennings can go dig up their own military experts to disagree with me, but at least I was able to put our best foot forward and get it on the record."

Billy Yancey, who understood the political aspects of the president's decision better than his counterparts, spoke first. "I believe the president recognizes the generals and admirals, speaking through you, have more experience on these issues than she does, or her politically oriented advisory team. She won't deny herself the benefits of your wisdom. What we can't accomplish is changing her core political belief that the best solution to dealing with a tyrant like Kim Jong-un is diplomacy. He doesn't care about diplomacy."

"And biding time," interjected Braun. "He learned from his father and achieved far more technologically than expected."

"Well, I think we can thank the Iranians for that," said Secretary Gregg.

Braun removed several folded documents from his coat pocket and handed them to Yancey and Secretary Gregg.

"What's this?" asked Yancey.

"New intel just obtained from our friends at MI6," replied Braun. "We believe these manifests establish a connection between Ukrainian-built rocket engines and North Korea via Iran."

Secretary Gregg studied the paperwork and looked up to Braun. "Tell me what all of this means."

"To bottom line it, the Security Service of Ukraine, or SBU, the country's successor to the KGB, were working with an informant on a sting trying to bust two North Korean spies while stealing rocket technology years ago. The SBU turned the spies, and they've been working for the Ukrainians since. The spies gave these manifests to the SBU, who in turn sent them to MI6."

"I see the translator's notes in the margins," said Secretary Gregg. "This appears to show the Ukrainians selling rocket engines to the Iranians."

"Exactly, and based upon our interrogations of the crew of the *FooChow*, it appears those same rocket engines have been traded to North Korea in exchange for the satellite technology."

"Is there an obligation to take this to the president?" asked Yancey.

Braun started laughing. "Did you seriously just ask that question, Billy? The president sees what we want her to see. Besides, my contact at MI6 is, shall I say, a *like-minded thinker* when it comes to *Whitehall.*"

Whitehall is a road in Westminster located in Central London. It's the recognized center of the government of the United Kingdom, including the Ministry of Defence and the Cabinet Offices.

"Silly me." Yancey chuckled. "Okay, so this intel is need-to-know as far as we're concerned. My feeling is that the president wouldn't change her position if she had access to this." He set the documents on the coffee table next to the fireplace.

"Agreed," said Secretary Gregg. "I don't think it should change our course of action. I need to address one concern of mine before we adjourn."

"What's that, Monty?" asked Yancey.

"It's the matter of the sister, Kim Yo-jong. Are you both certain she can be trusted? I mean, her reasoning for helping us is sound, but everything I've read about her is that she is fiercely loyal to her brother."

"I understand, Monty, so let me address your concerns, because I had them as well when Carl and I first broached the topic," said Yancey. "After our little dictator ordered the hit on his brother Kim Jong-nam in Kuala Lumpar, the National Clandestine Service decided to dig even deeper into his family ties. Ordering the death of his brother using the VX nerve agent was incredibly brutal, much worse than a quick and simple gunshot to the back of the head. Kim Jong-un was sending a message to his brother and the rest of his siblings—defy me and you will suffer immeasurable pain in your death."

The VX nerve agent, short for *venomous X*, used by the two female assassins was extremely toxic. A victim of a VX chemical attack usually died from asphyxiation due to not being able to exhale.

Yancey continued. "His other brother, Kim Jong-chul, has lived a life of exile outside North Korea. He seems to spend most of his time in London, attending rock concerts."

"Big Eric Clapton fan and quite the guitarist in his own right, we're told," interrupted Braun.

"He has an older sister, Kim Sul Song, who has never been photographed," continued Yancey. "She is rumored to be the father's favorite child. Our intel has revealed she has played a secretive, yet significant role in the propaganda department of Kim Jong-un's regime."

Secretary Gregg held up his hand, causing Yancey to pause. "Wouldn't she be the heir apparent after we kill her brother?"

"Not likely, mainly because of bloodlines," replied Braun. "Kim and his sister Kim Yo-jong have the same mother. The two studied together in Bern, Switzerland. When their father died, she was close by his side, and she was instrumental in helping him consolidate power. Like her half-sister, Kim Yo-jong has spent a considerable amount of time in the DPRK's propaganda department. Her elevation to the country's politburo five years ago sealed her position as his closest confidante."

Gregg added his copy of the Ukrainian documents to the pile. Braun gathered them up and tossed them into the fire. The three men sat in silence as the paperwork burned.

"What's the worst-case scenario if she's playing us?" asked Secretary Gregg.

"It won't matter if they're killed or captured. The team we've identified is deep cover, so we can easily disavow any knowledge or involvement," replied Yancey. "One of the men is of South Korean descent, which will point the DPRK's attention toward their own, or at least, in the direction of North Korea."

"What about the other operative?" asked Secretary Gregg.

Yancey nodded and smiled as he sat back in his chair. "Good man. Very reliable. And you'll like this. He's a fellow Texan."

Secretary Gregg smiled as well. "I've always said give me an army of West Point grads and I'll win a battle. Give me a handful of Texas Aggies, and I'll win a war. Maybe this young man from Texas can help us prevent one."

CHAPTER 24

November 8
The Moody Theater
Block 21
Austin, Texas

A jubilant crowd of twenty-five hundred Texans crowded the stage of the Moody Theater, home to the famed *Austin City Limits* music program, which had been running in Austin since the mid-1970s. Block 21, a hugely popular mixed-use development in downtown Austin, partnered with the Moody Foundation in Galveston to create the music venue, which became home to the longest-running live music television program in American history. ACL Live presented music lovers of all genres, especially country, the finest in performances. But, on this night, the Moody was packed full of supporters of newly re-elected Governor Marion Burnett.

Even though all the votes were not yet tallied, Governor Burnett's opponent had already conceded, just an hour after the polls closed. As the television monitors throughout the venue began to reveal the results, the Burnett faithful began to whip themselves up into a joyous celebration. After the local media reported that the concession call had been made, chants of *Texas strong! Texas free!* filled the hall.

Governor Burnett began her remarks with the customary condolences to her opponent and thanks to her team for their efforts. After several mundane remarks pulled directly from her stump speech about her vision for the future, she broached the topic her political handlers constantly reminded her to avoid during the campaign—secession.

"My fellow Texans, I did not run a campaign attempting to hide who I am. Y'all know my mouth is too big for that, right? While I'm committed to governing for the best interests of all Texans, I don't intend to compromise my principles for those who disagree with me. What I intend to do is disprove those naysayers who label my policies as isolationist, protectionist, or, God forbid—secessionist!"

The crowd roared their approval at the word *secessionist*. The chanting began again in earnest.

"Texas strong! Texas free!"

"Texas strong! Texas free!"

Governor Burnett continued. "Texans aren't un-American, and don't you let the media up East convince you that you are. I refuse to allow the media to define us. So if you people in New York City are paying attention, let me tell you about Texans.

"We're proud of our culture. Texans share a common way of life, which revolves around family, religion, and community. Our core beliefs may differ slightly, but in the end, we want Texas to be a great place to raise a family, start a business, and live free of burdensome laws that don't reflect our values.

"Texas has a proud history, one that reflects self-reliance, freedom, and a sense of pride that is unparalleled across the country. In every aspect of our lives, we choose freedom. My friends, God blessed Texas, and we thank Him daily, without hesitation!"

Again, the crowd erupted in cheers and celebration.

"Texas strong! Texas free!"

"Texas strong! Texas free!"

She allowed her supporters their moment. They'd worked hard year-round to push her over the finish line and election to another term in office. This party was for them as much as it was for her.

"Let me school the media and those folks in California who tried their darndest to influence this election. We Texans are a proud bunch, and we are also diverse. From El Paso to Brownsville and from Lubbock to Texarkana, this state is made up of all types of races, ethnic groups, religions, and cultures. Texas belongs to all of us, not just those who voted for me. It was given to us by God, and it will be enjoyed by our families for so long as we treat it with respect.

There is no us versus them among fellow Texans, is there?"

"Nooooooo!" shouted the crowd in response.

"But this election did send a clear message to outsiders who attempted to meddle in our affairs during this election, and in other ways daily. You stay out of our business and don't mess with Texas!"

The crowd cheered once again. Governor Burnett invoked an often-used phrase that had evolved as a battle cry of sorts for Texans. In actuality, *Don't Mess With Texas* was created as part of an antilitter campaign decades ago.

As the excitement subsided, Governor Burnett took on a more somber demeanor. "My friends, I'd like to take a moment to get serious about our future. The campaign is over, the election reflected the will of Texans, and now it's time for me to continue working on your behalf.

"I am a proud Christian, as I know most of you are. I've often been asked by the media, how can you reconcile being a Christian and working in the cutthroat world of politics? God has blessed me with this opportunity to help our state be a better place to live for all of His children. I believe the people of God should be a blessing to our culture, not be removed from it.

"Our Founding Fathers provided us the greatest country on Earth, one that is rare in history. We can be directly involved. We can vote and have a say in how we are governed, and the words of Peter, Paul, and Joseph confirmed in the Bible that we should.

"Like any political leader, I believe I have a vision for Texas that's in the best interest of every Texan. Now, in order to carry out that vision, I must get elected, and then like tonight, get re-elected. That requires gathering votes during the election process, which is a necessary result of being popular with the voters.

"I will tell you, I face a crossroads from time to time in my political values in which the right thing to do is not necessarily the popular thing to do. I try to inform the people of Texas on the issues, and I listen to their feedback. Then I turn to God for guidance.

"The Book of Proverbs says *if you are faint in the day of adversity, your strength will be small.* My friends, it is in our most difficult days that we must be strong. When evil tries to gain control over us, that is when we must stand tall. We must be heroes when life demands us to be heroes.

"I'm not necessarily talking about a war between nations. I'm talking a war between cultures with differing morals, values and core beliefs. Our nation is divided as it's entered a hyper-political climate. So-called blue states have become bluer, and red states have become redder as like-minded individuals relocate to be with others of their point of view. Sadly, we may never see eye to eye on anything except an external threat.

"My friend Reverend Tommy Nelson, pastor of the Denton Bible Church, said it best when he referred to it as a *continental divide among the American people.* The polarization of our nation is at an all-time high. My goal is to eliminate this rancid political discourse in our state by bringing all of us, regardless of race, sex, or whatever, together as Texans.

"We will be Texans first, if need be. And if Washington and a mouthy few in the northeast media or on the West Coast can't accept who we are, then they can learn to live without us! Because, make no mistake, my friends, under my stewardship, we can separate ourselves from the madness that has overtaken America. The solution is Texas strong! Texas free!"

CHAPTER 25

November 9
U.S. Naval Forces Central Command
NSA Bahrain

Duncan and Park had been airlifted from the flight deck of the USS *Jack H. Lucas* as it was en route back to US Naval Forces Central Command, NAVCENT, located at Naval Support Activity Bahrain. Two teams were left aboard the Singapore-flagged *FooChow* as it was taken into custody per Washington's instructions. The crew was being brought into NAVCENT for interrogation and further disposition.

Immediately upon boarding the Sikorsky SH-60 Seahawk, an ensign provided Duncan a sealed packet and access to a Microsoft laptop computer. When the men were notified by Captain Abbey that they would be returned to NSA Bahrain immediately, the adrenaline that had filled their bodies during the search of the *FooChow* returned out of apprehension.

The three-hundred-mile flight across the tip of the United Arab Emirates provided them plenty of time to review their new deployment orders. Anxious to learn about their new mission, Duncan booted the laptop. Inside the envelope, there was a note card with an alphanumeric code, meaningless to most people but one that had been established by Duncan before they left Langley months ago. It was a combination of the date Dallas had been killed in action and his brother's initials.

This code was a message advising Duncan that the information he'd be accessing was for their eyes only. It also indicated to him that he'd need to insert the 128GB USB drive that he kept in his possession. The flash drive contained software that allowed him to access the CIA's secure network designed solely for his benefit, and his superiors.

He responded to a series of security questions, and then he was able to review his messages on the secure server. The first message indicated he could share the information with Park.

"All right, buddy," started Duncan as he flexed his fingers and took a deep breath. He turned the laptop's screen so that both he and Park could view its display. The men cozied up in the back of the SH-60 as its twin turboshaft rotors propelled it at nearly ten thousand feet above the water at one hundred forty miles per hour. "Let's see what they've got in store for us."

"Looks like the first stop is Misawa Air Base," said Park. "I've never passed through there, have you?"

"Nope, not really familiar with it, either," replied Duncan.

Misawa Air Base was located in a remote location in the northeast of Japan. It was a joint installation of the Air Force, Navy, and Army, but it fell primarily under the purview of the 35th Fighter Wing.

"It has a long history dating back to the Korean War," Park said as he followed along with Duncan through their redeployment instructions. "It also acts as a staging area for special ops related to China. My guess is we're going into the land of the Red Dragon."

Duncan continued to read through the messages and then clicked a link marked logistics. Maps, images, and biographies of various people were made available.

"Park, have you actually been to Korea?" asked Duncan.

"Yeah, when I was like three years old with my parents. Why?" he asked as he leaned forward to study the monitor. "Wait. Really?"

"Really. We're going into North Korea," replied Duncan.

"Why? I thought our friends at Langley liked us."

Duncan looked at his partner. "To be determined. But why do you say that?"

"Because operatives who go into North Korea usually don't come back out."

CHAPTER 26

November 9
Undisclosed Military Command Center
North of Pyongyang
North Korea

Since the Korean War, the Kim regimes had become masters of putting their critical command and control facilities of the military underground. Many of their military command structures had been buried deep under mountains, oftentimes obscured by factories or transportation facilities. To avoid prying eyes from above, the buildings on the surface appeared unassuming, but underneath, a series of wide tunnels and cavernous openings built by political prisoners rivaled the underground facilities at Cheyenne Mountain.

North Korea was expert at keeping secrets from the outside world. Political dissent was met with immediate, oftentimes deadly punishments. Access to the worldwide web via the internet was forbidden and made impossible by the state's control over communications. Their technology and tight controls prevented outside media like Radio Free Europe and Radio Liberty from being piped into the country.

This veil of secrecy had served them well and was instrumental in allowing them to forge a close working relationship with another rogue nation who had the United States as a common enemy—Iran.

For decades, Iran and North Korea had shared missile and satellite technology. American intelligence also worked overtime to establish tangible proof of cooperation between the two nation-states in the nuclear arena.

It was the Iranians who taught the North Koreans to exploit the

West's penchant for interconnectivity. Pyongyang learned an enemy that had internet-connected banking, stock trading, critical infrastructure, and social media was vulnerable to cyber warfare. The Kim regime learned that the opportunities to wreak havoc via cyber attacks were endless.

North Korea had become experts at ransomware, including *WannaCry*, which had held online hospital records hostage until a fee was paid. Several years ago, North Korean hackers had compromised computers in Seoul, stealing a vast cache of data, including highly classified wartime contingency plans jointly prepared by the Pentagon and South Korea.

All of this information was routinely shared with the Iranians, with whom they'd shared a military alliance since the 1980s. Iran's Ghadir-class submarines were virtually identical to North Korea's Yono-class. The Iranians had recently tested missiles that were identical in design to the North Koreans'. And eight months ago, the Iranians launched a satellite into low-Earth orbit that appeared to be a copy of the North Korean KMS-4 launched by Pyongyang six years ago.

This collaborative military-to-military relationship was underscored when leaders from both countries met in open defiance of U.S. policymakers during the United Nations General Assembly vote on the sanctions package. The headline emblazoned across newspapers worldwide read *The Enemy of my Enemy is my Friend.* While the two countries were hardly enemies, these emerging regional powers had gained the upper hand in world opinion over the U.S.

Deep underground, in the mountains hidden behind an automobile parts factory, Kim Jong-un, through an interpreter, spoke directly to Iran's President Hassan Rouhani. They discussed their trade agreements, in violation of international sanctions. They agreed that the recent capture of the North Korean scientists and the satellite meant nothing. They pledged to escalate their own wartime military plans.

The two men, despite their vast differences in culture and ideology, truly enjoyed one another's company. They laughed together when a date was agreed upon for the demise of the *Great Satan*, as the Iranians referred to the United States. The Axis of Evil, hidden behind multiple layers of secrecy, had reached an accord— one that was decades in the making.

CHAPTER 27

November 9
The Oval Office
The White House
Washington, DC

President Harman joined Acton and Jennings in the Oval Office for coffee prior to the President's Daily Brief. PDB for short, the President's Daily Brief took place in the Roosevelt Room and focused on national security issues. The briefing usually lasted around thirty minutes and was attended by key members of the national security team, but not necessarily members of the president's cabinet.

President Harman routinely attended these briefings but mostly looked to her chief of staff and senior political advisor to discuss matters of utmost importance. Today, she wanted to address the issue of Iran and North Korea, but the initial conversation over coffee revolved around the national headlines out of Austin. Governor Burnett's speech the night before had struck a nerve with the media and political pundits.

"I personally don't understand what the big deal is," started President Harman. "She's clearly playing to her base. Did you watch the excerpts they showed on CNN?"

"Actually, I watched the entire acceptance speech," replied Jennings. "None of the midterm congressional races were nearly as intriguing as the governor's ability to fire up her supporters."

The president took a sip of coffee and shook her head. "True, but wasn't it just a lot of noise, especially when she constantly alludes to secession? They don't really buy into that garbage down there, do they?"

"Don't underestimate her message," replied Acton. "She has a clear and convincing state-centric nationalist approach to governing."

"Okay, Charles, that was a mouthful." The president chuckled. "Would you break it down for me?"

"Of course, Madame President. Typically, a candidate for president who advances a nationalism platform, like the prior administration, runs on five core issues—shared culture, proud history, common religion, everyday language, and national boundaries. She struck the same tones during her speech, but she applied these principles to Texas."

"It was if she were looking at Texas as its own country," interjected the president.

"Exactly. Here's an interesting fact about Texas that isn't known by a lot of people outside their state, but it's something that is taught in every elementary school there," started Jennings, the political whiz and a student of American history. "You've heard of Six Flags over Texas, right?"

"Sure, it's an amusement park," replied the president. "We have something similar in LA called Six Flags over Magic Mountain."

"Okay, that's true, but it's not what I'm referring to," continued Jennings. "It was originally used as a slogan to describe the flags of the six different nations that have flown over Texas. Throughout its history, Texas has been claimed by Spain, France, Mexico, the Confederacy, the United States, and in the mid-nineteenth century, it was its own republic. There are many Texans, led by Governor Burnett, who believe the days when Texas was its own republic, a sovereign nation, should be resurrected."

The president finished her coffee and set the cup on the table in front of them. "Listen, I was in San Francisco when they started talking that secession nonsense in creating the State of Jefferson. It went nowhere. Then, after the 2016 election, the pendulum swung in the other direction and the entire state wanted to split into several parts. They called it *Calexit*. It also faded away."

"I believe Texas is a little different, Madame President," said Jennings. "Last spring, they passed the Texas Sovereignty Act, which allows for overriding federal laws through the same process their legislature has for passing a bill in the State House. A request to nullify a federal law's enforcement in Texas would have to be proposed, pass through committee, and receive the votes in the Texas legislature. If the governor signed it, then the federal law would be avoided within the state."

Chief of Staff Acton nodded his agreement. "Madame President, Arizona and Maine have passed similar legislation. The concept is gaining traction in other Southern states."

"Yes, but that's a far cry from secession. Is secession even legal?" she asked. "I thought we resolved that after the Civil War when Lee and Grant met at the Appomattox Courthouse."

Acton responded, "It's my understanding that most constitutional scholars say no because it's legally impossible. The Constitution has no provision allowing secession. The Supreme Court, in a case dealing with Texas following the Civil War, called the United States an indestructible union. Justice Antonin Scalia once wrote the one constitutional issue resolved by the Civil War was that there is no right to secede."

"One thing is certain," said President Harman. "If they tried to secede, they'd have a heckuva legal battle on their hands all the way to the Supreme Court."

She checked her watch and stood, as it was time to walk across the hall to the Roosevelt Room.

"Madame President, before we go in, I wanted to let you know I've scheduled a meeting with the Chinese ambassador for Monday, as you requested."

"Good. It's time for us to exercise a little muscle on North Korea via their neighbors."

CHAPTER 28

November 9
The Armstrong Ranch
Borden County, Texas

The Armstrong family had gathered around the table for a breakfast of scrambled eggs, country ham and red-eyed gravy, and grits, of course. Major had turned over the early morning feed chores to Preacher once again, who'd been very successful at the cattle auction. The Armstrong steers had brought the high end of the weighted average, which was in the range of one hundred fifty dollars per hundredweight—roughly eleven hundred dollars per steer. The cow-calf pairs had fared well at sixteen hundred dollars.

In simple terms, most cattle ranchers went to the bank each year to borrow the money to operate their ranches until the calves were sold in the fall. If they bought their five-hundred-pound calves in the spring at a dollar a pound, and then sold them as full-grown steers at the end of the season in October through November before the coldest weather came, they'd double their money, or better.

The Armstrong Ranch no longer borrowed money to operate, having reached a level of financial self-sufficiency many years ago. Now Major managed the ranch's income to pay his labor costs and provide for his family. Running as many as two thousand head each year, the family was more than financially secure. It also enabled Major to invest in improvements to his property with an eye toward *darker times*.

"Daddy," started Palmer as she finished off her breakfast and pushed the plate away. She ate nearly as much as her brothers, unashamed to feed her big-boned frame. However, she was blessed with girl-next-door beauty, which had been bestowed upon her by Lucy. "I have to ask. That's a mighty big hole you've dug out back where the new barn is goin'. Are you plannin' a two-story condo for the new quarter horses?"

Riley snickered as he sopped up the red-eye gravy with a biscuit. Part of it dribbled down his chin, and he quickly caught it with his sleeve. Despite Miss Lucy's best efforts to instill manners in the boys, she eventually succumbed to their inherent cowboy nature and settled for simply having them potty-trained.

"Nah, Palmer, nothing like that at all," replied Major. "Your momma and I've been talkin', and we thought it was about time for you three to get a place of your own. So we designed an apartment out there under the barn."

"What? No way, Daddy!" protested Palmer. She looked around the table and then chose her mother. "He's pullin' our chain, right, Momma?"

Miss Lucy simply shrugged and smiled before Major continued.

"Honey, we'd thought you'd appreciate us puttin' you closer to your favorite chore—cleaning manure out of the horse stalls."

Cooper began laughing and slapped Palmer on the back. "You're so gullible, sis. Ain't none of us gonna have to live underground."

"You never know," said Miss Lucy dryly as she stood to clear the table. "This nuclear standoff with the North Koreans has gone to a new level that can lead nowhere good."

"Are you buildin' a bunker, Daddy?" asked Riley.

"We are, son, and I want all of us to be involved. In fact, a lot is gonna happen today."

Cooper got up from the table and grabbed some more dishes to help his mother. "I think it makes sense, considerin' what's goin' on. We could be firin' nukes at each other any minute."

"Come on, Daddy. Really?" asked Palmer.

Major decided to recall the history of the nuclear threat for Palmer's benefit. "Honey, ever since they used nukes on Japan, the world has feared a nuclear Armageddon where Russia and the U.S. shot at one another."

"I know, Daddy. Mutually assured destruction."

Major wiped his mouth with his napkin and pushed away from the table slightly to relax. "That's right, Palmer. That was a phrase that argued for slowing the proliferation of nuclear arsenals between the two countries. But then China obtained the technology, followed by India and Pakistan. Eventually, it was no longer a Russian-U.S. issue. It became a worldwide issue."

"The Cold War was between Russia and us, right?" asked Riley.

"Technically, it was between the old Soviet Union and the United States, but that's basically the same thing. Politicians want to declare the Cold War to be over, but there will always be the potential for the Cold War to become a hot war involving nuclear missiles."

Cooper returned from the kitchen and rejoined the conversation. "Whose bright idea was it to give nuclear weapons to those idiots in North Korea?"

"Yeah," chimed in Riley. "I wouldn't trust that fat kid over there to keep his finger off the button, would y'all?"

Everyone shook their heads from side to side.

"I think we're all in agreement that a nuclear North Korea is very dangerous, and I believe it's because they have nothing to lose. I'm not saying they'll ever attack us. My personal opinion is that they're building their arsenal to prevent us from attacking them. Personally, I don't know what their long game is, but I do know the threat is real."

"Daddy, do you think it's possible to get in a nuclear war with North Korea? I mean, you know, where we shoot at each other?" Palmer seemed genuinely concerned about the prospect of nuclear Armageddon.

Major leaned forward and looked his three youngest children in the eye. "As you guys know from growing up under this roof, your momma and I have placed great emphasis on self-sufficiency and protecting this family from potential catastrophic events. Now, there's not a whole lot we can do to prevent them from happening, whether they're naturally occurring, like a solar flare, or man-made, like a nuclear war. But we can take steps as our financial resources allow to be ready for worst-case scenarios."

"Daddy, isn't there a point where somebody might go a little overboard in prepping?" asked Cooper before adding, "We all watched that show *Doomsday Preppers*. Some of them folks were coo-coo for cocoa puffs, right?"

The group laughed and Major smiled to himself as he recalled some of the more elaborate preps portrayed on that show.

"I can't disagree with that, Coop," replied Major. "One good thing that came out of that series, however, is it raised awareness for the concept of prepping. You just had to keep in mind that they were trying to make good television, which is why they portrayed some of the preppers as whack-a-doos."

Riley started laughing and tried to contain himself. "Yeah, some of it was useful, but I'll be dogged if I'm gonna wipe my butt with some danged garden sprayer like that one woman suggested."

"Yeah, I could see it now," started Cooper as he began to laugh hysterically. "You'd be too uncoordinated to spray the nozzle in the right place, and then you'd holler for Momma. Momma! Would you please come hose down my butt!"

The table burst into laughter at the vision of Riley wandering around behind the barn with his jeans around his ankles, trying to hose down his backside with a garden sprayer.

After the hilarity died down, Major received a text. He read it and then held up the phone and announced, "That's a text from Preacher. Our delivery has arrived. Let's go see."

*****

After they hurriedly helped Miss Lucy finish up in the kitchen, the group descended into the cool fall air and marveled at the sight before them. Preacher was on a Polaris and was leading a caravan that consisted of two flatbed trucks and a crane kicking up dust as they approached.

"Are you kiddin' me?" mumbled Cooper without really expecting any type of rational answer.

"Daddy, you bought two of them?" asked Palmer.

"Come on," Major responded as he led the Armstrong entourage to get a closer look at the steel boxes that rode on the back of the flatbeds. "Let me get them started, and then I'll explain everything.

Major spent a few minutes speaking with Preacher and the installers from Rising S Company, an East Texas-based manufacturer of steel underground storm shelters, safe rooms, bunkers, and bomb shelters. Major had researched a number of companies and found Rising S to be trustworthy and skilled fabricators. He'd toured their plant southeast of Dallas about a year ago and earmarked funds from this year's cattle sales for this purpose.

After a moment, the men got to work, and Major returned to his still wide-eyed family. "Let me answer Palmer's question from earlier when she asked if it was possible to go overboard when prepping. The answer is yes, and I have no doubt some folks might look at this as overboard. But your momma and I see it differently. To us, prepping is like insurance. When we spend our family's money on advanced preps like these underground bunkers, we're basically insuring that there will be protection for our families in the event of a catastrophic event, from tornadoes to nuclear strikes."

"Daddy, you said families," interjected Riley.

"That's right, son. Do you see Preacher and all of his men? They're our family too. We provide them housing in locations throughout our ranch. Most of them have been with us for ten years or more. You've grown up with their kids, and their mothers have become friends of your mother's. When a major threat forces us into the shelter, we need to make room for them as well. Not only because it's the right thing to do, but because we'll need them to rebuild what's left and, more importantly, defend our homes against those who might want to harm us."

"Whoa, Daddy," said Cooper. "You think it could come to that? Gun battles with rustlers and such?"

"It's possible, Coop, and if it's possible, I intend to prep for it."

Lucy had been silent for most of the conversation until now. "Come here, kids," she started as she gestured for her three youngest children to gather next to her. She wrapped her arms around them and whispered, "Your daddy and I love you more than life. We'll be dogged if some dictator or a bunch of marauders will take one precious second away from us being together. We'd rather do without than lose any one of you to the threats we face. Do you understand?"

Everyone nodded and hugged their mother. For years, Major and Lucy had instilled the concept of self-reliance into their family. Now, as the children had grown into young adults, it was time to get them more involved in the Armstrongs' preparedness activities. They were mature enough to understand and respect the threats all Americans faced.

Cooper replied, "We do, Momma. The threats are real. Why not be ready, just in case? Right?"

"Right," responded Lucy.

CHAPTER 29

November 10
Midland-Odessa, Texas

While Major and the guys continued work on their underground bunker, Lucy and Palmer made the one-hour trek into Midland-Odessa to run some errands, which included taking advantage of the Emergency Preparation Supplies Sales Tax Holiday, which had been expanded to twice a year in Texas.

The Texas comptroller first instituted this opportunity for Texans to purchase emergency preparation supplies nearly ten years ago. Without quantity limits, the waiver of sales tax collection encouraged the public to purchase everything from generators to nonelectric can openers.

Once restricted to a particular weekend in April, the state comptroller added a second weekend in November following hurricane season. After Hurricane Harvey devastated the Texas Gulf Coast in 2017, then-Governor Abbott suggested the additional weekend be added to encourage Texans to prepare for disasters while the devastation was still fresh on their minds.

The program worked and was considered a huge success. Texas had a long history of encouraging its citizens to be ready for major storm events like hurricanes and tornadoes. In addition to protecting human lives, prepping reduced the burden on first responders, who could then focus their attention on the elderly and children, who were not capable of taking care of themselves in these cases. As one preparedness author once wrote, *It's the responsible thing to do.*

"Okay, Momma, what's our first stop?" asked Palmer as they approached Midland from the north on State Highway 349.

"Now that Daddy has his nuclear fallout shelter he's been swoonin' over since yesterday mornin', he wants us to stock it with supplies. We're gonna buy backups to a lot of things we already have and secure them in the bunker."

"Three is two, two is one, and one is none, right, Momma?" asked Palmer.

"Wow, you remember that?" her mother replied with a question.

"Yeah, I used to hear that so often when I was little that I thought it was a nursery rhyme. But it makes sense. If you only have one generator, and it breaks, then you have none. If something happens like Daddy was talking about yesterday, it's not like we can run down to Tractor Supply and pick up another generator. Which means having one is like having none."

Lucy laughed at her daughter's recollection of the prepper rule of threes. "I'm proud to have instilled something in that brain of yours."

"Momma, you've taught me more than you realize," added Palmer. "I just don't let on so your head doesn't swell up."

"Zip it, missy," said Lucy with a chuckle as she wheeled her Ford Expedition into KW Arms. "Here's our first stop."

"Of course, boy toys," quipped Palmer. "Why do they need so many guns?"

"Actually, there's a special order for your daddy, but I've also picked out a couple of handguns for us."

"Are we finally gettin' those matching Tiffany Blue ones?" asked Palmer with a laugh.

"No foo-foo, but we are going to pick up two weapons that are perfect for concealed carry. I have my concealed-carry permit, and your daddy wants you kids to get them as well."

"But I thought Texas is an open-carry state. We don't need the concealed-carry permit, do we?"

"Yes, but this is for when you travel as well," replied Lucy. "Texas, like many states, has entered into concealed-carry reciprocity. Most of the states you guys travel to have agreements with Texas."

They pulled into the parking lot, which was fairly busy for a Thursday morning. They walked in together and immediately realized they were the only women in KW Arms that morning except for the cashier. Lucy searched the store for Kirk Warwick, the owner and a longtime friend of the family who'd supported his store since it opened in 2010. Over the years, they'd become one of the best firearms dealers in West Texas.

As Lucy craned her neck to locate Warwick, he walked up behind her and announced himself. "Good morning, Miss Lucy."

This startled Lucy somewhat, who jumped a little.

"Oh, I'm sorry," Warwick apologized profusely as he stuck his hand out to greet Palmer. "Probably shouldn't sneak up on folks in a gun shop. You must be Palmer. I'm Kirk, the store owner."

"Nice to meet you, Kirk. Momma's just real excited to pick up her new toys."

Warwick chuckled as he gave Lucy a hug. "Well, y'all will be real pleased with what we have for you. Follow me into the presentation room and I'll retrieve your order. We don't want to make a big deal of what you've bought in front of these other folks."

"Okay," replied Lucy. She understood Warwick's suggestion of privacy. He always implored his customers to keep their weapons purchases under wraps. Your arsenal, he always said, was not something to brag about to your friends and neighbors.

After a few minutes, he returned with two pistol-sized cases and a box containing a rifle, which he set aside for the moment. He pulled the curtains closed and turned his attention to his customers.

"I believe you're gonna love these weapons," began Warwick as he popped open the hard plastic carrying case and presented matching Heckler & Koch VP9 Tactical handguns to Lucy. "As requested, Miss Lucy, we've equipped these with threaded barrels. The factory's cold-hammer forging process will guarantee you eighty to ninety thousand rounds without a problem through these barrels."

"How many?" asked Palmer as she cocked her head in disbelief. "Who shoots that much?"

"With training sessions included, you'd be surprised," replied her mother.

Lucy picked up one of the weapons and felt the weight. She was pleased with its light feel and balance. Palmer followed her mother's lead and expertly cleared the chamber. She and her brothers had been trained in the safe handling of firearms from the day they were old enough to pick up a BB gun. Major believed in teaching them to be comfortable around weapons and respect their capabilities.

"Also," began Warwick, "I didn't mention this in my voice mail to Major, but something else was approved for you guys."

He reached onto the chair next to him and showed Lucy their new SilencerCo Omega 9K suppressor, the smallest, lightest, and quietest silencer available under five inches.

"Wow!" exclaimed Lucy. "Already? I thought it would take nine months for approval."

Warwick smiled. "Do you remember when you and Major came in and placed your order? SilencerCo had just implemented a program where they provided an attorney to help jump through the federal logistical hurdles. The attorney eliminated some of the prepurchase requirements like obtaining written approval from local law enforcement and fingerprinting. The approval process for guns takes about twenty minutes in most cases, but a suppressor can take nine or ten months."

Palmer picked up the silencer and studied the threads. "It screws on to the end of my gun too?"

Warwick nodded. "Absolutely. They are designed for both of your weapons."

"Okay," started Palmer. "I have to ask. Why do I need a silencer, or suppressor? I mean, I'm not gonna go stalking somebody like a secret agent or something."

Lucy began to laugh because, in her mind, *one never knows.*

"I urge folks to practice using their weapons, Palmer," replied Warwick. "The suppressor reduces the risk of hearing loss, and it also acts as a muzzle break, allowing you faster follow-up shots when necessary."

Palmer shrugged. "Why not, right?"

Warwick nodded and then retrieved the box containing the rifle Major ordered. He opened the box and displayed a Daniel Defense

DD5V1 rifle. He handed it to Lucy, who held it gingerly in both hands.

"It's lighter than I imagined," was her first comment.

"Around eight pounds," said Warwick.

"Is that a machine gun?" asked Palmer.

"No, those are illegal," replied Warwick. "Basically, it's a more powerful version of the AR-15s your folks have purchased from me over the years. Only this particular weapon is chambered in .308."

"Like my hunting rifle, right?" asked Palmer.

Warwick nodded and smiled. "Miss Lucy might remember this, but from the first time your folks became my customers, I impressed upon them to purchase weapons in common calibers. For example, try to purchase all of your handguns in either nine millimeter or forty-five caliber. Your AR-15 rifles all use .223 Remington. Your hunting rifles all take .308."

Lucy handed the AR-10 platform weapon to her daughter. Palmer held it and then carefully pointed it away from the other occupants in the room to get an idea of how it felt in a shooter's stance.

"I like this. Can you hunt with it?"

"You can, and a lot more," replied Warwick. "With the right scopes, you'll find this weapon to be just as versatile as your AR-15s but with more firepower and a much longer range."

"Momma, I may have to arm-wrestle Daddy over this one," said Palmer with a chuckle. She looked over to her mother, who seemed to be oblivious to the conversation as she stared at her phone. "Momma, is everything okay?"

Lucy held up one finger indicating for Palmer to wait for her answer. She continued to type a message to someone. When she finished, she immediately removed her glasses and looked at Warwick.

"Kirk, Major wants you to order another one of these." Then she turned to Palmer with a grin. "One is none, right, honey?"

CHAPTER 30

November 11
Stockyard Championship Rodeo
Fort Worth, Texas

With the not-so-secret injury to Cooper's head on the forefront of Miss Lucy's mind, she insisted on checking the truck and trailer to make sure he'd left his gear behind as promised. She then threatened each and every one of them, reminding her rodeo kids in no uncertain terms, that if Cooper got within twenty yards of a bull, including the mechanical kind in a bar, she'd provide them a whoopin' they'd never forget. None of the three laughed at the prospect of their momma tannin' their hides. Despite the fact they were all bigger and grown adults, they honestly feared her *mama grizzly* side.

It took about four hours to drive to the Fort Worth Stockyards, where the season finale of the Stockyard Championship Rodeo was taking place that weekend. This was the next-to-last event before the PBR World Championship in Las Vegas. Had Cooper's head fully healed, he would have ridden at Fort Worth, although the prize money was insufficient to vault him into the top ten and keep him there. The event at the Calgary Stampede in two weeks was the date he'd circled on his mental calendar, and he had no intention of incurring a setback prior to then.

Plus, for once, this rodeo could be all about Riley and Palmer. After they got settled, they registered for their respective events, and Cooper made small talk with some of his fellow bull riders. Most were supportive, as they'd developed mutual respect for one another

137

over time. There were others, naturally, the *haters* as Cooper referred to them, who secretly wished Cooper would disappear into obscurity. He'd come out of nowhere to reach his level of success, and the haters wanted nothing more than to see Cooper fail. When he encountered these losers, he'd remember words that Pops taught him when he was young—don't worry about failing, but concentrate only on winning. Cooper did win, and often, which only exacerbated the jealousy among the haters.

The rodeo events calendar was full for both Friday and Saturday, although Riley's event was only scheduled for Friday evening as part of the day's final competitions. Riley was the perfect build for a steer wrestler. Speed and strength were the attributes found in champions, and Riley excelled in both. Steer wrestlers, also known as bulldoggers, used power and technique to wrestle the steer to the ground. That might sound simple enough, but then the real work began.

The steer weighed twice as much as his opponent, the bulldogger. Once the two entered the arena, the steer wrestler chased the animal on his horse, typically at thirty miles per hour. Riley would start on his horse confined in a box. The steer was given a head start, the length of which was determined by the size of the arena. The arena at the Fort Worth Stockyards was large, so Riley had plenty of room to work.

Cooper and Palmer stood on the rails of the box where Riley readied himself behind the barrier. As the steer reached a precise advantage point, the chase would be on.

"You got this, Riley," said Cooper as he shouted words of encouragement over the noise of the crowd.

Riley was getting hyped up, the adrenalin pumping through his veins. "He's a big 'un, Coop. Did you see the size of that boy? Heck, you should be ridin' that sucker!"

"Nah, he's a pussycat," said Cooper. "Remember, you're smarter than he is!"

Riley managed a smile despite his rapidly building intensity. It was almost time to release the steer from the breakaway rope barrier. Riley's muscles tensed, his brow furrowed, and he took a moment to pull his black felt cowboy hat lower on his forehead.

Riley glanced to his right and nodded to his hazer. In steer wrestling, the rider had the assistance of a *hazer*, another mounted cowboy who galloped his horse along the right side of the steer and kept it from veering away from the bulldogger. The top ten steer wrestlers in the world had a partner who acted as the hazer who could be nearly as important as those who wrestled the steer. Riley shared a hazer with several other steer wrestlers at this stage in his career, and usually shared a quarter of his earnings with the hazer.

His hazer nodded back and gave him a thumbs-up. Riley was ready. Steer wrestling differed from bull riding in which remaining on the bull eight seconds completed the event. In steer wrestling, the fastest time wins, so it was important to have a fast, responsive horse, and the bulldogger had to time his takedown perfectly. Riley had to be aware not to break through his barrier prematurely, for that would result in a ten-second penalty and likely keep him out of the money.

He waited patiently as the cowboys controlling the steer's breakaway rope watched him. Seconds later, the steer was released, and the chase was on. The chase resembled a drag race between the steer, the bulldogger, and the hazer.

Riley kicked his heels and his horse bolted forward. Within two seconds he was alongside the steer, even before his hazer was. As Riley pulled alongside, he slid down off the right side of his horse, which continued to race ahead, and then he hooked his right arm around the powerful steer's right horn.

In one simultaneous motion, Riley grabbed the steer's left horn, locked it in his grip, and using all the strength and leverage he could muster, slowed the steer and then leaned. However, Riley's work wasn't complete.

In order to stop the clock, he had to wrestle the steer flat on its back with all four feet pointed in the same direction. First, Riley stuck out his feet and slid with the steer's forward process, kicking up dirt but slowing the beast at the same time. With this leaning motion, Riley had gained momentum before he rotated his body, turned the steer and flipped him. With one fell swoop, Riley flawlessly dropped the steer to the ground, its feet flying upward, causing the clock to stop.

The announcer said it all. "Riley Armstrong's time of five point eight seconds vaults him into first place!"

He removed his hat and waved to the cheering crowd in the arena as the night's rodeo events concluded. Riley would go home with a fifteen-hundred-dollar check and a trophy in the form of a champion steer wrestler buckle sponsored by Wrangler.

After the arena was cleared, Cooper and Palmer jumped over the rail to celebrate with their brother. Cooper had already achieved notoriety around the Pro Rodeo circuit, and now Riley was making a name for himself.

Tomorrow would be Palmer's day, but at age twenty-one, she was still new to the National Barrel Horse Association circuit. In all of her shows, she competed with the best and typically earned top-ten finishes although she hadn't yet been in the money. Palmer was patient and knew she had to gain experience and pay her dues, just like her brothers.

"I think this calls for a celebratory Bud, don't y'all think?" asked Palmer, who despite having just turned twenty-one in recent months, was always the first to suggest a cold beer following an event.

"My mouth is still full of dirt," said Riley. "I need to wash it down with somethin'."

"Let's do it," said Cooper as he led his siblings out of the arena. "Y'all thinkin' Billy Bob's?"

Riley started to laugh. "We'd best not risk it. It's Friday night bull night there."

In the early years, Gilley's was a cowboy bar located just outside Houston that had become world famous when it was featured in the movie *Urban Cowboy*. When the co-owners had a falling out, the club closed and was relocated to Dallas, a move that included the original mechanical bull, El Toro, featured in the movie.

Not to be outdone, Billy Bob's at the Stockyards embarked on what turned out to be a brilliant marketing strategy. They installed an actual bull riding arena within their honky-tonk and adopted the slogan *Real Bulls, Not Steel Bulls.*

Bull riding at Billy Bob's became a regular Friday night occurrence and was run like a professional rodeo event. Points were awarded for the way the bull bucked, the degree of difficulty, and the technique used by the rider. Because the arena was located within the confines of the bar, the ring was tight, which encouraged the bull to buck fierce and spin tight.

Even as Cooper was rising through the ranks, he'd never considered riding at Billy Bob's, despite the notoriety he might have achieved. He thought it was too dangerous because bulls were unpredictable enough, much less in a confined space. In addition, Riley's point was well taken.

"I agree, Riley," said Cooper. "Would it surprise you that Momma has spies everywhere? They're probably following us now."

Palmer and Riley began to look around nervously, causing Cooper to chuckle.

"Where are we gonna go?" asked Palmer as she looked around at the crowd of people descending upon the Stockyards for a night of drinkin' and dancin'.

Cooper saw a neon sign that read *Basement Bar* pointing down a flight of stairs. A chalkboard sign on the inside of the door displayed the bar's specials. *No cover. $2.00 beer. $2.00 wells.* Cooper smiled, as all three specials met their budgets. The rodeo kids were not big drinkers. They usually enjoyed no more than two beers. Their interest in frequenting these cowboy bars at the end of the day was usually for the comradery of their fellow rodeo participants.

After the trio produced their IDs confirming they were twenty-one, they entered the small, but noisy bar, which billed itself as the world's smallest honky-tonk. They made the rounds and chatted with familiar faces. Riley and Cooper were catching up with two up-and-coming bull riders from San Antonio, Adriano Morales and Eduardo Pacheco. The guys were from Brazil, having immigrated to America with their parents in 2015 when political uprisings dominated the country and the economies of South America began to collapse.

Their fathers were employees of InBev, one of the world's largest beer companies, which had merged with Anheuser-Busch. With the completed acquisition of Corona Beer and Grupo Modelo, whose marketing arm was located in San Antonio, the boys' parents sought positions there and came to Texas on L-visas designed for intercompany employee transfers. Their parents worked to achieve their American citizenship, and the boys continued to pursue their dreams of being bull riders.

Cooper enjoyed talking with Morales and Pacheco because the Brazilians employed a slightly different bull-riding strategy in dealing with the rope and grip. They were comparing notes when suddenly Riley tapped Cooper on the chest and nodded toward Palmer, who was involved in a conversation with two cowboys at the bar.

Two guys, clearly full of themselves and probably several beers too many, were shouting at Palmer, who'd turned her back to them.

"Hey, girl! What's your problem? Me and my brother are just tryin' to be friendly."

One of the men reached for her arm to turn her around, but Palmer spun and said, "Friendly leads to conversation, and I don't feel like talkin'. Leave me alone!" She yanked her arm away from the man's hand and swung around, her ponytail swishing behind her.

The guy slammed his beer on the bar and growled. "Maybe you oughta learn a little respect, hussy." He began to follow after her, but he was immediately stopped by a charging bull in the form of Riley Armstrong.

It all happened so fast that Cooper couldn't recall if Riley was more steer wrestler, middle linebacker, or his nemesis, One Night Stand. In any event, a certified western bar brawl broke out.

Riley had knocked the wind out of the rude cowboy and immediately began to rain hail marys into the man's jaw. When the guy's friend tried to jump Riley, Pacheco kicked his legs, causing him to crash to the floor in pain.

Another bar patron, apparently friends with the two loudmouths, jumped on Cooper's back, who began to spin around in circles, emulating a bull trying to throw his rider. The man held on until one final spin when his face met the fist of Morales, causing him to loosen his grip on Cooper and fly onto, and then over, the bar.

Pacheco finally got Riley's attention and forced him to stop the beat down of the worst offender. Riley's hands were bloodied, but not near as bad as the other guy's face.

As others in the bar pushed and shoved each other just to be part of the action, the lights came on and the bouncers moved in to control the crowd.

Cooper grabbed everyone and whispered to them, "Quick, this way."

Several of the bar's patrons wanted no part of the fight and scurried for the exit. Cooper guided the group to blend in with everyone else so they wouldn't be identified by the guys who still lay on the floor, writhing in pain.

At the top of the stairs, they emerged into the cool, fresh air and then scampered down West Exchange to the White Elephant Saloon, where a line stretched around the block to get in. The five of them didn't say a word as they heaved in and out to catch their breath. Palmer kept a watchful eye on the street to see if they were being pursued by anyone, but it appeared they were in the clear.

All at once, the group began to laugh hysterically. Pacheco pulled a bandana out of his jeans and handed it to Palmer, who wrapped Riley's hand.

"We'd better get some ice on this before it swells up too badly," said Palmer.

"It ain't broke," said Riley.

"Maybe, let's see," said Palmer as she gave it a squeeze.

"Hey! Dang it, Palmer! That hurt worse than the punches I was landin'."

As the group had a good laugh, two Fort Worth patrol cars drove toward the bar with their blue lights flashing, reflecting off the walls of the Stockyards as they passed.

Cooper laughed and then got serious. "Quit your squallin'. We need to get off the streets anyway."

Morales laughed and patted Riley on the back. With his heavy Spanish accent, he said, "I see why you wrestle the steers. You are the baddest cowboy I've ever seen."

"Thanks," said Riley. "And thanks, guys, for pullin' me off that jackass. I was out of my mind. I might have killed him if ya'll hadn't stopped me."

"No problem, my friend," said Pacheco. "We have to ride tomorrow and must get some sleep."

Cooper shook their hands and slapped them on the shoulders. "I wish I could ride with you, but I'm out. Thanks for your help tonight. If we ever need to return the favor, I promise we'll have your backs."

CHAPTER 31

November 12
The Oval Office
The White House
Washington, DC

Washington, DC, was full of diplomats. Some wielded authority and real power, including the authority to bind their countries to verbal agreements. Others were simply figureheads and mouthpieces for their government. One person likened it to the husband who claimed he couldn't make a decision on a car without consulting his wife, who was at the other end of the showroom, hiding from the salesman.

While administrations came and went, as did the power between political parties, one rule remained constant in the duties of Washington's diplomats—*think twice before you say nothing*. Ambassador Ho Lin of China was an expert in listening, analyzing, and saying nothing. For nearly three decades, he'd infuriated State Department officials and presidents with his shrewd poker face, careful choice of words, and ability to say nothing in the midst of said diplomacy.

He unconsciously caressed the folded leather pouch that rested in his lap as the Lincoln Town Car made its way through the security gates at the White House. His hands trembled slightly, but not out of nervousness, but rather, from becoming old. Very few people in Washington knew that Ambassador Lin was approaching eighty.

A cold rain continued to fall outside, causing his view to be obscured by the rain-streaked windows. Not that it mattered, he'd come to the White House many times in his career to do battle. He'd learned the art to say the nastiest things in the nicest way, much to the chagrin of others. During his tenure, he'd always won these battles, even if his opponents didn't realize it.

As the car approached the final one hundred yards to the White House entrance, he managed a slight smile. China had been winning since that historic visit by President Richard Nixon in 1972. That seven-day trip ended twenty-five years of no communication or diplomatic ties between the two countries.

Dubbed by Nixon to be *the week that changed the world* because of how it isolated the Soviet Union further geopolitically, it also opened up world markets to the Chinese. The result had been fifty years of economic dominance, which had built China into a communist superpower, dominating world trade with its exports, and manning one of the most powerful military machines on the planet.

Ambassador Lin was proud to say that most of this success for China happened on his watch and was due to his unparalleled diplomatic skills.

Despite his successes and an innate ability to read the American political tea leaves, he was puzzled by the scheduling of this meeting. Had it been a matter of import, he would not have been given five days advance notice.

As the car pulled to a stop, Ambassador Lin fidgeted with his coat buttons and drew the collar tight around his neck. The cold, damp air didn't suit the elderly gentleman, even for the brief time it took to enter the White House. Then again, it was the lack of knowledge concerning the subject matter that troubled him most, leaving a cold spot in his gut.

He had no idea what the Americans were going to say, and how they were going to say it, so he readied himself for a variety of scenarios. Ambassador Lin had become a student of American protocol. Today's meeting was a perfect example and was rich in *tells*, a poker term that described a player's behavior or demeanor that gave off clues as to their intentions.

The first such tell was the presence of President Harman, especially on a Saturday morning. He'd only met her once before, during a state visit by the Chinese president. Her presence today represented a disturbing twist in the normal diplomatic channels.

Meeting with ambassadors was usually entrusted to the State Department.

The second tell was the invitation itself. Ambassador Lin had been instructed to come alone. Under all circumstances, he would be accompanied by his deputy chief of mission. He made this his customary protocol to protect him from being misquoted to his superiors. In China, any traitorous activity would result in an instant recall and likely death. By their explicit instructions, the Americans were forcing him to come alone, which was within their right, but rarely exercised except under extreme circumstances.

Finally, the tell was the choice of location. Protocol dictated a neutral location for diplomatic meetings, such as the Roosevelt Room, where a majority of the sessions took place. A meeting scheduled in the West Wing Lobby, located on the ground floor, indicated that the Americans were angry with your government. One could expect that to be a one-sided, brief conversation.

Ambassador Lin entered into the warmth of the foyer and was escorted by Secret Service toward the Oval Office. This represented the third and easily the least common site for conferences. If the president wanted to ask for a favor of some magnitude, he'd call on the ambassador to meet in the Oval Office because it was seen as a rare privilege and a sign of respect.

However, as Ambassador Lin surmised because he couldn't think of any, there were no favors to be granted. Which led him to believe he was summoned alone to the Oval Office and a direct meeting with President Harman because she was very angry with China.

Two topics ran through his mind—the brutal vote in the United Nations and North Korea's upcoming missile test. He was prepared to respond to both matters. His instructions on the sanctions were clear. He was not to equivocate or concede any involvement in turning the other nations against the sanctions, which resulted in the landslide vote.

With respect to North Korea, the answer would be the same as always. China was doing its best, but the DPRK was a sovereign nation with a will of its own. As he was led through the West Wing to the Oval Office, he thought of the final tell that would reveal the attitude of the Americans—the parties in attendance.

If they were pleased with China and were looking for an important favor, he'd be greeted by the deputy Secretary of State for China affairs and the National Security Council officer assigned to China.

As the door was opened for him, he was greeted by a young woman whom he'd never met. This concerned Ambassador Lin, but he steadied his nerves. It was a ploy, but it would not work on him.

"Madame President, may I present Ambassador Ho Lin, ambassador extraordinary and plenipotentiary of the People's Republic of China to the United States of America."

President Harman stepped forward and extended her hand. "Good evening, Ambassador Lin."

He reached forward and shook her hand. "I'm honored to be of service to you, Madame President, and naturally, I bring greetings on behalf of the government of the People's Republic of China."

Several people were in attendance, but none of them would speak, per protocol. The president would be the sole voice of the United States on this day.

"Ambassador Lin," began President Harman, as she gestured for the older man to take a seat as she did. "I'd like to discuss the matter of the rumored launch by North Korea of another ICBM missile. I hope you agree that Kim Jong-un has crossed the line in the sand agreed upon between China and the United States many times."

"Madame President, our country is committed to placing all the pressure it can to prevent such hostilities by North Korea, but as we've stated, they are a sovereign nation and China can only do so much."

Ambassador Lin relaxed in his chair, although he continued to rub his hands across his black leather pouch. China was very much aware of the DPRK's intended missile launch and had no intention of instructing Kim Jong-un to do otherwise. North Korea was a useful tool in keeping the United States at arm's length from any potential attack on China. Further, a divided Korean Peninsula was preferred by Beijing, as opposed to a unified Korea under the control of Washington via its puppets in Seoul.

"Mr. Ambassador, this upcoming launch has dire consequences for stability in the region," said the president.

"Madame President, although I have no knowledge of any proposed missile test, might I say that the prior tests by North Korea were conducted safely without incident or threat to life."

"Without incident, perhaps. But not necessarily without threat to life. These missile launches routinely pass over Japan, and that must stop."

"Yes, Madame President, of course I understand your position. Again, let me reiterate our position. North Korea is a sovereign nation, and China's capabilities and influence are limited."

President Harman leaned forward and smiled. "I understand your position as well. We see two alternatives, then. Here's our first proposal. We'd ask that you use your considerable influence over Kim Jong-un, which you so deftly downplay, to redirect his ICBM missile test in the direction of the South China Sea."

For the first time in Ambassador Lin's diplomatic career, he managed a smile and a spontaneous laugh. He really didn't know how to respond.

President Harman continued. "Mr. Ambassador, I can see by your reaction that you consider my request foolish. Perhaps you think that I'm crazy to ask the People's Republic of China to allow an ICBM test over its sovereign territory. I can respect that, but I need you to relay this to Beijing. The days of talk are over. Japan will no longer tolerate intercontinental ballistic missiles flying over its citizens. The United States will no longer allow the DPRK to threaten our nation with nuclear annihilation while they launch ICBMs toward our shores. If China cannot fix this problem and convince Kim Jong-un to stop these tests, then efforts at diplomacy end right here, right now. I hope you understand my meaning, Mr. Ambassador."

Ambassador Lin stood in silence as President Harman's words hung in the air of the Oval Office. He nodded to each of the attendees and then finally to President Harman. "I will relay your message to the president immediately upon my return to the embassy, Madame President. Thank you."

President Harman rose and shook the ambassador's hand. "Thank you for coming. Please extend my warmest regards to President Jinping and the esteemed members of the politburo."

CHAPTER 32

November 12
35th Fighter Wing
Misawa Air Force Base
Japan

It was day four after they'd received their orders and redeployed to a specially designated, secure compound at Misawa Air Force Base. The base was shared with elements of the Japan Air Self-Defense Force, which had occupied the area as a military stronghold since 1870 when it was established as a stud farm for the Japanese emperor's cavalry. Although the bulk of the facilities were utilized by the U.S. Air Force's 35th Fighter Wing, a secured, high-clearance complex was set aside for the 373rd Intelligence, Surveillance and Reconnaissance Group, or ISRG.

The ISRG provided Misawa and the Pacific Command with strategic intelligence and real-time monitoring of operations within the theater. Today, ISRG was hosting the deputy director of the Korea Mission Center, a division of the CIA dedicated to dealing with Kim Jong-un and North Korea. He was conducting a private briefing with Duncan and Park.

"Gentlemen, my name is Walter Campbell, deputy director of the Korea Mission Center. I'm meeting with you in private for a reason. Over the last four days, you've been expected to familiarize yourself with your insertion point, the timetable and locales of your mission, and your extraction. Do you feel adequately prepared for what's about to be asked of you?"

Park and Duncan looked at one another and shrugged. Duncan, who'd learned from his father to hold his tongue, resisted the urge to respond with, *yeah, I can now go sightseeing in North Korea. Other than that, the answer is most likely no.*

"Yes, sir," responded Duncan, appropriately. Campbell looked to Park, who nodded as well.

"Gentlemen, in three days, our source within the DPRK has provided solid intelligence that the North Koreans will be launching an ICBM test at Kusong. Do you know where that is?"

Duncan bristled at the unnecessary question meant to ferret out whether they were prepared. He and Park had studied and drilled one another on the geography and history of the region, including the importance of the DPRK's military base at Kusong as an ICBM launch facility. He decided to throw it back at the condescending spook.

"Forty degrees north, one hundred twenty-five degrees, ten minutes east is the location of the ICBM launchpad, which was constructed in 2014, July," replied Duncan smugly.

Campbell didn't reply or acknowledge Duncan's obvious snarky response. "At 8:00 a.m. local time on the fifteenth, the DPRK has scheduled a launch of an ICBM missile. Kim Jong-un will be there to observe. Your orders are to assassinate him while he is available in a semipublic setting."

Duncan leaned back in his chair and allowed the directive to sink in. Killing a member of the Kim dynasty of leaders in North Korea had always ended in failure and ruin for the assassins. The Kim regime and its predecessors had fought off challengers since the days of Japanese colonialism on the Korean Peninsula in the 1930s. When communist regimes were collapsing around the world in the 1990s, the Kims' hold on power continued.

Despite geopolitical challenges and lethal attacks from within and without, the Kim dynasty had always managed to dodge would-be assassins using their uncanny survival skills and an elaborate network of bodyguards, informants, and undercover secret police.

"I've assumed this possibility," said Duncan. "A direct assault on the capital, whether covert or via special ops, would be suicide. Even if we could breach the defenses of their 3rd Corps or 4th Corps, he and his family would have more than enough time to escape."

"Why don't you just drop a bunch of missiles on his head using the B-1Bs flying up and down the coast?" asked Park.

"Mr. Park, that would be considered an overt military act," replied Campbell. "Your successful mission will provide Seoul and Washington plausible deniability. The agency has a disinformation campaign ready to make Kim's assassination appear to come from his own people."

Duncan pulled out a map of the Kusong base and studied the aerial of the ICBM launchpad. "I've seen images in our materials provided by Langley of Kim Jong-un watching his missile tests. Do we have one specific to Kusong?"

Park began thumbing through the images. He slid out an eight-by-ten image, which was provided by the North Korean state media. He pushed it into the center of the table.

"This image was from last summer. It appears to be at the edge of some woods overlooking the launchpad."

The image depicted Kim Jong-un sitting at a table with his fingers clasped on top of a map. He was in a jovial mood, grinning from ear to ear with two of his senior level officials dressed in their black politburo suits, and five tickled-pink generals, all smiling for the camera.

"We have to assume that this position is somewhere near the base facilities," said Duncan. "If we can get a closer look at satellite recon images, we could pinpoint this spot."

Park pulled the picture back in front of him and pointed toward the mountain behind Kim. He then unfurled a large topography map of the Kusong area and laid it out for Duncan to see.

"Let me find a ruler," said Park.

"Don't bother," started Duncan. "This will be close enough."

Duncan used a pencil and measured in increments against the scale of the map. "Two inches per quarter mile," he mumbled. "This mountain range appears to be about a mile away, with plenty of elevation to take the shot."

"Are you accurate from a mile away?" asked Campbell.

"I'll need the right tools," responded Duncan. "Can our British friends get me what I need?"

"Most likely," replied Campbell. "That doesn't answer my question. Can you make the shot?"

Duncan studied the image and the map again. He tapped his fingers on the pine trees and a dirt embankment behind the observation area. "There are always variables to contend with, including the fact that this location may be moved elsewhere around the launchpad. These pine trees pose a problem, as does this embankment. It's something we'll have to address when we're on the ground there."

"What about the distance?" asked Campbell.

"Park and I have successfully made longer shots. Thirty years ago, the thought of hitting a target at a mile or more was the stuff of legend. As the Barrett fifty-cal rifles became more sophisticated, and the optics more precise, even two-mile shots were attained. Out at the ranch, I could peg empty water barrels with my .308 at nearly a mile, but that required a lot of practice. In this case, hitting Kim from a mile or so will require the perfect combination of cartridge, rifle, optics, and accessories."

"And skill," added Park. "You'll have to pull this off using a never-seen-before rifle and a single well-placed shot. There won't be any second chances, cowboy."

Campbell pulled out his phone and opened up his notes app. "Tell me your first and second choices of the tools you need, and we'll get the message to MI6."

Duncan began to make some notes, and Park looked over his shoulder. He muttered a couple of suggestions, and Duncan incorporated them into the list. After a minute or two, Duncan's list was complete, and he read it aloud.

"First option is the Barrett assembly. Using the fifty-caliber Barrett cartridge, any of the bolt-action model rifles compatible with fifty-BMG such as Robar, Steyr, McMillan, or, of course, Barrett will do.

"The second option is the .338 Lapua Mag cartridge. The Lapua is used by tactical law enforcement units in the States. My daddy's Texas Ranger Company C had some dang fine shooters who could nail two-thousand-yard targets with their .338 rounds. If the Brits can rustle me up a Bushmaster chambered in the .338 Lapua, that would work well."

Campbell typed in the details and then looked up from his phone. "Will the optics choices be interchangeable between the two rifle platforms?"

"Yes, because these rifles will have similar sixteen- to eighteen-inch rails for mounting scopes. I need a reticle with around 20X magnification. Anything larger is rough on the eyes and can mess with my adjustments. For a one-mile shot, I need a scope with a wide range of windage and elevation adjustments, especially for this time of year. We've been tracking the weather, and a front is moving in. If it arrives before we take the shot, it's most likely gonna be a bust."

"Okay, give me some options," said Campbell.

"Leopold Mark 4, Nightforce NXS, and, um, Park, what's that scope we used in Belarus?"

"Horus. It's spelled H-O-R-U-S, like hours, sort of, but

pronounced ore-us. They're based in Idaho and are great if we have wind issues."

Campbell made his notes, and then Duncan added a final item to the list. "Horus also offers a ballistic range system that would be a huge help. See if he can pick up their Vision Sighting System. We can input everything from atmospheric conditions to the size of the cartridge. I know that's a big ask, but it could help us achieve success."

"Bipod?" asked Campbell.

"No, thanks," replied Duncan. "We'll create a makeshift sandbag rest of some kind. Oh, add a spotting scope that has a range of a mile. Pentax, Nikon, Swarovski. Any of those three will do."

Campbell finished his notes and then sent a message to someone to put in the wish list for fulfillment. He appeared to be readying himself to leave before Duncan decided to ask a few more questions.

"I have to ask this question since we're the ones that may not come out of there alive," started Duncan. "How reliable is your intel on this? Who are we relying upon to set this up?"

"Armstrong, you know the drill," replied Campbell with a gruff. "Need-to-know basis only."

"It's our asses on the line, Mr. Campbell. Give me something."

Campbell hesitated and looked into Duncan's eyes. He appeared to give the best answer possible, without breaking protocol. "She is as close a confidante to Dear Leader as they come, without being married to the man. She's very uncomfortable with the direction the country is headed and especially with respect to human rights violations. She's made it clear the time to act is now."

"You do realize this is a suicide mission, don't you? This close confidante better be right."

Campbell leaned forward with both hands on the table. "Gentlemen, you knew the risks of these operations when you signed on. You've never failed before, and we have one hundred percent confidence this mission will be successful. Get your head on straight, hit your mark, and then get the hell out. Now, are we good?"

"Good as gold," replied Duncan.

"Good, get your gear together because you ship out in an hour," said Campbell as he headed for the door. Then he spun and added, "Gentlemen, you're dark from this point forward. No conversations with anyone, family included. Clear?"

"As crystal," replied Park.

PART THREE

CHAPTER 33

November 13
The Yalu River
Sinuiju, North Korea

The Chinese-flagged ferry left the United Nations freighter, which had anchored in Korea Bay. The freighter was part of a prescheduled humanitarian mission by the Food and Agricultural Organization of the United Nations. The FAO-UN, an agency of the United Nations, was created to lead international efforts on behalf of developing and third-world countries to lessen poverty and hunger.

Recognized worldwide as a politically neutral opportunity to help impoverished countries, even those like North Korea, FAO-UN modernized their farming operations and improved nutrition for all of its citizens. This particular relief effort was organized out of the FAO-UN regional office in Bangkok, Thailand. Duncan and Park took the positions of two preapproved aid workers on the ship's manifest. Their documents were expertly created, and their records changed to allow their cover to pass muster.

Duncan had been told that the North Korean border guards at Sinuiju were not considered the A-Team. The highly politicized and media-recognized Korean Demilitarized Zone, or DMZ, along the 38th parallel was protected by the DPRKs top soldiers. Sinuiju was a busy port because of its proximity to Dandon, China, across the Yalu River. It was not surprising to have the North Korean guards be negligent in reviewing travel documents.

As the ferry was approaching the docks, Park added his final thoughts.

"You weren't understating it, Duncan," said Park. "This is

suicidal. Here we are, a couple of Americans strolling into our fiercest enemy's clutches. Walk in the park? Nope. Capture results in death."

Duncan furrowed his brow and grimly nodded. "I get it. They could chuck us into the concentration camp here at Sinuiju, or even haul us to Kaechon, the worst of the worst."

"For the rest of our lives," added Park.

"I think we're getting closer to the docks," interjected Duncan. He pointed along the shore to a series of broken-down ships tethered to equally ragged-looking wooden docks. This was a country that spent as little as possible on day-to-day infrastructure, but military spending had no limits.

"Seriously, Duncan, these guys will fire off nukes before we can run down the side of the mountain," continued Park as the two men stood on the rail of the ferry puttering up the Yalu river. "They're crazy enough to use them too. If we pull this off, they'll feel like they've been embarrassed and will have nothing to lose. They're not gonna turn the other cheek. It's gonna be bad, right?"

"Armageddon," mumbled Duncan. His mind raced to his days in church and sermons from Revelations. He often fantasized what Armageddon would look like. Park was right. They might be lighting the fuse by killing Kim Jong-un. *Is it the right thing to do?*

"Exactly! I'm less concerned about the North Koreans finding us than I am one of our own nukes falling on our heads as we try to escape."

Duncan and Park had worked on many dark-ops missions in the past, and they certainly were aware of the ramifications of this one. This would easily be their toughest challenge. North Korea was difficult to get into and even harder to get out of. The DPRK was infested with paranoid citizens who lived in fear of hiding secrets from the military. Their lives required that they spy on one another for fear of their loyalty being tested and the ramifications of lack of disclosure to the authorities.

The language barriers were minimized by virtue of Park being fluent in Korean, but the cultural differences prevented the two Americans from blending in. The one overriding concern was the lack of a backup plan or assistance. They would be on their own from the moment they stepped off the ferry in Sinuiju until they were extracted the afternoon following the assassination.

Duncan had confidence he could make the shot. He knew they could pull it off, but would they be able to escape once the hornet's nest had been kicked?

The ferry slowed to an idle as it coasted toward an available slip at the seaport of Sinuiju. Their instructions were explicit. Do not speak unless forced to. Park could speak Korean, as his cover allowed it. However, Duncan was to reply in simple German phrases, most of which he'd learned for prior European missions.

The men returned to the rest of the relief workers and separated from one another. Duncan had identified an attractive, young German woman who would garner a lot of attention from the North Korean border guards. His hope was to be passed through quickly while they spent more time with his traveling companion.

Because he was of Korean descent, Park would be closely scrutinized. He intended to pass through their brief interrogation process first alongside the team leader of the FAO-UN group of twenty-two aid workers. The team leader, who was British, was also an operative for MI6, having been inserted into the FAO-UN organization shortly after its formation. She was fluent in Korean and would be able to handle any complications regarding Park's entry.

If Park was rejected for some reason, Duncan would fall back and re-enter the ferry. He and Park would find an alternative means of entry. They had six hours before they were to meet their handler from MI6.

After a few tense moments in which Park was carefully scrutinized, he was allowed in, and the rest of the FAO-UN contingent followed. Most were carrying duffels carrying personal items such as clothing and bathroom sundries. A second set of North Korean guards rifled through these bags, often dumping the contents on the dock and kicking through clothing to see what the bags contained.

If a camera or laptop computer was found, the scrutiny became more intense and, for some, lasted two hours. Park and Duncan were briefed on this in advance, and therefore did not bring any form of electronics with them.

Naturally, Duncan and Park packed light, but believably. While the North Korean guards were not as thoroughly trained as TSA agents from the U.S., they were capable of pulling someone out of line for closer scrutiny on a whim. It was important for the two men not to draw attention to themselves because once they entered the country, they planned on separating themselves from the group.

There was precious little time to waste in getting to Kusong and their goal of looking at their options for establishing a sniper hide.

While the men waited on the rest of the FAO-UN team to clear, they took some time to study their surroundings. North Korea was known as the world's most isolated country. What was not commonly known was that travel to North Korea was possible, as was working and investing in business. While China is the country's largest trading partner by far, there are European business interests that have invested in North Korean industries such as software, shipping, and mining.

In addition to humanitarian aid workers, the most likely people to be seen in North Korea were exchange students, tour guides with their guests, businessmen and of course, diplomats from other countries, although the latter two groups were most likely found in Pyongyang.

Ordinarily, tourists would be abundant in Sinuiju because of its proximity to Dandong, China, across the Yalu River. Very few travelers could be observed due to the closing of the China-North Korea Friendship Bridge between the two cities. While not open to pedestrians, vehicular traffic between the two cities remained steady on most days, but Beijing's most recent attempts to bring pressure on North Korea to stop the upcoming ICBM test included closing the Friendship Bridge for *repairs*. The move was largely symbolic because the New Yalu River Bridge had just opened a mile upriver after ten years of construction.

Periodically, a uniformed patrol would randomly stop apparent travelers and request to see their travel permits. Duncan and Park had rehearsed their responses to being detained during their preparations to comport to their visas and passports as well as their connection to FAO-UN.

It was a charade they'd carry on for less than forty-eight hours. After the assassination of Kim Jong-un, none of their rehearsed answers would likely help them.

CHAPTER 34

November 13
Dongrim Hotel
Dongrim, North Korea

Dongrim was located about thirty miles southeast of the seaport, about halfway to Kusong. The Dongrim Hotel, which housed the aid workers, had the exterior appearance of a block and stucco warehouse, but on the inside, the furnishings rivaled that of a Hampton Inn or Marriot Courtyard hotel. The staff was friendly, and the accommodations more than adequate, especially at a price tag of twenty-nine dollars per night.

The room contained a flat-screen television, plush bedding, and a marble enclosed shower. Duncan checked his Apple Watch, a detail overlooked by the North Korean border guards. While internet connectivity was not available, the apps loaded on his version included satellite access to maps, GPS tracking, and weather radar.

After a one-hour power nap, the alarm on his watch woke him, and he took a quick shower. He finished dressing in clothing suggested by his CIA advisory team. In North Korea, the citizens were too poor or hungry to think much about clothing and fashion sense. However, based upon a North Korean's employment, their uniform might vary.

The FAO-UN team suggested their team members wear blue jeans or khakis, along with shirts and jackets befitting the weather. It was the onset of winter, and most North Koreans wore a form of black or dark blue felt coat. Duncan and Park had packed predominantly black clothing to be worn, as they intended to travel to Kusong in the early nighttime hours.

As the sun began to set, the men walked out into the cold evening air with a map, putting on their best tourist impressions. Even though the Dongrim Hotel had a nice dining room, the men sought out a restaurant where their contact from MI6 would be waiting.

It was dark when the two tourists entered the Jade Stream Pavilion and sat at the dining bar overlooking the well-lit waterfalls outside the building. They were to remain seated, enjoy their dinner, and the MI6 operative would approach them toward the end of their meal.

Halfway through dinner, a lanky Brit was seated next to Park and immediately began studying the menu. He sat in silence for several minutes until his order was placed. When he'd been served a glass of North Korean wine, he took a sip and grimaced.

"Porter Kensington," at your service, he said under his breath. The MI6 operative was dressed in a pin-striped suit to lend the appearance of a businessman. Working under a New Zealand passport, Kensington's cover allowed him free travel through the country, as he was considered a valued investor in the North Korean's magnesite mining operations in Tanchon.

"How's the wine?" asked Park, keeping his eyes forward on the dancing lights appearing through the waterfall.

Kensington mumbled his response. "Shameful. Horse swill."

Park and Duncan finished their meal without further conversation. After the check was delivered, Kensington slipped a piece of paper to Park with an address on it. Then he mumbled, "Twenty minutes."

With their tab settled, they walked into the street, which was devoid of traffic. "Park, it's going to be hard for us to travel at night with the lack of traffic. We'll stick out to any military patrols."

"I agree," replied Park. "Waiting until morning to move is like losing half a day. It's gonna be cold, but I'd like to be set up in those mountains when the sun rises so we can identify a spot."

"Maybe our new friend can help," added Duncan.

The men found their way to another hotel in Dongrim and waited in the karaoke bar as instructed. They suffered through several poorly performed American songs before they were approached once again by Kensington. This time, with no conversation, he passed Park a room key and abruptly left.

Duncan and Park waited several minutes and then left the bar. "That was brutal," said Duncan with a laugh. "I bet that's what they do in these concentration camps, listen to terrible renditions of old Elvis Presley songs."

"No doubt," said Park as the men entered Kensington's hotel and climbed the stairs to the second floor.

They made their way to Kensington's door. Just as Duncan was about to insert the card key, the door swung open and an arm motioned them into a pitch-black space. Duncan subconsciously reached for his waist to pull his sidearm and then remembered where he was. His body tensed, preparing for a physical assault.

He moved into the dark room, followed by Park, and the door shut behind them. Kensington, in a British accent that could just as well have been New Zealander, spoke to reassure the American operatives.

"Sorry about the cloak-and-dagger, gentlemen. There are prying eyes through the peepholes of my neighbors. This country is awash with paranoia, even among the visitors."

Kensington removed his jacket and threw it onto a chair next to a desk. His room was furnished similar to the Dongrim Hotel. Duncan only noticed one suitcase, which lay open on the still-made bed. He glanced around the room, hoping to see signs of the weaponry he requested.

"My name's Park, and my friend is Armstrong. I'm sure you know as much about us as we know about you."

"Good point, Mr. Park, but none of that will matter by morning. In a few minutes, the three of us will depart Dongrim for the Panghyon Airport, which is thirteen miles from the Kusong missile launch site."

"What happens then?" asked Duncan.

"There, a Sungri truck will be waiting for you. It contains a false bed that will withstand cursory inspections by the DPRK roaming patrols. The truck will be loaded with grain sacks containing winter wheat and rye, consistent with your visas as FAO-UN humanitarian workers."

Duncan began to relax. Kensington was all business, and that suited him just fine. "Do we require travel papers to approach Kusong?"

"Yes, and those have been arranged. They'll be in the truck's dashboard compartment. I must caution you upon your approach. Once you cross the bridge at the Taeryong River, the level of scrutiny rises substantially near the entrance to the military base at Kusong. Your travel permits will allow it, but the risk is great."

Park approached the window and carefully parted the curtains to look at the streets of Dongrim. "Traffic is sparse. Any attempt to approach the proposed site would be met with resistance every step of the way."

"That's correct," said Kensington. "Your best attempt at ingress is the early dawn hours. Delivery trucks from Dongrim and the coastal villages along the Korean Bay will fill the road, and you'll be able to blend in."

"That puts us behind schedule," said Duncan. "Any other options?"

Kensington thought for a moment and pulled a map out of his suitcase. "You could travel along the river, which would require you to steal a small skiff. The other alternative is to hike. It will take you several hours to avoid detection, but you will be able to approach the launch site through the mountains."

"Okay, we'll figure it out on the ride up there," said Duncan. "I assume nothing has changed since our last intel briefing yesterday morning."

"Correct," said Kensington as he zipped up his suitcase. "An inflatable will meet you both at the village of Sinmi-do at dusk that evening. Let me confirm for you that the target launch date is the fifteenth. The weather system will move in that afternoon, which would require them to abort the launch for at least a week if not longer."

"There's no chance the launch has been moved up, is there?" asked Park.

"No, I'm assured of this by our resource."

"Let's talk about her for a moment," Duncan insisted. "Are you one hundred percent confident in your intelligence?"

Kensington pulled his suitcase off the bed and extended the handle in order to roll it behind him. He smiled slightly as he responded, "I'm sure. The two of us are intimate and will be together after this is all over. I fly to Pyongyang on the last flight this evening, where I will be picked up by her personal security detail. Rest assured, gentlemen, our intelligence is as good as it gets."

Park shrugged, and Duncan nodded his acknowledgment of the new information. Kensington was excited about accomplishing this mission for more reasons than changing the balance of power in the world. Duncan thought to himself, *If this guy's sleeping with Kim's sister, or aunt, or one of his female advisors, he's as close as any operative has ever been to the dictators of North Korea.*

CHAPTER 35

November 13
Armstrong Ranch
Borden County, Texas

Yesterday, the last of the dirt was pushed on top of the Armstrongs' new underground bunker. One of the ranch hands maneuvered their Bobcat around the six-inch-square barn poles that had been set in cement. Stacks of lumber, roofing material, and paint awaited the completion of the dirt moving.

Cooper slapped his dad on the back. "Daddy, you'd never know it was there except for the air vents sticking up through the ground, and the hatch, of course."

"I agree, Coop," said Major, who then pointed toward the air vents sticking up through the ground. "Do you notice how I've positioned those to come up in between the barn supports?"

"Yeah, do you plan on building around them?"

"Exactly. This setup is relatively impenetrable, but why make it easy on someone who's trying to attack us. I plan on extending that metal ductwork through the walls of the barn and cover them up on the inside as well. I doubt anyone would notice them protruding through the roof."

"What about the hatch?" asked Cooper.

"It will be in one of the horse stalls, probably dedicated to a pony. We'll cover it with hay, and once we're inside, a pony will replace the hay by pushing it around with his hooves. It's just another form of concealment."

Lucy and Palmer emerged from the house and joined the guys. Riley had taken the new Daniel Defense rifle out for a test drive. On

171

the eastern edge of the Armstrong Ranch, a ravine opened up as the plateau began to break up slightly. It was an ideal place to practice shooting targets from both short and long distances. Major impressed upon the kids to keep their shooting outside the ravine to a minimum. Even though they were isolated, sound carried, and he didn't want any passersby thinking they were running a gunnery range.

"Did you guys go inside to see what Palmer and I accomplished?" asked Lucy as she grabbed her husband around the waist. The Bobcat was parked, and a crew of a dozen men began to bang on the boards. Within minutes, the precut Texas red oak planks were creating walls on two sides of the barn structure.

"Not yet," replied Major. "You wanna give us the nickel tour?"

Palmer led the way and groaned as she lifted the heavy steel hatch. A rush of new-home-smelling air hit them as they climbed down the metal stairs to the bottom.

"We've tried to stock the shelter with two weeks for starters because we weren't sure how much room we'd have," started Lucy. She walked over to a control panel and started the generator, which was in a separate underground container, complete with its own air intake and exhaust system.

The generator was a tri-fuel model, which used propane, natural gas, and solar power. The propane tanks were behind the house, and the solar panels were to be installed on the roof of the barn. A natural gas well was two hundred feet away, but a trench was created and a flex-pipe attached to the well. It was then run into the bunker's hole to power the generator. This provided three fuel options to keep the power on while underground.

"Our meals will consist of a two-week supply of primarily compact, nonperishable foods," continued Lucy. "We also have protein, vitamin, and mineral supplements, including meal-replacement shakes. I tried to focus on the dietary supplements to make up for the lost calorie intake that we're used to."

Palmer added, "Daddy, we've also stocked up on medical supplies, especially potassium iodide, which everyone will take in the event of a nuclear attack. Potassium iodide blocks radioactive fallout from entering the thyroid. It basically fills up the thyroid with good iodine and prevents the radioactive iodine from coming in."

"Whoa, sis. I'm impressed!" exclaimed Cooper, who reached into a cabinet and pulled out a packet of IOSAT potassium iodide tablets.

"Thanks, Coop. Momma's got me hooked on this preppin' thing. Those IOSAT packets provide us fourteen days of protection, more than we need, from what we've read."

Cooper returned the box to the cabinet, looked around and began walking through the two interconnected structures. He found the closets and cabinets stocked full of water, food, guns, and ammo. "I see that you guys have thought of everything."

"We haven't put in any extra clothing yet," said Lucy. "Because our seasons vary greatly here, we'll rotate out winter and summer clothes in the fall and spring. Your daddy says we won't have a lot of time once we receive notice of a nuclear attack. Right, dear?"

"Most likely less than thirty minutes," Major replied. "Here's the good news. Borden County is not likely to be a target of a nuclear strike."

The group chuckled as he motioned for them to sit around a small dining table surrounded by an L-shaped bench seat and two folding chairs.

Major continued. "Even though Riley's not here, I think this is a good time to talk about what is possible. We won't have much time once we receive word of an attack. Think about how we spend our days. We're scattered all over nearly ten thousand acres. In some parts of the ranch, cell service is spotty. So we need to do some planning and even have some dry runs."

"Like a fire drill, right?" asked Palmer.

"Pretty much," replied Major. "If we lived in a major city like Dallas, we'd only have about ten minutes to get away from the blast. Here, the bigger problem is the lethal fallout of radiation, which may fall on our ranch due to the prevailing winds."

"But you said we wouldn't be a target," interrupted Cooper.

"That's true, son. However, there are major military installations to our south and west that might be targeted. Depending on the time of year, the positioning of the jet stream, and wind currents, we might get dusted."

"Is it like dust?" asked Palmer.

"The most hazardous fallout particles are visible to the naked eye and resemble fine sand. That's what you have to avoid."

Cooper added, "Daddy, when the wind blows here in the spring and summer, you'd think we're in the desert."

"That's true, and so I don't put everyone in a panic, I ordered personal radiation detectors for everyone to carry in their wallets or pockets. They're more reliable than nothing, but to provide us an extra comfort level, I ordered several different types of radiation-monitoring devices to help overcome false readings."

Lucy added this, "Here's the way we look at it. If there's a possibility of a nuclear attack, we can gather everyone up and get into the safety of the bunker. If nothing happens, we had a good practice drill and go on about our day. If there is an attack, we'll live while, sadly, those who are unprepared won't."

CHAPTER 36

November 13
Armstrong Ranch
Borden County, Texas

"Are you impressed at how well the kids have taken to our plans?" asked Major as he and Lucy headed into Midland again. They had requested KW Arms order the second AR-10 for rush delivery. Also, Major wanted to stop by Walmart and pick up some more ammunition. Their last stop was to conduct some *prepper banking*.

"Very," replied Lucy. "Now I kinda regret not getting the kids more involved in the detailed plans you and I have implemented over the years. In a way, I still look at them as teenagers who were only interested in ropin' calves and killin' rattlesnakes."

"I agree, but I think they're getting involved at the right time. If we pushed it on them as teens, they might've accused us of cryin' wolf and dismissed the whole concept of preparedness."

Lucy sat quietly for a moment as they drove the final few miles into Midland. Finally, she asked the question that had been troubling her.

"You pay attention to the news more than I do," she began. "Also, you just said they were gettin' involved at the right time. Dear, why do you think this is the right time? And don't you dare try to protect me, okay?"

"Okay, deal," Major replied. "You've got your woman's intuition thing, well, a man gets a feeling in his gut, you know?"

"Of course."

"I've been around politics enough to know that you can't trust any of them regardless of whether they label themselves with an R or a D.

Both sides have an agenda, which would surprise the public if the politicians were honest about it."

Lucy chuckled and stated her feelings. "I wish they'd all stay home and do nothin'. We'd be better off."

Major slowed for the first red light entering Midland and turned on his right blinker to head towards Walmart.

"I think there's a bigger problem that most people in America sense as well, but they can't quite put their fingers on it."

"What's that?"

"I firmly believe our government is being run by wealthy and powerful individuals or business interests that have their power in Washington regardless of who's in charge of the White House or Congress. Some folks call it a shadow government."

"Sounds mysterious and conspiratorial," added Lucy. "Have you been reading too many internet articles on InfoWars or by that crazy Dave Hodges guy?"

"No, seriously. I know the difference between what's real and what's fake. Just follow me on this. Neither one of us has ever held a position in the government of Borden County, nor have we wanted to, right?"

"Yup, thanks but no thanks," said Lucy with a laugh.

"That said, though, is there any doubt I could drive up to Gail and tell any one of those county officials what I wanted, and they'd jump to give it to me, wouldn't they?"

Lucy sat up in her seat and nodded. "Of course. You donate to their campaigns, you're the largest taxpayer, and the biggest landowner by far. They should jump when you come callin'."

Major continued. "You've made my point, although the comparison is on a much smaller scale. I've never been elected to anything. I earned a little respect as a lawman, and I've treated the folks who run the county well. But I shouldn't have any real power, yet I do."

Lucy pointed to an available parking space and Major found his way into it. Walmart was packed with shoppers seeking early Black Friday deals and fixin's for Thanksgiving.

"I see your point. There are people around the country who are like you, but their influence is on Washington and the people who work there."

Major shut off the truck and sat there for a moment. "Right. It doesn't matter who we elect, the people who control the levers of power could live in Boston or Silicon Valley or even Texas."

Lucy then asked, "What does this all lead you to believe? Why are you suddenly stepping up our preps?"

"Again, it's just my gut feeling, but I get the sense somebody is pushing us toward a war with North Korea. Regardless of what the president may want, I think powerful people would benefit from a war with Kim, regardless of the consequences to all of us."

*****

Major and Lucy loaded up on more supplies for their new bunker, and each of them made separate ammunition purchases in the gun department. The rash of lone-wolf terrorist attacks and random violent assaults by mentally disturbed people had raised awareness for retailers when selling large amounts of ammo to a single purchaser. For that reason, Major spread out his purchases between KW Arms, Walmart, and half a dozen online ammunition retailers.

After picking up the second Daniel Defense rifle, they stopped by the bank and withdrew nine thousand dollars, intentionally staying under the ten-thousand-dollar withdrawal amount that triggered the filing by the bank of a currency transaction report with the Internal Revenue Service. The Armstrongs hadn't been audited in many years, and Major was careful not to garner their attention.

Their last stop was The Vault, a statewide precious metals dealer who had recently opened a branch in Midland. Major had begun to do business with them shortly after they opened, occasionally purchasing bags of junk silver—pre-1965 dimes, quarters, and half dollars.

Prior to 1965, the U.S. Treasury minted coins that contained ninety percent silver and only ten percent copper. To save money, the U.S. Mint changed the mix, and soon coinage became a mix of aluminum and copper.

Major's concern was the potential collapse of the economy in the event of a catastrophic event. If the economy were to falter, the value of the dollar would plummet, creating an inflationary environment. He believed the public would turn to a barter economy, where goods and services were traded based upon their perceived values to one another.

For example, Major might trade a calf for a horse. Or a farm tractor for another Bobcat. Over time, a fair price would be established in trading posts around the country, much like it was done in the eighteen hundreds.

Many online prepping resources discussed using ammo or guns as valuable barter items. Major had laughed at length about this with Lucy one night before bed. He'd told her the last thing he was gonna do was give another man a gun in trade just so he could use it to come back and kill his family someday.

Major liked the concept of pre-1965 silver because it would be universally recognized as real, and its value could be easily established. The only downside, depending on the size of the purchase he planned on making, bags of silver were bulky and visible. He needed to purchase some gold as well.

Major had phoned ahead to request half-ounce American Gold Eagle coins. He'd researched the options extensively and found the American Gold Eagle, the official gold bullion coin of the United States, to be the most widely circulated.

He checked gold prices, and they'd dropped slightly to eighteen hundred dollars an ounce, making the value of each half-ounce gold coin nine hundred dollars. Major took the cash inside and suggested Lucy wait in the truck. He said it wouldn't take long.

When he returned, he provided her a small ziplock bag with ten gold coins in it. She turned it around and around and then upside down. She began to laugh.

"Um, do you want me to count it? Major, is this it, really?"

He started the truck and pulled out of the parking lot. "Yes, ma'am. You are holding nine thousand dollars in your hand. Don't spend it all in one place."

"Ten coins, nine thousand dollars?"

He replied proudly, "Today, yes. Tomorrow, after the end of the world as we know it, it might be worth ten times that, or more."

"What are you gonna do with it? Bury it in the backyard?"

"Miss Lucy, as a matter of fact, that's exactly what we're gonna do. Let me tell you about my plans for buried survival caches around the ranch."

CHAPTER 37

November 13
The Taeryong River
Near Kusong, North Korea

It was ten in the evening when the men reached the bridge at the Taeryong River. They'd stuck to the road into Kusong as far as they dared before Duncan began looking for locations to hide the truck. He slowly eased the dark green Sungri farm truck off the paved road. The nearly forty-year-old garbage truck turned farm vehicle rattled and creaked as it descended a slight embankment towards a rutted trail created by farm tractors. The four-tire rear axle barely fit in the deep tracks as Duncan moved the steering wheel back and forth to avoid low-lying branches.

They'd encountered no problems on their way to Kusong and commented more than once at how desolate the landscape appeared. Most rural areas of North Korea did not have power.

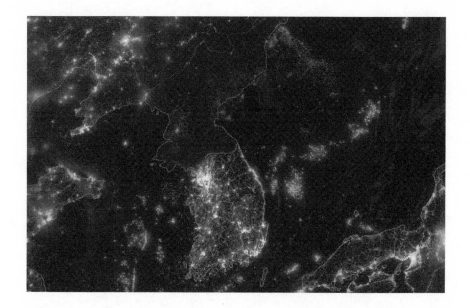

From satellite images, it was apparent that the despotic dynasties of North Korea had done nothing to advance the living conditions of their people. When asked about the lack of power and electricity for their people, the North Korean ambassador to the United Nations once responded that North Koreans were a proud and resilient people whose worth was not measured by flashy lights.

In their brief period within the DPRK, Duncan and Park observed sadness and despair in a world of quiet poverty. The people of North Korea existed, but they did not live. The men reaffirmed their commitment to succeeding at removing the obstacle that stood in the way of providing the people of North Korea a better life.

Duncan etched a visual of the next few hundred feet into his mind and cut off the headlights to avoid detection. Shortly thereafter, Park jumped out of the truck and led Duncan deeper into the woods until he found a place to back the truck in for safekeeping.

Satisfied they'd avoided curious eyes, the two men walked deeper into the woods along the path to see where it led. It eventually narrowed and became more overgrown. It was the proverbial road to nowhere, which suited their purposes perfectly.

They returned to the truck, and Park began to toss the grain sacks over the sides to get to the secret compartment hidden underneath the truck bed. Duncan powered up the display on his Apple Watch to check their coordinates on the global positioning satellite app. They were four miles northwest of the launch site and approximately twenty-two miles from the extraction point on the island of Sinmi-do in the Korean Bay. His days of running the USS *Jack H. Lucas* with Captain Abbey would pay off in the next couple of days.

"Okay, I'm there," announced Park as he leaned over the wood rails of the truck to get Duncan's attention. Park returned to his hands and knees on the steel bed of the truck, fumbling around for the latches to open the hidden compartment. Duncan climbed into the truck bed and illuminated his watch's display. In the darkness, it worked like a floodlight.

"There," said Duncan, pointing toward two rusted hex-nuts near Park's feet. "See the pattern? There's three on each side."

"Great," said Park, pointing toward Duncan's watch. "Does that thing turn into a wrench, too?"

Duncan ignored the question and tried one of the hex-nuts. With a little elbow grease, he got the rusted nuts to turn. Park tried as well, and within a minute, the compartment lid was loose, and they carefully lifted the steel plate out of the way.

Using his watch to illuminate the truck bed, a space large enough to hide two adults was revealed to the men. Inside were duffle bags and a rifle case. Also included were two handgun cases and another hard plastic case that held rifle optics, a spotting scope, a GPS device, and a two-way radio set for short-range communications.

"Well, looks like the Brits hooked us up," said Park. "Let's see what's in the duffle bags."

The guys simultaneously unzipped the dark, olive drab green duffels and peered inside. Park pulled out peasant-type clothing and a couple of rolled-up wool blankets. Duncan produced two Cryovac-sealed bags containing ghillie suits. The Cryovac shrink film process reduced the bulky sniper gear to a fraction of its size, making them packable in the rucksacks provided by MI6.

A ghillie suit was a luxury in Duncan's eyes. For the purpose of this shoot, he'd planned on breaking apart some brush and debris and creating a hide. With each of them having a ghillie suit, which was already made up of basic camouflage materials, including loose straps of burlap, cloth, twine and plastics made to look like twigs, their exposure to North Korean recon patrols would be minimized.

He typically created a custom ghillie for his sniper activity. The sniper team wore heavy ghillie suits designed to obscure their position. Together with strategically placed vegetation, the suits made them nearly undetectable to the enemy, and their target. Prior to deployment, the team spent a considerable amount of time customizing their ghillies. There was always the potential of spending long hours or even days in these outfits as they waited for the perfect opportunity to complete their mission. A bureaucrat's idea of a one-size-fits-all suit wasn't acceptable. Their lives depended upon comfort and concealment. With the unusual insertion for this operation, Duncan was pleased to get this one.

"We've got MREs, water bladders with Katadyn water purification tabs, and compressed toilet paper," said Duncan with a laugh.

Park didn't think it was funny at all. "Do you get the feeling they know something about that restaurant that we don't? I better not get the runs from that crap. I couldn't identify it and should have left it on the plate."

"You'll live," said Duncan as he tossed Park his rucksack. The operatives quickly stuffed their extra clothing and the ghillie suits into the packs. They tucked the provided paddle holsters into their belts and checked the Colt 1911 service models used by British intelligence. The forty-five-caliber weapons packed a punch. They each had four magazines and another box of fifty rounds. This added a lot of weight to their rucksacks, but neither man complained.

Each of the weapons had threaded barrels to allow for the supplied silencers. A suppressed weapon would allow the men to strike when needed, silently.

Finally, Duncan reached for the rifle case to reveal the weapon he'd use to kill Kim Jong-un. It was the new Barrett MRAD, which stood for *multi-role, adaptive design.* It was chambered in .338 Lapua Magnum rounds, which suited his purpose. The MRAD had a foldable stock, which made it portable and more readily concealable. Its barrel was interchangeable by simply loosening two bolts with the provided Torx wrench. With these upgrades, the Barrett sniper rifle could be changed to a serviceable battle rifle quickly. Duncan was provided one box of ammo and five fully loaded, ten-round magazines.

"Park, I couldn't ask for anything more except a little warmer weather," said Duncan as a chill came over his body. There was no wind and the night was clear, allowing for a frost to settle in over this portion of North Korea.

"Well, as far as I can tell, we've got about a four-mile hike over the river and through the woods that will surely work up a sweat for us both."

"Let's pack up our gear and put everything back the way we found it," started Duncan. "I'm gonna remove the distributor cap and hide it close by so nobody can run off with our truck. If they come upon it, it'll look broken down."

"What about the gun cases?" asked Park.

"We'll carry them for a while, hiding them in the woods as we go. I wanna leave this truck without a trace of anything out of the ordinary. Let's not give them a trail straight to us, right?"

"Right!" agreed Park as he hustled to cover the now-empty compartment.

CHAPTER 38

November 13
Near Kusong, North Korea

Duncan and Park donned the peasant garb provided by MI6 and smudged their faces with dirt. Park wore a set of earmuffs, and Duncan, attempting to hide his sandy blond hair, wore a peasant cap with fur ear covers. Under close scrutiny, he'd never pass as a local. But from afar, he was only slightly out of place because of his nearly six-foot frame. Most Koreans were five feet nine inches tall, like Park.

The men hoisted the empty duffle bags over their shoulders, which concealed their rucksacks and the Barrett slung over Duncan's shoulder, but under his coat. Although they were hyperaware of their surroundings, they couldn't appear to be in a battle mindset. Despite the darkness and the desolate location, the men were never certain who might be watching them.

They took the path deeper into the woods. Duncan moved along the left side of the road closer to the river, and Park paralleled his movements through the edge of the forest on the right side. To the untrained eye, they looked like typical North Korean farmers walking along a path.

An hour later, the outer perimeter of the Kusong military base lay ahead of them. After a review of the topography map provided by the Brits, Duncan determined they'd need to pass through the camp's perimeter fence and cut through a mountain pass to reach their proposed shooting site. He plugged the coordinates of the site into the handheld GPS device and led the way.

185

Duncan looked behind him and then darted across the narrowing path to join his partner. "Park, we're getting close to the perimeter fence according to the GPS coordinates. If it's too tall, or manned, we'll have to find a way around it to the south, but that'll cost us a lot of time."

"Let's see what we run into," said Park. "We might be able to avoid the fence by using the riverbank. I don't think breaching it is the best idea, especially if it appears to be patrolled on a regular basis."

Duncan nodded and led them through the woods as the path came to an end. The clear skies allowed him the full moon to navigate by. The stars were extraordinarily bright, reminding him of the views during clear evenings at the Armstrong Ranch, where ambient light didn't distract the naked eye from the beauty of the universe.

They soon reached the outer perimeter fence of Kusong's military base. The ten-foot-tall fence was roped with razor wire at the top. A quick examination of the structure revealed that this stretch of fencing was not electrified. On the inside, a well-worn ten-foot-wide path indicated it was regularly patrolled.

"Whadya think?" asked Duncan.

Park studied the simple chain-link fence. It was stretched from post to post without regard for the terrain. "We could follow it until we find a low spot in the ground where we can slip under. Or there is the river option."

"I don't like the riverbank because we'll be exposed to the other side, which runs along the highway. If they have night vision, we're toast."

They made their way along the fence into the woods. Duncan carefully moved underbrush out of the way to clear the way for his partner. As they crept forward, they saw a burst of light. Duncan raised his fist into the air, and Park crashed into him in the dark.

"What?" Park whispered.

"A flash of light up ahead a hundred feet," said Duncan.

The men found cover and studied the area where Duncan had

seen the flash. A small red glow appeared.

"A cherry," said Park. "That's the lit end of a cigarette. You must have seen him light up."

"Yeah, and this sucks for more than one reason. Look at the gap up ahead. It's perfect to crawl through, but this guy would be all over us."

"We could wait him out," Park suggested.

"We could also take him out, but he'll be discovered missing at some point tomorrow. That'll draw too much attention."

Park craned his neck to look over the underbrush. "Is he alone?"

"Best I can tell. What are you thinking?"

"A distraction. When I was a kid, my father taught me how to throw my voice. You know, like a ventriloquist."

"Yeah, I get it," said Duncan. "How's that gonna help?"

"I practiced making animal sounds to mess with my sisters," he replied. "When they were playing in the backyard near the woods, I'd scare them by growling. I could sound like a dog, a bobcat, and even a badger."

"Seriously, a badger? Do they have badgers in North Korea?" asked Duncan.

"Probably more of them than dogs. You know what they say about Koreans eating dogs? That's true in the North. These people are starving. I'm pretty sure a badger wouldn't let itself get caught. They're mean and awnry sons of bitches."

"Go for it," said Duncan. "If we can lure him away, we can sneak in behind him and keep working our way toward the mountain."

"All right. Get into position to cross. I'm going to make a wide arc through the woods to draw attention up a ways. Then I'll double back to join you. Worst case, better silence that sidearm. We don't want him to get off a round first."

"Agreed. Good luck, Mr. Badger," said Duncan as he patted his partner on the shoulder. Duncan crawled on his belly to reach the low spot in the forest floor. The gap between the dry creek bed and the bottom of the fence was just enough to crawl through.

Park slipped off into the darkness, keeping a constant eye on the smoking cigarette, which provided just enough of a red glow to mark the soldier's position.

Over the years, he'd continued to practice the *distant effect*, the technical term for throwing your voice. It required a series of inhales and exhales to take a large amount of air into his lungs.

Park took several breaths to simulate the breathing pattern and to help him relax. He placed the back of his tongue against the roof of his mouth, effectively closing off his throat. Pulling his stomach in at the same time, he tightened his diaphragm to apply pressure below his lungs. Finally, he slowly exhaled, letting out a guttural groaning noise as his breath left his throat.

The low-pitched, rumbling sound of a badger was used as a warning to intruders near its territory, or when they were defending their young against a predator.

By stretching out the exhale when he groaned, and finishing it off with an extended *aah* sound, the effect of the noise was to appear like it came from a distance.

Park mustered all of his recollection from childhood and years of practice and gave an Academy Award performance. The badger-like sound was one of his best and quickly grabbed the attention of the soldier, who raised his weapon and darted away from Duncan's position after tossing his cigarette to the ground.

Park knew he had to hustle back to the fence before the soldier realized it was a false alarm. Park also realized the soldier would likely be back to retrieve his still-burning cigarette, a precious commodity to a young North Korean in the military.

By the time he reached the opening, Duncan had passed. Park surveyed the perimeter road one last time and shimmied under the fence. He quickly darted to the woods on the other side, where Duncan reached an outstretched hand to grab him from behind a large Korean red pine, which dominated the forests in this part of the country.

"Good work," whispered Duncan. "There's a trail that leads in the general direction we want. Let's put some distance between us and the badger hunter."

The guys walked heel-to-toe, making steady time as they traversed the forest and began a steady incline up the side of the mountains that separated the Kusong Base from the surrounding farmlands to the west.

The men took another three hours to crest the top of the ridge and begin their slow descent to the other side. By two in the morning, they'd found a place suitable for sleeping in their ghillie suits, which provided some warmth in the thirty-five-degree frosty night.

CHAPTER 39

November 14
National Military Command Center
The Pentagon
Washington, DC

Defense Secretary Gregg spent a few minutes with the chairman of the Joint Chiefs of Staff as they entered the National Military Command Center, commonly referred to as the war room within the Pentagon. In this command and communications center, all activities of the U.S. military are directed.

Both men were en route to a briefing but had several minutes to interact with the troops who manned the computer stations and monitored U.S. military operations worldwide.

Secretary Gregg was extremely popular with the troops. He was a soldier's soldier, born and raised on a military base and, as a result, dedicated his entire life to the defense of the United States. His network of close allies stretched around the globe and through every aspect of the military. Even the chairman of the Joint Chiefs considered Secretary Montgomery Gregg a close friend and confidant.

After some pleasantries were exchanged, they entered the briefing room and introduced themselves to Colonel Kimberly Sterling with the Air Force Space Command. Based at Peterson Air Force Base near Cheyenne Mountain in Colorado, the U.S. Space Command coordinated a variety of satellite and cyber operations in support of the U.S. military.

They were also responsible for monitoring space situational awareness via the Air Force Satellite Control Network. AFSCN provided tracking data to the Pentagon, which helped catalog space objects and low-earth orbit satellites launched by other countries.

This briefing was suggested by AFSCN the day before, and Colonel Sterling, the head of the satellite reconnaissance team, flew to Washington to conduct it herself. Everyone took a seat, and Colonel Sterling powered up the four wall monitors at the end of the briefing room.

Her first graphic provided a timeline of events to set the stage. "On February 7, 2016, North Korea launched a satellite into orbit. NORAD tracked the missile on a southerly trajectory over the Yellow Sea and immediately determined it was not a ballistic missile threat to the U.S. mainland or its allies.

"An hour following the launch, North Korean officials formally proclaimed their mission a success. USSTRATCOM confirmed two new space objects were detected. One was confirmed to be a Kwangmyongsong-4, or KMS-4, satellite. The other object was likely the rocket's first stage, which was later detected falling harmlessly through the Earth's atmosphere over the Indian Ocean."

"The so-called Super Bowl Satellite," added Secretary Gregg. "If I remember correctly, Kim Jong-un was so proud of the accomplishment that he orchestrated a massive fireworks display over Pyongyang to commemorate the launch."

"Exactly, Mr. Secretary," said Colonel Sterling with a nod. "North Korea further boasted that it could fly a nuclear-equipped satellite over any position in America with its technologically advanced navigation systems."

Secretary Gregg added, "At the time, the executive director of the task force dealing with electromagnetic pulse attacks warned that North Korea may have launched a satellite-borne EMP. He warned that the DPRK was capable of placing a nuclear warhead aboard one of these satellites, which could be dropped on our heads."

Originally established at the urging of Speaker of the House Newt Gingrich, the EMP Commission in Congress conducted extensive research, tirelessly conducting tests, identifying risks, and performing statistical probabilities concerning the immediate and long-term impact of an EMP attack on the United States. Their findings were startling.

This unpaid group of scientists, engineers, and security experts agreed. An EMP attack on America would likely result in the destruction of the nation's power grid and civil infrastructure, including dangers to nuclear facilities.

The abilities of our government to function at local, state, and federal levels would be hampered or shut down altogether. The corresponding economic collapse and resulting societal unrest would ravage the country unchecked as first responders would be overwhelmed, or abandon their posts altogether to protect their own families.

As General John E. Hyten, commander of USSTRATCOM, said, *It's more than a dangerous threat. It is a total game-changer—an event to end life as we know it. A high-altitude EMP detonation would turn off every light, burn up every kind of computer, fry every cell phone, and stop virtually every vehicle within the blast's reach. That's what an EMP does. It brings our world to a screeching halt and throws us back to the 1800s technologically, for years.*

Despite these dire warnings over the last three decades, the suggestions of the EMP Commission have gone largely ignored and opposed by the energy industry. Some federal regulators, such as FERC, the Federal Energy Regulatory Commission, and most electric utilities have sought to maintain a status quo, which, the EMP Commission argues, leaves ninety percent of Americans at risk.

Eventually, due to lack of additional congressional funding, the EMP Commission was abandoned in 2021 with President Billings's new budget. The commission's paltry appropriation of under a million dollars was deemed excessive. Ironically, the EMP Commission's budget fell under the overall appropriations of FERC, the very agency that pushed back against the commission's findings.

There was one statistic that remained unrefuted and was therefore cited repeatedly by the media and those who encouraged the government to take action to harden the power grid—*ninety percent of*

Americans would die within one year of an EMP attack.

Colonel Sterling continued. "As always, the U.S. and its allies in the region roundly condemned the launch. At Peterson, we immediately established tracking of the KMS-4 satellite, which we redesignated as NORAD 41332. As promised, NORAD 41332 passed over the Super Bowl in Santa Clara, California, during halftime, indicating North Korea's ability to plan and control the satellite's path."

The USAF colonel tapped a few keys on her keyboard and pulled up a monitor depicting the satellite's current positioning. The split screen depicted the earth from high Earth orbit, or approximately twenty-two-thousand miles above the planet. The left side of the screen was a closer view of the planet using a traditional map identifying countries and major bodies of water.

NORAD 41332 had just traveled over Australia, travelling toward the north and China.

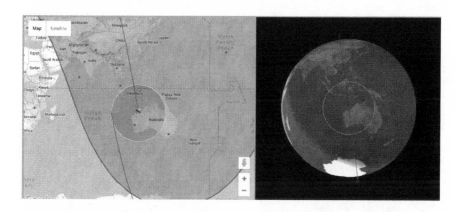

"As you can see, in the time it took me to introduce this screen to you, the satellite has now traveled hundreds of miles and is currently over Mongolia."

"What is the second line to the left of Australia?" asked Secretary Gregg.

"Sir, the line overlaid on the map represents its projected trajectory. After NORAD 41332 passed over the Arctic, it will travel across the western hemisphere and eventually return to the line of trajectory indicated, in the Indian Ocean just west of Australia."

"Thank you, Colonel. Does the projected trajectory ever deviate?"

"Rarely, sir," she replied. "After the initial launch in 2016, the trajectory remained the same until July 27, 2017, when the Iranians launched its most advanced satellite to date aboard the Simorgh rocket. This satellite carried the same technology as the North Korean KMS-4, which sent alarm bells throughout the world."

Secretary Gregg stood and walked up to the monitor. NORAD 41332 had crossed over Russia and approached the Arctic Circle. "Iranian state television called the rocket Phoenix, and the satellite was determined to be a near-clone of the DPRKs launch of eighteen months earlier. As was typical, we denounced the launch and even claimed the rocket had suffered a catastrophic failure and blew up."

"That's correct, sir," interjected Colonel Sterling as she turned on another monitor and revealed a second satellite being tracked. "The Iranians, like Kim Jong-un, immediately issued threats and warnings. They said if their interests were ever violated, they'd issue a *proper answer* to the United States."

The Iranian satellite was tracking a much westerly orbit of the Earth. As NORAD 41332 passed over Greenland, the Iranian satellite travelled in a southerly direction over Canada.

"Colonel, are you suggesting that these satellites are capable of carrying nuclear warheads?" asked the chairman of the Joint Chiefs.

"Sir, the technology was there in 2016," replied Colonel Sterling. "We have now confirmed that the Iranians adjusted the trajectory of their satellite to match the geosynchronous orbit of NORAD 41332. The two have adopted an identical geostationary orbit twenty-seven-hundred miles apart."

"Explain the difference, please," Secretary Gregg requested.

"Geosynchronous follows the direction of the Earth's rotation. Geostationary adds an additional element that assures a satellite returns to the same point in the sky at the same time each day."

"Why is this significant?" asked the chairman of the JCS.

Secretary Gregg didn't need to ask. He now understood where this briefing was going. He returned to his seat with a grim look on his face.

"Sir, with the adjusted flight path, the Iranian satellite will pass over America's West Coast at the precise time NORAD 41332 passes over the major population centers on our East Coast."

The room grew quiet at the implications of this revelation.

The chairman of the Joint Chiefs asked a follow-up question. "At what altitude will they pass?"

"Roughly one thousand miles above the Earth's surface, sir. The worst-case scenario for an EMP detonation would be around two hundred fifty to three hundred miles above the Earth's surface. A three-hundred-mile altitude would create an EMP impact radius of nearly fifteen hundred miles. The lower the detonation altitude, the smaller the radius, but the impact would be felt by all electronic devices."

"Colonel, why do you think the Iranians and North Koreans have timed their trajectories in what appears to be a perfectly choreographed orbit?" asked Secretary Gregg.

"Our working theory, sir, is that they want to time their satellites to be over Northern California and our population centers in the northeast, including New York and Washington, at the same time."

"A simultaneous attack would damage us from coast to coast, would it not?" asked Secretary Gregg.

"Yes, sir, depending on altitude and location of the detonation."

"How often does this perfect alignment occur?" asked the chairman of the JCS.

The colonel hesitated and returned to her seat. As she sat, she looked at both men directly. "Every day, sir. At multiple times every single day."

Secretary Gregg took a moment and closed his eyes, assessing the threat from above to America's soft underbelly below. Every day, at the given moment, the United States could be attacked from the sky without warning or ability to defend itself. He leaned back in his chair and stared toward the ceiling.

Then he glanced at the monitors. The North Korean satellite, now labeled NORAD 41332, hovered ominously over St. Louis, Missouri, the heartland of America.

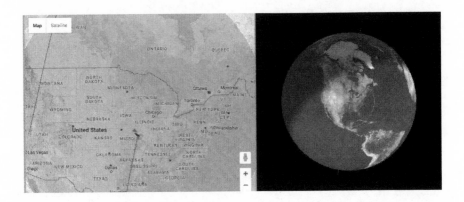

Chapter 40

November 14
Central Luxury Mansion
Ryongsong Residence
Pyongyang, North Korea

In the early 1980s, the Korean People's Army constructed a fortified compound to be the primary residence of then-ruler Kim Il-sung. When Kim Jong-un succeeded his father as supreme leader, he adopted the Ryongsong Residence, also referred to as the Central Luxury Mansion, as his main residence.

The complex was far more than his primary residence. Above ground, the buildings were protected by numerous military units stationed with a broad array of weaponry. Multiple layers of electric fencing, minefields, and security checkpoints deterred any type of ground assault of the residence.

Aerial assaults would likely fail as well. Beneath the Ryongsong Residence, an underground wartime headquarters existed. The cavernous space was protected with walls reinforced by iron rods and concrete coated in lead to protect the headquarters from nuclear attack. A myriad of secured tunnels ran to an underground train station, which stretched to various points in the North Korean countryside. Pedestrian tunnels led to large houses, beautiful gardens, and man-made lakes within the secured perimeter.

One of these residences, Changgyong Residence, was home to his beloved sister and new member of the politburo, Kim Yo-jong. She had been instrumental in convincing her brother to become a *man of the people* by making more public appearances, from his early interaction with American NBA basketball star Dennis Rodman to frequent appearances at fairground attractions, state-run factories, and of course, high-profile displays of North Korea's military might.

He'd just completed an official state visit from the Chinese ambassador, who carried a message from Beijing. Officially, he was advised the Americans had threatened retaliation if he followed through with his scheduled missile launch the next day. Unofficially, both men agreed that the Americans were just posturing, as they always had for decades. The entire world knew they would not undertake a first strike unless the DPRK attacked the U.S. or one of its protected allies first.

Kim's sister sat in on the meeting but remained quiet throughout. She knew her position was to remain stoic, standing by her brother in public, but capable of speaking freely to him in private. The two descended into the war room below the Ryongsong Residence together and stopped in an opulent parlor to have tea before they continued with their day.

He'd just instructed his military leaders to reach out to their back-channel liaisons in Japan and South Korea to be prepared for military drills to be conducted by the DPRK's military. These conversations routinely occurred behind the scenes to avoid his actions being mistaken for military provocation.

The United States had just flown several B-1B bomber missions along the edge of North Korean waters as a show of force. Kim Jong-un was concerned because his radar units had failed to pick up the bombers until they were a hundred miles away from his coastline. He went into a rage with his generals, who immediately snatched up two radar operators and hauled them to another room.

The actions by the U.S. military were similar to the attempts to provoke Kim five years ago when they flew multiple B-1B missions over the South Korean half of the peninsula below the 38th parallel. The veiled threats didn't stop the scheduled missile test then, nor would it stop the one scheduled for tomorrow.

"Sister, they are a weak bully," started Kim as he calmly sipped his tea and settled into a chair. He continued to gain weight, resulting in the removal of all couches from areas he frequented. He'd suffered an embarrassing moment the year before when he'd settled into a couch on the residential level and was unable to get off it without help.

He continued to make his point. "Do they have nuclear weapons? Yes, but so do we. Unlike them, I have the courage and strength given to me by our father to use them."

"Dear Leader, my brother, they have much to lose," said Kim Yo-jong, referring to her brother as Dear Leader as a show of respect. "We may be smaller in size, but we are bigger in heart. That is why they cower at your shows of force and run away like the mice they are."

"Yes, sister, you do understand. What the Americans do not understand is that we desire this confrontation. We want to prove to the world once and for all which country is mightier."

"Indeed, Dear Leader, I know this. I also know that the only words from our comrades in Beijing and Moscow that are expected to be abided by are *don't shoot first*. It is a smart political move, and only one which someone of your patience can observe."

Kim Jong-un reached for an Ovomaltine biscuit cookie from a plate adjacent to his chair. He dipped it into his tea, as he'd learned to do in those two years in Switzerland with his sister. The brand outside of Switzerland was usually called Ovaltine, the powdery drink mix many Swiss and American kids grew up on. The Swiss division of Ovomaltine made a crunchy biscuit, which was frequently dipped in milk or hot tea.

Kim Jong-un cherished the memories of Switzerland with his sister and had ordered thousands of cases of the product to be available to him in each of his residences and work spaces. Calories, obviously, were not a consideration.

"Sister, we will not strike right away unless provoked. But when we do, the world will never forget. We will cement our position in history and gain the respect of leaders that has eluded our country for decades."

Kim Yo-jong sipped the hot tea and peered over her cup as her brother spoke. She smiled as she admired his spirit and resourcefulness.

"You deserve this, my brother. Dear Leader, I know your day in the spotlight will come!"

CHAPTER 41

November 14
Central Luxury Mansion
Ryongsong Residence
Pyongyang, North Korea

Following their tea time together, Kim Jong-un and his sister entered the war room, where his generals stood awaiting his orders. The technology available to the DPRK was advanced, although perhaps a year or two behind that of the United States.

Unit 180, Kim Jong-un's online army consisting of six thousand of the country's best cyber warriors, had mastered the ability to infiltrate the U.S. Departments of State and Defense for more than a decade. What they couldn't learn from hacking the Americans, they were easily capable of obtaining from its allies—Japan and South Korea.

The world once laughed at the DPRK's ability to engage in cyber warfare, but that all changed in 2014, the day of the SONY Pictures cyber intrusion. When Kim Jong-un learned of SONY Pictures' new film project *The Interview*, a comedy that shed the Dear Leader in a bad light, Unit 180 deployed a malware known as *Shamoon Wiper* to erase Sony's IT infrastructure.

In addition, the hackers of Unit 180, who cleverly called themselves the Guardians of Peace, or GOP, began leaking confidential emails of top Sony executives, A-list Hollywood stars, and their agents. The contents of these emails threw the media into a frenzy, and Sony demanded action be taken against the DPRK.

Within the next several years, Unit 180 stole millions from banks, brought the National Health Service of Great Britain to its knees, and infiltrated the details of top-secret military planning exchanged between South Korea and the Pentagon.

But their high-profile hacks paled in comparison to the amount of proprietary software and design they stole from international companies every day, including from their closest ally—China. These products and technologies were reverse engineered by North Korean scientists and internet technology specialists before being incorporated for the benefit of the Korean People's Army.

Kim's war room closely monitored the United States as it escalated its forces in the region. When the third carrier strike group entered the Sea of Japan, his generals sounded alarms, which placed their military apparatus on its highest alert.

Today, the military loaded two Stormpetrel antiship cruise missiles on a newly-placed-into-service Wonsan guided-missile patrol boat. The vessels were ordered to patrol North Korea's east coast along the edge of its territorial waters.

The Wonsans were intended to be highly visible to the Americans. They would be closely monitored and, hopefully, distract them while Kim released his newest weapon, one that was far more stealthy than the Wonsan patrol boats.

"Sister, today is a momentous one for us as well," started Kim Jong-un as he approached his always eager group of generals, most of whom were in their seventies. Impeccably dressed, the men always awaited every word out of Dear Leader's mouth, and stood with pen in hand to jot down every directive. "This is our greatest naval achievement, sister, the Pukkuksong-1 submarine, codename KN-11. This underwater demon carries an advanced nuclear warhead that can reach America's West Coast, Hawaii or Guam. But I will use it to punish Seoul for their alliance with the Americans. If they attack us, we will attack Seoul as the first step in reunifying the Korean Peninsula under our rule."

"Dear Leader, this is a magnificent achievement by you and your generals," started his sister, much to the delight of the generals, who appreciated being recognized. Her brother didn't praise his military leaders. Their father had told him it was a sign of weakness. "It is a shame that reunification can't be achieved without loss of life to our distant cousins."

"Yes, sister, but that has been their choice," he quickly replied in a tone that shut down the conversation. This moment was about achievements, not the shortcomings of his regime's policies. He turned to his generals and gestured for them to proceed.

"Dear Leader," one of the generals began to explain, "the KN-11 is diesel powered and will therefore leave a footprint for the Americans to track as it drops to its lowest depth. To mask and confuse their devices, we will also launch three Sang-O II submarines with it in a cluster formation. Initially, it will appear as one or two vessels being launched. Then we will split into two groups. Once the KN-11 is at its lowest depth, we will divide into three distinct paths leading away from your great achievement's location."

Kim Jong-un stood a little taller and smiled. He had learned the art of deterrence over the years from his father. When it was his turn to lead the regime, he'd mastered a level of political prowess to go along with his nature's military might.

While the entire world was singularly focused on his nuclear proliferation, he was building a massive ground force together with a respectable navy. With the addition of Russian technology, he'd transformed his Air Force from one using outdated MIG-21 and MIG-23 technology to the more modern and capable MIG-35Ds, a dual-seat fighter with advanced avionics and weapons systems capable of competing with any American aircraft.

His father, Kim Jong-iL, had sought to reunify the Korean Peninsula, a goal which would satisfy his people and establish a legacy for Kim Jong-un's regime. After his father's death in 2011, he knew the world expected this to be his goal. However short he might be in stature, Kim Jong-un's lofty goals would make him a giant among men.

CHAPTER 42

November 14
The Situation Room
The White House
Washington, DC

The weight of the world weighed upon President Harman as she sat in the end seat of the conference table of the Situation Room. The Situation Room was born out of frustration on the part of President John Kennedy after the Bay of Pigs debacle in Cuba. President Kennedy was angered by the conflicting advice and information coming in to him from the various agencies that comprised the nation's defense departments. During the Truman presidency, a bowling alley had been built on the lower level of the West Wing, but it was ordered to be removed and replaced with the Situation Room by President Kennedy.

Initially, before the age of electronics, President Kennedy required at least one Central Intelligence analyst remain in the Situation Room at all times. The analyst would work a twenty-hour shift and sleep on a cot during the night.

Other presidents, like Nixon and Ford, never used the Situation Room. In most cases, a visit from the president was a formal undertaking, happening only on rare occasions. President George H.W. Bush, a former CIA head, would frequently call and ask if he could stop by and say hello.

When there had been a foreign policy failure, such as when the shoe bomber boarded a flight on Christmas Day in 2009, the Situation Room became a forum for a tongue-lashing of top-level intelligence and national security personnel. Today, it was the scene of a tense standoff between the world's major superpower and a gnat that had been flying in out of America's ears for decades.

President Harman was joined by Chief of Staff Acton, her national security advisor, and the head of the CIA. Defense Secretary Gregg was unable to attend so that he could continue to monitor the scheduled war games with the South Koreans.

"Gentlemen, how certain is your intelligence regarding this launch?" asked the president as she twirled a pen through her fingers. She continued to stare at the satellite feeds provided by the Pentagon, which focused on her carrier groups positioning themselves in the Sea of Japan and the missile launch site in Kusong. "This could either be a momentous occasion where our final attempts at diplomacy work, or it could be the start of world war three. Either way, I wanna be in the room when it happens."

Acton looked at their CIA chief. "Is the intel rock solid?"

The longtime CIA director nodded. "Rock solid, sir, within a twenty-four-hour time period. Years of intelligence have brought us to the point where we can identify with relative certainty when the missile launches will take place. Because of weather patterns across that portion of North Korea, the launch must take place either today or tomorrow. It will be sunny and thirty-five degrees today and tomorrow, but after that, a cold front moves through, bringing plummeting temperatures, wind, and snow for days."

The president nodded and checked her watch. It was approaching six thirty in the evening in Washington, but eight o'clock the next morning in Kusong, North Korea, a thirteen-and-a-half-hour difference.

President Harman had aged since entering the Oval Office following the death of President Billings. When she was tapped for the VP slot, she knew there was the possibility of his taking ill, or even dying. He was the oldest president ever elected to the office.

As president, like her predecessors, she had to make decisions that would have a profound impact on the world. In many ways, the demands and pressures were more than any one human being could carry out, but the Constitution required the post be manned by only one person.

The room remained quiet as they studied the grainy images from the satellite. The rocket stood upright, ready for launch. Occasionally, a vehicle would scurry across the open space surrounding the launchpad. To the west of the launch facility was the military base and the small town that serviced the soldiers who occupied the facility. Open fields stretched for nearly a mile to the east until a mountain range rose out of the valley. North of the missile launch site, the mountains were closer, allowing for a protective ring to be placed around the launch site in the event of a catastrophic test failure.

President Harman let out a long breath and mumbled under her breath to her chief of staff, "This better work, Charles."

"It will, Madame President, and the world will be much better for it," he replied. "When you and I first sat down and discussed the issues on our platter, the DPRK problem and Iran were numbers two and three behind our intent to help those Americans who've been left behind in our own country. In some respects, this could've been considered number one on our priority list."

"Because of the nuclear threat?" she asked.

"Absolutely," Acton replied. "Iran wanted them and so did North Korea. Now they're working together to achieve nuclear parity with the second tier of nations like Pakistan and India."

President Harman looked at her watch again. Five minutes until launch time. "I'm also concerned about the advancements they've made in their delivery capabilities. With each test, they prove to the world their ICBMs can reach the U.S. mainland, Europe, or virtually any target they choose."

"Madame President," said Acton reassuringly, "if you pull this off, believe me, the mullahs in Tehran will sit up and take notice. With your diplomatic maneuvering, we may have solved both problems at the same time."

The group sat in silence again, staring at the digital clock's tick down to the fateful hour. As the clock struck 8:00 a.m. in Kusong, and the minutes started to tick past the appointed hour, the president grew nervous. She wanted to believe her pressure on the Chinese worked. There was little or no activity at this point. The missile sat alone, pointed upward toward the sky and the watchful eyes of the U.S. satellite.

Today was not the day. Perhaps tomorrow.

CHAPTER 43

November 14
Mountain above Missile Launch Site
Kusong, North Korea

Duncan and Park had reached the summit of the mountain ridge overlooking the Kusong Military base at four o'clock in the morning, allowing them three hours of restless sleep. The mountain ridge overlooking the launch test site was rocky. Their trek was made easier by following a mining road that traversed the face, connecting tunnels to a series of abandoned uranium mines. The sound of wolves howling in the distance discouraged the men from taking up residency in the mines for the night. An abandoned shaft made for a perfect den for the wolves.

The sun began to rise just after seven and warmed Duncan's face. He and Park had gathered twigs and crunchy grasses to incorporate into the ghillies provided to them. They had settled into a swale of soft dirt in between two large boulders that still retained some heat from the prior day's sunshine. By avoiding a soft bed of grass or lichens, they prevented moisture from entering their suits and bodies. Dirt and rocks were the best insulators of heat.

Park began to stir, and Duncan reminded him to keep his head down. In the darkness, with only the faint moonlight for them to get their bearings, the men ran the risk of positioning themselves within view of base activity in the valley below them.

Duncan had spent many years growing up hiking throughout the desert southwest. He'd taken trips as a teen through Utah, Nevada and Colorado, where the mountainous terrain was very similar to North Korea's. The climate reminded him somewhat of the Rockies as well. The famous 38ᵗʰ parallel, which formed the border between North and South Korea, split the United States in half as well, running from the Pacific Northwest, through northern Nevada, Utah and ultimately through West Virginia.

Duncan peered over the rock outcropping that separated the two boulders. The view below was striking. He took in a panorama of prairie land, complete with tall grasses and the occasional pine tree. It was desolate except for one thing—an eighty-foot-tall intercontinental ballistic missile rose over the next ridge below him, which stood in stark contrast to the peaceful grasslands surrounding it.

"Rise and shine, Comrade Park," said Duncan jokingly.

"Very funny, cowboy," Park shot back as he made every effort to work out the kinks from sleeping on the uneven ground. He rose to his knees and shook his ghillie suit like a shaggy English sheepdog. Dust flew off and settled around him. Duncan immediately got the visual of Pigpen in the Charlie Brown cartoons.

"We did a pretty good job of finding our way in the dark," said Duncan. "The main base is to our right, tucked around the mountain. I can see the tip of the missile from here, but this is still too far away to see the observation area. We're gonna have to make our way to the ridge below us."

Park moved forward to get a better view. "So weird, right? I mean, what's wrong with this picture?"

"The Hwasong-18 is wrong in every picture," replied Duncan. "It's their newest technology, a hybrid of their prior successes in the portable Hwasong-class of ICBMs with the larger nuclear warhead provided by the Taepodong. This missile can reach any point in the U.S. or Europe with ease."

"I wish we could take it out, too," quipped Park.

"It would take a lot of C-4 to topple it, but besides, they'd just build another one. They probably have a couple more in waiting."

Park shook his head in disgust. "Sadly, they'd rather build missiles than feed their people."

Duncan pulled back between the boulders and searched through his rucksack for a protein bar. He didn't want to feel full as they made their way through the rock formations today.

"I'm gonna trust the bosses on this one. You don't just take out a despot like Kim Jong-un because you don't like him. Clearly, the scumbag deserves to die, and I'm gonna deliver the bullet. I just hope they have a plan in place to keep the nukes from flying. Talkin' a bunch of BS back in forth in the media is one thing. Intentionally instigating a nuclear war would make zero sense."

"You're still up for this, aren't you?" asked Park.

"Yeah, of course. I'm just sayin' that I don't want us to be responsible for world war three. Wars have been started on less provocation than this."

Park settled in and ate his breakfast MRE consisting of apple maple oatmeal warmed with a flameless ration heater. The packet contained thirteen hundred calories, which would provide him energy for the morning.

"What's the plan?" asked Park.

Duncan took another look over the rock ledge. "It's impossible to see anything from up here. There are no mining roads to assist us this time, so we'll have to find our way down to the next ridge without being seen. As we move closer to the base, we've gotta move slowly and keep our heads down. I'm sure there are patrols that scan this ridge from time to time."

"First, we'll establish our hide. Then we better think about how we're gonna get the heck out of Dodge after the shot."

"I have an idea for that as well," said Duncan. "Let's move out."

CHAPTER 44

November 14
Mountain above Missile Launch Site
Kusong, North Korea

Working their way down the ridge in their ghillie suits was no small feat. Between the suit itself and the added layers of natural foliage, it was like rock-climbing while carrying a greenhouse. As they reached the valley below the tallest ridge, the base at Kusong came into full view. It was bustling with activity, no doubt making sure they'd pass inspection if Dear Leader requested one.

"I'm glad they're spending their time and attention on tidying up for tomorrow's big day," said Park as a truck raced across the concrete launch site in the opposite direction of their position.

He pulled the spotting scope out of his rucksack and surveyed the grounds surrounding the missile. Other than the buildings on the outer perimeter of the base located to his right, there were no other structures except for the supposed location of the observation stand beneath a stand of pine trees below them.

Duncan used his binoculars to study the area as well. The launchpad sat in a bowl between two mountain ridges before it opened up into a valley. The dual ridges gave them two possible vantage points. The ridge opposite their current location gave them a couple of advantages.

"Park, if we could make our way to the ridge on the other side of the observation stage, I'd have a better shot without the pine trees negatively effecting the trajectory. Plus, there is the added benefit of our escape route."

"Okay, let's talk about that first 'cause I really don't plan on dying in North Korea."

Duncan settled in behind a rock and gestured for Park to do the same. He retrieved a map from his pack, along with the GPS device.

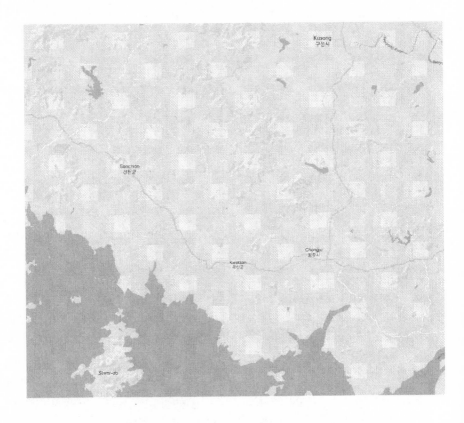

Duncan laid out his plan. "Our extraction point is here, at Sinmi-do, to our southwest. The island is connected by this small land bridge, which allows vehicular traffic in and out to the fishing villages."

"Our calculations put the distance at twenty-one miles from our current position," added Park. "If we move to the ridge on the other side of the test site, we cut off a mile or so."

"At a twenty-minute pace, that could make all the difference. Launch is scheduled for eight in the morning, we bug out along the south side of the test site instead of backtracking to our vehicle as planned."

Park leaned back and studied the map for a second. "You wanna abandon the truck? Whadya mean about twenty-minute pace?" he asked hesitantly.

"That's the first thing the patrol guards will be checking. Traffic will be snarled as vehicles are inspected, and I really don't think our cover will withstand scrutiny. We're better off walking to Sinmi-do."

"Twenty miles? With all of this gear?" asked Park with trepidation in his voice.

"You can handle it. I'm only talking about carrying our weapons, binoculars, and the GPS. I'll carry the rucksack with ammo and the rifle. At a steady pace, we can make it before dark."

"Duncan, seriously. That's almost like walking a marathon. I walked eight miles once, ten years ago. There's gotta be a better way."

Duncan thought for a moment. "The only other option is to identify and prepare our hide, then double back tonight to retrieve the truck. We can bring it to this mining town on the other side of the ridge at Anch'ang-dong. We'll ditch it and then try to make our way through the roadblocks."

Park began to calculate the time associated with retrieving the truck. "I don't think that'll work either. We don't have enough time to double back, retrieve the truck, and still have our wits about us to take the shot in the morning. Let's do it your way, but after we get settled in the hide, let's study this map again. Maybe we can come up with another mode of transportation."

"Saddle up but keep your head down," said Duncan as he began to move through the rock formations and descended closer to the valley at the next ridge.

The terrain was treacherous and required them to be careful with their footing to avoid a sprained ankle. All of the variables with this mission raced through his head as they worked their way around the launch site. He wondered if there were any circumstances under which he'd call off the mission. This had never been addressed during their brief meeting with Campbell at Misawa. He got the sense a lot was riding on his successful takedown of Kim Jong-un.

Two hours later, the men emerged atop the ridge facing the far side of Kusong and the launch site. At the lower elevation, the rocket towered into the sky, standing alone waiting its orders. The view of the observation area was much better from this direction with one disadvantage—the shot would have to come from behind their target. If Kim Jong-un was surrounded by his entourage of generals and politburo members, they might effectively shield Dear Leader from Duncan's shot. The other side of the ridge afforded him a direct, frontal shot, albeit through a stand of pine trees.

The men studied their options and moved to a rock ledge that dropped nearly a hundred feet to the side of the ridge below. The more Duncan studied the options, the better he liked the ledge.

"I don't know, Park. This is pretty dang good right here. It's like a platform. No obstructions. Also, it gives us a clear path out of here down the other side of the ridge."

Park nodded. "I agree. The report from the Barrett will send them in all directions chasing their tails. We'll get a decent head start out of the camp before our hide is discovered."

Duncan looked around and found an area of soft sand and dirt. "Look, we can sleep there tonight. After we take the shot, throw our stuff in the shallow space and dump some rocks on top. In their frenzy, they might just miss it. That'll help."

Park pointed over the edge of the rock ledge toward the observation platform. "Look, we've got some activity down below."

Duncan slipped the ghillie hood over his face and slithered like a snake to the edge. He shook his head to remove a piece of dead grass that had stuck into his ear. He'd taken shots in a ghillie suit before. They were a distraction and required an inordinate amount of concentration. He wondered if the suit was worth the concealment effort in light of the lack of patrols.

He morphed into a near-motionless shape and studied the activity through his binoculars.

"I guess our intel was right. They're adding a table and chairs to the platform. They're placing flags behind the table as well as some more chairs. A photographer is milling about, checking various angles to take photos."

"Everything is a photo op for this guy," said Park. "Anytime he can show off his military hardware, he appears in his spiffy pin-striped commie suit, black hair slicked back, and a big old grin to match that big old frame of his."

Duncan didn't respond to Park's comments, but instead studied the furniture layout. "It looks like he'll be walking up a few steps nearest to us. Park, I can't wait until he's seated because the flag might affect the shot. If there's even the slightest breeze, the flag will flutter behind his chair."

"Do you wanna take him before he gets on the platform? Maybe after he emerges from the car?" asked Park.

"Either that, or after the launch when he's being congratulated by his buddies. We'll have to make the call as the scene develops."

"Duncan, this sucks. You've got no margin for error. Do you think you'll be able to take a second shot if necessary?"

Duncan took a deep breath and looked at the target area again. "Doubt it. It's gonna have to be one shot, one kill."

CHAPTER 45

November 15
Mountain above Missile Launch Site
Kusong, North Korea

Duncan had another night of uncomfortable sleep mixed with bouts of restlessness. At times, both men found themselves awake, and they rehashed their plan. Preparation for a shot like this one would usually take weeks at any number of U.S. military installations that matched the terrain. North Korea was an enigma in many ways, which prevented planning. Duncan and Park had to rely upon their experience and common sense to successfully strike their target.

Just before sunrise, Duncan's watch vibrated, which brought him out of his semi-slumber. The launch was scheduled for eight a.m., but they expected Kim to arrive earlier for his usual photo-op session.

Both men had their positions ready. Park, as the spotter, positioned himself close enough to Duncan to provide him accurate information without crowding his movements. Neither man expected to take the second shot, but if they did, Duncan would need to insert another .338 round through the bolt action of the Barrett.

After filling his rucksack full of sand, Duncan rested the barrel of the rifle on top and sighted in the general area where he expected Kim Jong-un to emerge from his vehicle. The afternoon before, he and Park had determined the optimal position that provided the best line of sight to their target. They had cleared the ground of stones and debris to provide a comfortable place to lay on their bellies as they waited.

Once again, the nighttime temperatures had dropped into the upper thirties. As the sun rose, the combination of their faces thawing and anxiety brought beads of sweat to the foreheads of both operatives.

The atmospheric conditions couldn't be better. The sky was clear, the air was not particularly damp at this early hour, and there wasn't a trace of wind. It was ideal for a missile launch, and a sniper's bullet.

The men completed their range card and made the necessary adjustments. Duncan took one final look through his scope at the observation platform as well as the stairs leading up to it.

Duncan checked his watch. Ten minutes 'til eight. "Where are they?" he muttered aloud.

Park didn't respond but took the binoculars and began to survey the launchpad area. From the far end, closest to the base, he saw vehicles moving from behind a concrete blast wall similar to those used in airports to protect buildings from jet engine noise.

"Vehicles approaching. Two military escorts. A black sedan of some kind. Another black—"

Duncan interrupted as he saw the vehicles come within the field of vision of his scope. "Mercedes. Of course, Dear Leader rides in style."

Duncan's heart began to race as Park announced, "Showtime."

The vehicles pulled to a stop, and several armed guards exited to quickly check the perimeter. Their focus was under the platform's decking and behind a thatch-roof-type structure near the pine trees on the far side of Duncan's position.

Moments later, they waved to their superior, who ordered the doors to be opened for the dignitaries. Several generals in their customary olive drab uniforms poured out of the vehicles. They scurried about to position themselves near the stairs, most likely according to rank and position.

The occupants of the Mercedes remained in the car for nearly a minute, causing Duncan to become concerned.

"What's the deal?" he asked aloud.

"Hold on," replied Park, who continued to look through the scope. "Of course. They're waiting for the photographer to get into position. Be ready."

Duncan exhaled and relaxed his mind and body. Real time stands still for the sniper, but his mind races at lightning speed. Duncan reconfirmed the adjustments he'd made to the rifle he'd never fired. Once the target was identified, Park would call out the final numbers.

Park, as instructed by Duncan, began to describe what he saw aloud. "Two men emerging from the Benz. Nope. Nope. Not yet."

"Numbers," muttered Duncan as he focused on the men who'd emerged first.

"Three mils head to crotch, dial four hundred."

Duncan carefully turned the knob on his scope to conform to Park's sighting.

"Zero wind. Hold zero mil. Repeat. Hold zero mil. Target emerging. Duncan, they're gonna swarm in behind him as he climbs the stairs."

"Roger that," Duncan whispered. The trigger's factory setting on the Barrett MRAD was two and a quarter pounds—light, smooth, and crisp the way Duncan liked it. When he was growing up on the ranch, his dad had taught him to treat his long rifle gently and with respect. His words passed through his mind. *Don't jerk the trigger, son. Nice and easy.*

Duncan focused on his target as he received assistance walking up the stairs, knowing there would only be one opportunity to make the kill shot.

Ready. Set. Squeeze. Boom.

The recoil hammered the folding stock into his shoulder. The ground vibrated beneath him. The feeling was exhilarating, powerful.

The long-range, high-velocity .338 round left a slight vapor trail as it flew through the air, creating a distortion in the atmosphere. The crack of his rifle reverberated throughout the valley and off the walls of the surrounding ridges.

Time stood still for Duncan as he awaited Park's report.

PART FOUR

CHAPTER 46

November 15
The Situation Room
The White House
Washington, DC

Once again, almost twenty-four hours later, the group had gathered in the Situation Room to watch via satellite the scheduled missile launch at the Kusong launch facility in North Korea. This time, they were joined by Secretary Gregg, whose interest went far beyond the launch. He knew this would be the first, and best, opportunity for his operatives to end Kim Jong-un's life.

"This is nerve-racking," quipped the president as she settled into her chair and crossed her legs. Once again, she nervously fidgeted with her watch, her pen, or anything else within her grasp.

Secretary Gregg watched her for a moment. He held no contempt for her although he disagreed with many of her policies. In a way, she was the perfect occupant of the Oval Office for him to accomplish his purpose. The deep state that stood behind the secretive work undertaken by Secretary Gregg's assassins would've never tried this bold action if President Billings were still alive. Say what you will about the man's advanced age and gaffe-prone statements, he was dialed into world affairs, especially as it affected the military.

"Did you see those trucks pulling away from the missile?" asked President Harman.

"Yes, Madame President, it appears they are readying for launch," replied her national security advisor. "It appears to be a lot more activity than yesterday, which leads me to believe the launch is imminent."

"The incoming weather pattern, as predicted, forced the launch for today," added the CIA director. "In fact, the front has accompanying high winds. If the launch doesn't go as planned, they might need to remove the missile from the launchpad for safety reasons."

Secretary Gregg sat in silence toward the rear of the room, periodically scrolling through his messages from the Pentagon. He knew today's launch would happen because the intel received from Kim Jong-un's sister had confirmed it. A slight smile came across his face.

A student of military history, his mind wandered to the decisive victory achieved by US Naval Forces over the Japanese at Guadalcanal on this date in 1942. It was the first major offensive and a decisive victory for Allied forces in the Pacific theater.

Building on their success at Guadalcanal, the Allies continued their campaigns against Japan, which ultimately ended in their surrender. President Roosevelt, when he learned of the success of the combined forces at Guadalcanal, said, *It would seem that the turning point in this war has at last been reached.*

Secretary Gregg saw today as a pivotal point in world history, one that he was a major part of. Within minutes, Kim Jong-un would likely be dead, and North Korea would be on the path to freedom and an accepted country on the world stage. He envisioned millions of grateful North Koreans streaming into the streets in jubilant celebration as the dynastic, oppressive regime collapsed.

"It's almost time," said Acton as all attention was directed to the screen. No vehicles were moving. There appeared to be some activity near an observation tent at the fringe of the concrete launchpad.

"What's happening?" asked the president as trucks began to streak across the paved roads in the valley without choosing any discernible point of interest. "It looks like somebody kicked an ant pile."

"Have they scrubbed the launch?" asked the president.

The director of the CIA walked up to the screen and studied the activity. "Something has happened. There is too much activity for the launch to occur now. Let me contact Langley."

He pulled out his cell phone and walked to a remote corner of the room and placed a call. The national security advisor watched the activity as well and then turned to Secretary Gregg.

"Monty, what do you make of this?"

Gregg leaned back in his chair and tried to look as confused as the others. He held up his cell phone to indicate he'd contact the Pentagon for more information. In this moment, silence was his best ally.

Then Acton spoke up with his opinion. "Maybe the Chinese backed him down? Who knows what they told Kim Jong-un, but it clearly appears the launch is not going to happen. Madame President, I think you can declare this a success."

"I don't know, Charles, it does appear that he has changed his mind for some reason," said the president. "I want to believe that our diplomatic efforts made the difference. Let's go back to the Oval and contact the Chinese ambassador. Hopefully, he can shed some light on what happened."

"I agree," said Acton, who began to gather up their things from the conference table.

The president turned to her three top national defense advisors. "Gentlemen, find out what happened, and when you have a consensus, contact Charles and set up a briefing for me. Thank you."

Secretary Gregg pushed himself up out of the chair and returned his cell phone to his jacket pocket. He knew it would be some time before confirmation of the kill shot would be received, unless the North Koreans announced it first.

Most likely, the new head of the regime, *Miss Dear Leader*, or *Dearest Leader*, whatever, would be moving quickly to consolidate power and take control. She'd have quite the battle on her hands with the generals, who'd insist on striking back at the assumed perpetrators, most likely the United States.

Whether she gained control or not, Secretary Gregg and the rest of the deep state had what they wanted—a war.

223

CHAPTER 47

November 15
North Cascades National Park
Washington-Canada border

Ceremoniously standing with one foot within the United States and one foot in Canada, Kyoung-Joo Lee, a commander in North Korea's Lightning Death Squad, waved two dozen of his elite commandos to duck through the crooked fence posts with loose strands of barbed wire running through them. One by one, they ducked under the wire and slapped the concrete monument marking the international border between the two countries.

Commander Lee smiled with pride as his special operations forces gained another boost in manpower. Throughout his nine years working in Canada on a temporary work visa, he'd coordinated the entry of fourteen thousand four hundred commandos within his charge across the porous border between the countries.

He laughed with delight as one American administration after another lamented the influx of Hispanics into their country through Mexico, all the while ignoring a much larger border with little or no oversight.

All across the northern border, especially from Washington State to Minnesota, vast expanses of prairie grass with no checkpoints or visible signs of security provided illegal aliens access into America with welcome arms. From terrorists posing as Syrian refugees to Commander Lee's highly trained and motivated operatives, Canada had become a gateway, a stopover, into the nation that prided itself in being the most secure on the planet.

Repeatedly, for years, he'd proven them wrong. The Canadian

government was extremely helpful in issuing student and work visas to Korean nationals, but were horrible at keeping track of their whereabouts. After several months of briefing and training, the commandos were escorted into America at various insertion points in the North Cascades National Park in Washington, where they were handed over to Commander Lee's subordinates.

The North Koreans were particularly adept at creating false paperwork for his operatives as they were assimilated into American society. Soon, cities like Los Angeles, New York, Seattle, and Chicago were infiltrated by North Korean commandos as part of their Lightning Death Squads.

Kim Jong-un began the relocation program of his best soldiers into the program led by Commander Lee in early 2016. He took advantage of the political divide in America surrounding the relocation of refugees and the open borders policies adopted by the Canadians.

Kim was never sure how and when these sleeper cells would be activated, but he was a forward thinker when it came to hostilities with the United States. While U.S. administrations came and went, changing policies like the shifting wind, Kim Jong-un focused all of his attention on defeating his nation's arch enemy.

Over time, his special operations forces had increased to two hundred thousand soldiers. Coupled with Commander Lee's insertions, another six thousand had immigrated to the U.S. via phony South Korean passports. Now ten percent of his commandos resided in the U.S., waiting for their moment to shine.

A 2020 Pentagon report called the Lightning Death Squads *the most highly trained, well-equipped forces in the rapidly ascending North Korean Army*. They quickly gained a reputation for being lethal when a South Korean patrol boat made the mistake of entering North Korean waters in the Sea of Japan. The commandos responded quickly to the perceived threat, boarded the ship, and executed the South Korean sailors, which almost caused a major international incident.

Numerous, mysterious, yet formidable, the death squads were treated as royalty at home. In America, they were sworn to secrecy except when talking among themselves. They spent their days performing menial tasks, learning English, and studying American military maneuvers.

In the last year, they'd begun to test the fences. From time to time, they'd breach perimeter security at U.S. military facilities to gauge the reaction of U.S. forces. They were instructed to take down critical infrastructure like electricity substations and telecom connections to determine how utilities reacted.

As a small group by comparison to the population, they'd been trained in insurgency operations. Each was responsible to gather the gear they'd need to conduct this type of terrorist activity, including weapons, explosives, and safe places in which to regroup.

They'd even procured chemical weapons such as anthrax. Commander Lee was a proponent of instilling fear in the enemy with the offensive use of biological weapons. While a biological agent like smallpox or other airborne viruses like pneumonic plague were difficult to control, bacteria like anthrax could be. Anthrax had the added benefit of ease of production. For less than three thousand dollars, the necessary equipment could be purchased on Amazon or at a farm supply store to produce anthrax in a garden shed.

Commander Lee was always requesting more operatives as his plans for America grew more ambitious. Pyongyang readily obliged. Soon the border between British Columbia and Washington in the wilderness of the North Cascades National Park became but a speed bump for the influx of North Koreans.

This was Commander Lee's ninth day in a row of escorting his commandos to their new home in America. Their handlers eagerly awaited them, and soon they were whisked away into the paths worn between the evergreens, giving little or no regard for the delicate ecosystems the Americans fought amongst each other to protect.

He continued to stand defiantly, looking at the open span of forest beyond the border. The dewy mist had fallen on the ferns and lichens, plant species that were protected by the American court systems, ensuring that no border fence or perimeter security would encroach upon the beautiful forest. It was quite beautiful to behold in more ways than envisioned by those who cherished the forest's biodiversity—a word that didn't translate into Korean because it had no purpose in his homeland.

One thing that Commander Lee had learned in ten years of studying the American culture was that the enemy seemed willing to fight each other with more hate and vigor than they would their real threat from across the Pacific. He imagined the day when his country would use this character flaw against America.

CHAPTER 48

November 15
Mountain above Missile Launch Site
Kusong, North Korea

"Hit. Head shot, stand by," said Park. The target collapsed in a heap, generating a smile from both men. For a moment, Duncan watched through his scope as chaos ensued. Orders were shouted and screams of agony could be heard from a mile away as the target's lifeless body bled out on the platform. Random gunfire in the direction of the ridge across the valley brought Duncan back to the task at hand.

"Let's blow this joint," said Duncan as he scooted backwards on his belly until he was out of view of the soldiers below, who'd been frantically searching for the source of the gunfire. "Time's awastin'."

"Great shot, cowboy!"

Duncan patted his partner on the back. "Thanks for the spot. I would've loved to have seen the look on his face before it exploded. It always bothered me to shoot a man from behind. In this case, he wouldn't have extended me the same courtesy."

Within minutes, Duncan and Park had changed into their North Korean peasant clothing and buried any trace of their gear. Duncan switched out the barrels of the Barrett MRAD to turn it into a battle rifle and slung it over his shoulder. After one final look around their sniper hide, the two set out in a hurry along the path they had identified the day before.

With adrenaline pumping through their veins, the men bolted away from the scene and hopped over rocks like mountain goats fleeing a wildfire. After they reached the top of the ridge, they found the tree-lined cover they planned on using to avoid detection. Time would tell if their advance planning would give them the head start they needed to avoid capture.

They fled down the back side of the ridge and in the direction of the nearby mining town. This area was beyond the perimeter fencing of Kusong. Based upon their intel, Kusong was the home to twenty-five hundred soldiers, some of which were supposedly deployed as spy-hunting teams in the surrounding mountains. Thus far, the men had only encountered the patrol sentry on their first night. As they descended the mountain toward the mining town of Anch'ang-dong, Duncan began to notice the activity on the road passing through the valley.

"Park, something doesn't feel right," Duncan began as he pulled Park's arm to slow his descent. "This is more than a quick-reaction team. This looks like they're preparing for an attack. I've counted ten troop carriers passing below us, all full of soldiers."

"How long has it been? Ten minutes?"

Duncan checked his watch. "Fifteen. They've responded much faster than we anticipated. Either way, the roads are not an option. We're gonna have to move southward through the base. If we travel outside the perimeter, we'll meet a lot of resistance because they're more mobile."

Park caught his breath and then weighed their options. "If we follow the top of the ridge around the missile site, we'll have the high ground and be moving in a southerly direction. At some point, we'll have to breach their perimeter patrols, but we can deal with that when the time comes."

"Yeah, let's go back to the top and move along using the tree canopy as cover. At least they haven't deployed any choppers yet."

"Fine," said Park with a chuckle. "You get your marathon hike after all. Keep in mind you may have to carry me across the finish line."

"This will teach you to lay off the fast food, my friend."

"Whatever," said Park with a shrug as he passed Duncan and led the way back up the ridge.

Duncan glanced to the mining town one last time and shook his head in disbelief. *They were onto us awfully fast.*

After they reached the top of the ridge, Duncan retook the lead. He was more familiar with traversing uneven terrain than Park was. He'd pick a route that would be easier on his partner considering his lack of upcountry hiking experience and his physical condition, which was not up to Duncan's.

A half hour later, Duncan and Park heard the sounds of helicopters performing a grid search across the area where they'd taken the shot. Gradually, the choppers spread out in all directions, eventually crossing over their heads. While they were able to easily avoid detection, the game of cat and mouse was slowing them down.

Duncan was constantly checking his watch and calculating the time to the extraction point. He was beginning to realize their escape was going to require a vehicle at some point, even if it was for a few miles.

Thirty minutes later, after the helicopters veered off toward the woods where they hid their truck, Duncan and Park reached the flatlands of the valley, which would allow them to pick up their pace considerably. They had only traveled a mile in an hour and a half, and Park was already showing signs of fatigue.

Duncan knew the trek through the mountains was the difficult part of their escape physically. It was also the most crucial period to avoid detection. If they weren't discovered in that first hour, then the North Koreans would begin to extend their search and focus on vehicular traffic. Now it was a matter of making better time than the first portion of their escape.

"Let's take a break so you can catch your breath," said Duncan as he found a lean-to shed with several empty drums in it. Park immediately leaned against a post and slid down to the ground, where he propped his arms on his knees. The next few miles would determine if Park could make it all the way to the extraction point at Sinmi-do.

Duncan studied the GPS and then pulled out the map. He studied the area for a moment and then confirmed their coordinates.

Satisfied with their route, he repacked his rucksack and offered Park a bottled water.

Park readily gulped the water down before standing. "Thanks. I'm done hiking. Walking, I can handle. Just tell me it's a straight, flat shot to the Korea Bay."

"It is," Duncan responded. "We're gonna head toward the Taeryong River where it comes out on the southeastern side of the base. There's a road we can follow that will take us due south. However, somewhere between here and that road will be their perimeter fences and likely beefed-up patrols."

"I don't think my voice-throwing trick will work in the daylight."

"Not to mention the fact these guys will be on high alert for anything out of the ordinary."

Park adjusted his gear and gave a thumbs-up to Duncan, who led the way once again. He was walking at a quick pace as the two men talked about the reality of their mission for the first time since leaving their sniper hide.

Park began the conversation. "How long do you think it will take for them to let the world know what happened?"

"That's a good question," replied Duncan. "Everything they do here is carefully orchestrated. Plus, Kim wasn't seen in public all that often. It was kinda like bin Laden back in the day. They'd release some pictures or video to Al-Jazeera for distribution, but you could never tell when or where they were taken."

"So they might hide it until they get their ducks in a row," added Park.

"Most likely. There are no other sons in the Kim dynasty except whatever little kids that guy had. Remember, he had one of his brothers taken out in Malaysia, and the other brother spends all of his time out of sight and out of his mind at Clapton concerts in Europe."

They moved swiftly along the pine-needle-covered forest floor. The sounds of the helicopters were way off in the distance, and no other vehicles could be heard, as the pine trees blocked sounds from outside the woods.

"Maybe his sister is next in line?" asked Park, before answering his own question. "Do you think our chap Kensington is playing footsies with Dear Leader's little sis? Wow, that would be close to the top."

Duncan checked his watch and subconsciously picked up the pace. *We have to make some time along the way.*

"He was pretty confident in his source. I'm surprised her brother would let a Brit anywhere near his sister, much less to be sleeping together, as he implied."

The men continued and came across a dry creek bed, which enabled them to move quickly toward the river ahead. They pushed through a thick area of underbrush. Duncan could see daylight and what appeared to be an open area. They were almost out of the camp.

Just as they were about to exit into the clearing, they immediately dropped to their knees.

Duncan and Park had found the river and the road that would take them to the extraction point. They'd also found a North Korean patrol of a dozen men searching the banks for the killers of their Dear Leader.

CHAPTER 49

November 15
Kusong, North Korea

"What are they saying?" asked Duncan over his shoulder in a whispered voice. He carefully walked backwards on his hands and knees to join Park. Their visibility was limited by the thickness of the natural vegetation along the river. The shouting of orders and hurried responses indicated the North Korean soldiers were under pressure to find the shooters.

"Just typical commands," replied Park. "But one officer continues to urge his men upriver. Where is the road from our current position?"

Duncan studied the GPS and then showed it to Park as he replied, "Two klicks to the south of here along the river."

The voices began to fade, and Duncan crawled to a large pine and stood up behind it. He was only able to make out the helmets of the soldiers, but they were all moving to his right, upstream toward the camp.

Duncan waved Park over, who continued to listen. The voices grew fainter.

"Let's go for it," Duncan suggested. "I'm guessin' there were a dozen men in that patrol. Most likely, they parked their truck at the road and began searching up the river, probably looking for our footprints on the banks. If we can stay along the edge of the woods, we can make good time to get to the road."

Park was on board. "Yeah, then we'll jack their truck. We may not be able to talk our way through their checkpoints, but we can pick up a lot of miles before they notice their truck missing."

"Let's roll," said Duncan without hesitation. The men slowly made their way to the clearing and the river's edge, which was slightly damp, possibly hampering their progress. Choosing the more stable high ground along the bank next to the underbrush, they began running at a steady pace toward the road.

Nearly two miles and fifteen minutes later, they saw a truck parked in front of a short concrete bridge. It was a standard military troop carrier with a green canvas cover on the back and the red star of North Korea painted on the doors.

Park slowed and then abruptly darted into the woods. He motioned for Duncan to join him.

"Duncan, they've left a man behind to watch the truck. He may be the driver."

Duncan studied the bridge and the area around the truck. "That transport could carry more than the dozen soldiers we saw. They may be searching downriver from the highway. Park, we've got to move quickly."

"All right," said Park. He pulled his sidearm and affixed the suppressor. He handed Duncan his rucksack and his earmuffs. "Here, trade hats with me. I'm gonna wander over there like I'm a lost local."

"But we're still inside their base perimeter fence," cautioned Duncan. "He may not buy it."

"It won't matter," said Park, who was lightning fast when drawing his concealed weapon. "He'll be dead before he has a chance to raise his rifle."

Duncan looked back upriver, wondering when the patrol would return. "Gotta go for it. I've got your six."

Park nodded and slowly made his way toward the riverbank and stopped thirty feet from the truck where the woods ended. He pulled his weapon and stretched the sleeve of his oversize jacket, allowing him to conceal his forty-five.

The soldier was smoking a cigarette as he wandered aimlessly at the truck's tailgate. Park waited until the guard turned to pace in the other direction before he emerged from the woods. He was able to close the gap to twenty feet before the guard noticed his presence and promptly swung his rifle around.

"*Nongmin-eul, meomchuda!*" the guard shouted as Park emerged from the woods. *Stop, peasant!*

Park didn't respond or hesitate. Appearing to raise both hands in surrender, his right arm emerged from his sleeve and fired a single round into the throat of the guard, knocking him backwards until his body crashed onto the pavement.

Duncan burst out of the woods with his weapon drawn to cover Park in the event another soldier emerged from the back side of the vehicle. Park carefully rounded the rear bumper and cleared the bed of the truck while Duncan checked the cab and the driver's side.

Satisfied they were clear, Duncan walked toward the river and looked for any signs of the troops returning.

"We're good," Duncan announced as he caught up with Park at the tailgate.

"More than good," said Park with a smile. "Look what I found!"

Park held back the canvas cover to reveal the interior of the troop carrier. Three long rectangular boxes lay before him, one of which had already been opened by Park.

"RPGs! Sweet!" exclaimed Duncan. He hoisted himself into the covered truck bed and rummaged through the contents, where he found the coats and caps of the soldiers. "We can put on these coats and bluff our way through."

"One step ahead of you, Comrade Armstrong," said Park with a laugh. He'd stripped the soldier of his jacket and pants and found them to be a perfect fit. "I pulled his body out of the pool of blood from his throat. Throw me a cap."

Duncan tossed him a hat, and Park immediately put it on before standing at attention. "What say you?"

"You look better than the dead guy," said Duncan. "Come on, let's toss him in the woods. We can't do much about the blood."

The men unceremoniously pitched the dead soldier into a thicket of brush and made their way back to the truck. Without hesitating, they fired up the big diesel and lumbered southbound toward the coast.

Park turned on the military comms mounted to the dashboard of the truck. The antiquated technology resembled an American-made CB radio from the seventies. As he drove, he scanned through the channels.

Duncan checked his watch. It was just past noon. "We're seven miles from the crossroad where the camp perimeter is located. There will be a manned security gate there. We'll have to make—"

Loud static from the radio interrupted Duncan. Men were shouting at one another in a clearly excited tone.

Park held up his hand and listened.

"Did they find the dead guy?" asked Duncan.

Park shook his head side to side as he leaned over the steering wheel to concentrate on what was being said. He finally relaxed and leaned back in his seat after turning down the volume.

"Sorry, but I had to concentrate. Although we share a common language with the North, the dialects are different. South Koreans have adopted a number of Japanese words and phrases into their language. American words too. In North Korea, there is a commonly used dialect called *Pyongyang*. Those guys were worked into a frenzy, making it difficult to follow."

"What could you decipher?"

"I gather they've found our abandoned truck. They're diverting resources to the west side of the camp."

"Good. Listen up. We're only two clicks from one of the base's main entrance points. It will be fortified and heavily manned."

Park looked down at the dashboard. "We've got half a tank of fuel, more than enough to make it to the extraction point."

Duncan continued. "We'll still have a dozen miles or so to Sinmi-do. We've got six hours to get there. One option is to ditch the truck short of the checkpoint, find our way through the fence, and continue to hoof it as planned. It'll take us four hours, getting us to the extraction point at dusk, barring unforeseen problems."

"Plan B?" asked Park.

"Try to bluff our way through, but that could be shot down before we arrive if those patrols return to find their truck missing and their comrade dead."

Park grimaced. "That's a real possibility if they're diverting manpower to the other side of Kusong. They may have called the patrols back already."

"There's a third option," started Duncan as a grin came across his face. "We've got three RPGs and our own firepower. We could blast our way through 'em and make a run for the coast. At the checkpoint, there are three options for them to follow us. We could be in Sinmi-do in twenty minutes, even in this rust bucket."

"If they chase us and descend upon the coast, which is a natural course of action, we could get caught before the boat picks us up."

Duncan took another look at the GPS when sirens began to wail from all directions. The radio chatter began again.

"What, Park? What?"

"They found the dead guy. We're gonna have company!"

CHAPTER 50

November 15
Kusong, North Korea

"Stop the truck!" said Duncan as he started to open the passenger door. He'd rummaged around in the glovebox and under the seat. He found a rusted, flat-head screwdriver that suited his purposes. "I'm gonna load the RPGs and tear through the canvas so I can stand. We're gonna blast our way through and figure it out on the other side."

Park squealed the big tires as he brought the transport to a halt. The forward momentum threw Duncan against the dash and slammed his door wide open. He quickly kicked out his leg to hold it there and jumped out.

Duncan ran around the side and climbed into the covered truck bed. Park was slamming his fist on the window, shouting for him to hurry. Duncan found an area in the canvas that had been repaired previously and drove the flat-head screwdriver into a patch, easily reopening the hole. With all his muscle, he grabbed the opening with both hands and tore the seam wider until it stretched to the wooden sides of the truck.

Within seconds, he'd emerged with the RPG locked and loaded. "Wait here for them to round the bend in the road," he shouted to Park. Duncan familiarized himself with the trigger mechanism. He recognized the model. Several years ago a freighter was boarded, bound for the Suez Canal. Concealed under bins of iron ore was a cache of thirty thousand RPGs destined for Egypt. A UN investigation revealed Egyptian businessmen were using their companies as cover to buy the rocket-propelled grenades for use by the Egyptian military in violation of the UN ban on DPRK weapons exports.

Duncan steadied the weapon and waited. He could hear the approaching truck rounding the curve. He marked the spot where it would appear.

There it was, a vehicle very similar to the troop carrier he occupied. Duncan took aim and fired. The RPG round blasted through the air and hit the truck just above the radiator, tearing through the hood and imbedding in the cab before exploding.

Debris and body parts from the blast flew hundreds of feet into the air. The resulting explosion of the truck's gas tank also sent a ball of fire skyward, accompanied by black smoke.

Duncan pounded the roof of the truck. "Go, go, go!"

Park gave it gas and the two-and-a-half-ton vehicle lurched forward. The debris covered the road, but Park was able to drive through the grass on the shoulder and avoid large truck parts or bodies on fire.

The firing of the RPG had revealed their position, and now it was time to take advantage of their shock and awe approach. Park continued driving, and Duncan leaned around the cab and reached his arm through the window.

"Hand me the rifle!"

Park didn't slow down as he passed the Barrett to Duncan. They were now in view of the main checkpoint, which consisted of a center gatehouse flanked by steel gates and concrete barriers that stretched forty feet on both sides of the entrance.

A Humvee-style truck was approaching them. A gunner was scrambling to man a machine gun that was mounted in a turret on the truck's roof. Duncan never let him get into position.

The Barrett, which he'd converted to a battle rifle by exchanging barrels, was now fully automatic and drawing ammo from its magazine. The powerful .338 rounds shattered the windshield of the truck, instantly killing the driver.

The vehicle swerved toward the shoulder, causing the gunner to reach for the trigger, but he was only able to shoot wildly into the air.

The truck careened down an embankment and flipped onto its roof, crushing the gunner underneath it.

"We're gonna blow-n-go!" shouted Duncan as he prepared another RPG.

Bullets started flying at them, pinging off the bumper and skipping along the road beside their tires. Duncan took aim and fired at the guardhouse. It exploded in flames, and the gates creaked as the metal succumbed to the intense heat.

Through the carnage, Duncan could see men on fire running in all directions. Some bodies were intact; others were missing parts as they burned to death.

He switched to his rifle as Park prepared to burst through the flames and into the intersection. Sporadic fire came at them from Duncan's right. Two soldiers were crouched behind a concrete barrier. Duncan kept their position in his rifle's scope as the truck passed through the obliterated security gate.

As soon as the soldiers rose above the concrete barrier, Duncan used two perfectly placed shots to drive .338 rounds into their chests.

Park continued southbound, and Duncan took up a prone position at the tailgate to fire upon any vehicles that gave chase. He readied his rifle and waited for several minutes. When it appeared they were clear, he finally exhaled and allowed his tense body to relax.

Their escape was far from over, but they'd just accomplished two things. One, they'd escaped from Kusong. Second, they'd just bought themselves hours of valuable time, which provided them more options.

He allowed Park to drive another mile or so before he leaned into the window and told him to continue on this course and stop short of the next intersection. Then he heard it.

The *whump-whump, whump-whump* sound was obvious. A North Korean helicopter had been diverted to hunt them down.

Duncan had studied the intel on the People's Army Air Force while at Misawa. Kusong was not an air base for their military. Their closest air combat division was at Kaechon, forty miles to their east. The base was the primary location for their older MIG-17 fighter jets but would most likely have Russian-made MI-24 attack helicopters.

Duncan hoped the helicopter hunting them down was a utility chopper along the lines of the Polish Mi-2. While it was likely armed with a twenty-three-millimeter cannon, it's maneuverability wasn't in the same class as the MI-24. Duncan could take it down with their last remaining RPG. However, if the approaching chopper was an MI-24, he and Park would be burnt toast riding in this truck.

He whacked the roof and yelled to Park, "Chopper! We've got to get out now!"

Park slammed on the brakes without warning, tossing Duncan around the rear like a rag doll. He regained his footing, grabbed his rifle and slung it over his shoulder. He unpacked the final RPG and made his way onto the paved road.

"I've got our gear!" yelled Park. "Dude, we're so close!"

"I know, but if the wrong kind of chopper is tracking us, it'll be bad news, buddy."

The men ran for the edge of the woods and waited. Duncan found a fallen tree to hide behind, and he waited for the helicopter, which was most likely following the road. He quickly surveyed the grounds around them. There wasn't enough room for the chopper to land, not that it mattered, he was soon to learn.

Within seconds of the Polish Mi-2 rounding the tree-lined curve, two fifty-seven-millimeter cannons released from the chopper's sides. Their escape vehicle exploded, sending a ball of fire into the air and causing a hole to form in the melting asphalt.

The pilots of the Mi-2 hovered for a moment to admire their handiwork, a fatal error. Duncan steadied his aim and took advantage of the stationary target.

He fired the last RPG. The munition burst from the launcher and maintained a perfectly straight trajectory. Instinctively, the pilot attempted to turn to the right to avoid being hit, providing the RPG the broadside of the proverbial barn as its target.

"Bingo!" shouted Duncan as the Mi-2 burst into flames after a series of detonations of ammunition and fuel cells caused a mushroom cloud of smoke and fire to soar upward.

"Yeah!" exclaimed Park as he joined his partner. "They'll know where we are now. We've got a couple of small towns to avoid up ahead, but even walking through the fields, we've only got a few miles until we reach the land bridge to Sinmi-do."

"Piece of cake, right?" asked Duncan with a nervous laugh.

"Yeah, sure. Let's go. Those suckers will be on us like white on rice."

Duncan laughed. "Racist."

"What? No, it's not. It just means they're about to be up our—"

"I know, just kiddin'."

Duncan didn't wait and began jogging into the woods. Park was close on his heels as the men started the final stretch to going home.

CHAPTER 51

November 15
Coast of Korea Bay
Sinmi-do, North Korea

Sinmi Island sits off the coast in West Korea Bay. At twenty square miles, the mountainous island is the largest within North Korea's territorial waters. Known for its small fishing villages and steep jagged peaks, the extraction point was chosen because the island has nearly a hundred small inlets and miles of coastal shoreline to choose from.

A single road encircled the sparsely populated island. On the western shore, a small peninsula that was completely uninhabited jutted out into the shallow water. The white sandy beaches were ideal for their extraction by the thirty-five-foot-long Naval Special Warfare Rigid Inflatable Boat, or RIB.

These high-speed watercraft were capable of reaching sixty-mile-an-hour speeds with four passengers. The dual Caterpillar in-line diesels were turbocharged, making them perfect to encroach into North Korean territorial waters and make a fast retreat without being detected.

Exhausted from running the final stretch of beach to the appointed extraction point, Duncan and Park sat in the woods in the event a fishing boat or wayward soul happened by their position. Their bodies began to relax, and their mood was upbeat.

"Twenty minutes to spare," said Duncan as he checked his watch for what seemed the millionth time since setting foot in the Hermit Kingdom.

Despite the rapidly dropping temperatures and a light mist blowing off the bay, both men were sweating. Park still wore the dead soldier's uniform, which was made of heavy green felt. It helped him retain heat, but the additional sweat was pushing him towards dehydration. Duncan still resembled a North Korean local when observed from a distance.

Their clothing choices had served them well as they crossed the final two miles over the land bridge connecting the North Korean mainland with the island. Remarkably, during those stressful twenty minutes as the two men ambled along separate from one another, not a single North Korean patrol came onto, or off, Sinmi-do.

Nor had they detected any patrol boat activity. There were numerous fishing ports along the mainland, and Duncan surmised their pursuers were concentrating on those first.

The wind picked up slightly, and the mist turned to a steady drizzle. Both men adjusted their hats and clothing to stay dry. Duncan checked his watch again. It was fifteen minutes past the hour. If he was nervous about the delay, that meant Park was about to lose his mind with anticipation. He wasn't as flexible as Duncan was during a mission. He believed in planning, timing, and wasn't much for adapting in the field.

Duncan decided to make some small talk. "A week ago, we were sittin' on the *Lucas* and you were squallin' about being bored. Are you happy now? Did you get your adrenaline fix?"

Park started laughing. "Screw you, cowboy. I guess I would've preferred an operation that blew up a bridge or strong-armed a Russian spy instead. You know, a little appetizer before they threw us into the fray."

"A warm-up op. That would've been nice."

Park shuddered as he wrapped the coat around his body. "You're gonna be famous, you know."

Duncan laughed. "Why? Because I'm the one that pulled the trigger? This was a team effort, buddy. There's no way to pull that off without you."

"Seriously, Duncan. You're gonna need to hire an agent and stuff.

244

I see book deals, movie rights, appearances on all the news networks. You'll be just as famous as that guy who killed bin Laden."

"Maybe," said Duncan with a shrug. "What was his name, anyway?"

"I don't remember," replied Park dryly with a laugh.

"Me either. Listen, they told us to keep our mouths shut about this op. I seriously doubt the United States government wants to take credit for the assassination of a world leader, even if he is a stooge. My guess is the agency is already starting a disinformation campaign pointing fingers of blame at some poor sap, you know, an up-and-coming general of some kind."

Park nodded. "Yeah, probably right. We won't even get a medal."

"Heck, Park, we probably won't get Thanksgiving Day off."

The two men sat in silence for a while as minutes suddenly turned to more than an hour. Occasionally, a boat could be heard in the distance, but it wasn't the high-pitched whine the powerful diesels would produce on the RIB.

"I hate not having comms," said Park.

"Me too. Listen, you don't think our boys would disavow this mission so much they'd leave us hangin', do you?" asked Duncan.

"I gotta say, a couple of things bothered me. First, our buddy James Bond seemed in an awful big hurry to catch a flight the other night. It was as if he handed us the key to a stolen car, patted us on the head, and dashed into the terminal to flee the scene of a crime."

Duncan shook his jacket to repel some of the moisture that had begun to soak it. The coat was not meant for protecting him from the elements, but rather it was merely a useful prop to complete the mission.

"The other thing was the mining town after we left the hide," said Duncan as he recalled the scene in his mind. "We hadn't been gone ten minutes and the place was crawlin' with soldiers. I suppose I could've underestimated their response time, but I found it strange they'd be deployed to that half-abandoned place."

"That too," added Park. "What time is it now?"

"After eleven."

Park was getting antsy. "Dude, five-plus hours late. They're not comin'."

"C'mon, man. Don't panic. They may be held up by patrol boats."

Park shot back his response. "Have you heard or seen any patrol boats? Look around. It's pitch black out there. Patrol boats would be shining their lights around the bay, looking for any type of vessel in the water. There would be choppers buzzin' the coast. Even if they were dispatched from Pyongyang, they would have joined the hunt."

Duncan didn't have a response, but he was getting the sinking feeling that Park was right. He was beginning to feel *expendable*. He too was puzzled by the lack of pressure being placed on all parts of the Korea Bay coastline. The military could've deployed their million-man army to this region by now. *Why haven't they?*

"Let's give it 'til midnight—*zero hour*. If they're not here by then, we'll find our own way out of the country. Got any cousins in South Korea?"

"Yeah, actually, quite a few. You get us to South Korea, and I'll have us treated like heroes before we head home. Deal?"

"Deal!"

CHAPTER 52

November 16
Sinmi-do, North Korea

It was zero hour. Temperatures had begun to plummet, and the drizzle had turned to a steady rain. Duncan and Park had moved up the hill to seek any form of shelter from the conditions. A rock outcropping provided them some relief from the moisture, but not the cold, which had now soaked through their clothes into their bodies. The predicted cold front had arrived slightly early. By tomorrow afternoon, the winds and blowing snow would hit North Korea, making travel by water impossible for as long as a week. Both men agreed that avoiding capture, especially under these circumstances, would be impossible for that length of time.

"China's closer," said Duncan as he and Park weighed their options. "It's at least ninety miles to the Northern Limit Line from here."

The Northern Limit Line was a disputed territorial boundary that separated the Yellow Sea from the Korea Bay. Since it was drawn as part of the 1953 Armistice Agreement by both North Korea and the United Nations, numerous conflicts had occurred as North Korea refused to acknowledge the demarcation line as agreed upon.

Although the U.S. Navy didn't maintain a presence in this part of the Yellow Sea, the South Koreans did. If they could commandeer a boat and make their way into international waters, then hopefully Park could talk their way onto one of their patrol boats or even a frigate.

"Do you think we'll even get the words *U.S. embassy* out of our mouths before the PLA busts us in the chops?" asked Park. "I don't think so."

"What's your plan?" asked Duncan as he studied his wrinkled fingertips. His hands were beginning to get numb.

"The closest point of safety is back on the UN freighter," replied Park.

"How are we gonna explain that to the captain?" asked Duncan sarcastically.

"Who cares? The captain has an obligation to hoist us up out of the sea. And besides, we'll be on board doin' the explaining. What's he gonna do, throw us back overboard?""

"Good point," replied Duncan. He thought about Park's suggestion, and it began to make sense. At this hour, stealing a boat would be easier. Navigating through the small islands that dotted the coastal waters would provide them some cover. "I wish I had marked the GPS coordinates of the freighter before we left. I just never imagined we would be returning to it."

Park stood and shook off the cold. He was rejuvenated now that they had a plan. He patted Duncan on the shoulder. "C'mon. I'm done with North Korea. Let's go find a ride. We'll sail a heading of due west, which should take us in the direction of where they anchored. Hopefully, they're still there."

Duncan stood and readied himself for the trek back to the nearest fishing village. "They should be. The UN crew had a lot to unload, if I remember correctly."

"Hey, I feel pretty good," started Park. "Why don't we go up and over to save some time? The terrain's nothing like we had to deal with at Kusong."

"Sure, I'm up for it. Lead the way, Ranger!"

The men began the hike up the six hundred feet of elevation until they reached the top. The colder air hit them as a wind gust crossed the more barren landscape. They meandered through the pines and began their descent when they came upon a small road barely wide enough for a Jeep. The road was made of gravel but was a welcome relief for two tired operatives who had struggled to keep their footing on the uneven forest floor.

They'd traveled a few hundred yards down the mountain when their backs were illuminated with flashlights.

"*Jeongji! Jeongji!*" yelled a North Korean soldier, ordering Duncan and Park to halt.

Duncan responded by leaping for cover down the side of the road, but Park was a second too late. The gunshot tore through his left shoulder, causing Park to spin around and tumble down the embankment.

"Park!" shouted Duncan as he reached to help his friend. Automatic fire tore up the pine needles near Park's body, striking him in the foot.

Duncan scrambled up the embankment, twice losing his footing in the wet grass soaked by the now steady freezing rain. He returned fire, which created a thunderous boom of the Barrett's muzzle echoing up and down the trail.

The shouting continued, and the soldiers desperately looked to find the source of the return fire. One of the soldiers fired widely above Duncan's position, but Duncan didn't shoot back. He returned his attention to Park's lifeless body, which lay sideways against a tree stump.

He scrambled down the bank and immediately felt for a pulse. His breathing was slow and shallow, but at least he was alive. Duncan frantically looked around to assess his options. He heard the crackle of a radio and then running footsteps in his direction.

Are there more? If not now, there will be soon.

"Park, are you with me?" asked Duncan as his head swiveled from the road to his unconscious friend. "Crap!"

Duncan couldn't hold them off. Even if this patrol of what seemed like two men could be neutralized, the sound of radio chatter reminded Duncan that he couldn't outrun a two-way. He needed to get Park out of there. *But to where?*

The small road wasn't an option. Most likely, any additional patrols would come roaring up the hill right towards him. Plus, being in the open left him no cover against the soldiers pushing their way towards their position.

He bent down and hoisted Park onto his shoulders. Park's good arm was draped over Duncan's left shoulder, and his right leg was slung over the right shoulder. Duncan quickly contemplated grabbing his rifle, but he simply couldn't juggle Park and the weapon. He'd have to rely upon his sidearm and the magazines stuffed in his back pocket.

After kicking the Barrett under a fallen tree and pushing some pine needles to obscure it from view, Duncan, slowly at first until he got his balance, made his way through the forest as quickly and quietly as possible. The flashlights illuminated parts of the forest but not in any discernible search pattern. He was working his way down toward the beach when he heard a vehicle sling gravel as its tires spun during the ascent uphill.

More voices. More soldiers. Too many to make out a number, but the flashlights told the story. They were running down the hill in his direction.

Duncan picked up the pace, now moving at a slow trot with the weight of Park pushing down on his shoulders. His muscles ached from the cold damp conditions they'd endured. Now, at four in the morning, he was fatigued, cold, and out of energy.

Yet he continued his descent. The soldiers were getting closer. They began to fire off rounds in his direction, which were deflected by the pine trees. The number of rounds tearing off the bark began to increase. It was a matter of time.

No man left behind!

Duncan continued as he began to slip and lose his balance before crashing into a pine tree like a pinball banging against a post. More gunfire. The flashlights became one. Duncan caught his breath and began to run along a sandy creek bed leading toward the sound of running water below.

He grimaced. He'd veered off course away from the beach and toward a small valley that held a narrow creek. The creek was rising from the cold rain, which had now fully penetrated his body and added twenty pounds to Park's.

Then the final volley came. They'd caught up to him. Despite the darkness, their rounds found their mark. The DPRK Type 88s, their version of the Russian-made AK-74s, ripped through the forest, and five powerful rounds embedded into Park's back.

The impact forced Duncan forward, causing him to lose his grip on his now dead friend and tumble head over heels, over and over down the creek until he reached a thirty-foot-tall cliff. Unable to gain his footing, he slid toward the edge until he careened over the side. His body contorted in the air as he tried to right himself, to no avail.

When he landed flat on his back in the shallow creek, the blow knocked the wind out of him. A barely conscious Duncan Armstrong was floating face up in the icy waters toward the tiny village of Jai-do.

CHAPTER 53

November 16
Armstrong Ranch
Borden County, Texas

Intuition had no real scientific explanation. To be sure, scientists tried when they defined the phenomenon as a process *that arises within a circumscribed cognitive domain.*

What?

Mothers know the meaning of intuition, even without the guidance of a phrase created by words that don't seem to match. Some called it a gut feeling, others understood they're tapping into something extraordinary, but they were not sure what. For a mother, intuition was one of the impenetrable mysteries of humanity, a protective mechanism that guided her as she cared for her children.

Lucy Armstrong awoke just after four o'clock that morning by sitting straight up in bed. Her pillow and nightgown were soaked with sweat, and her body was covered with goose bumps. Major was pleasantly snoring his way until dawn, but Lucy bolted out of bed and immediately ran to the bathroom to look at herself in the mirror.

She began to cry. Gentle tears streamed down her face at first, and she forced a laugh to calm herself down. She ran water in the sink to mask the sound from her sleeping husband, but when she looked in the mirror again, the waterworks came in earnest.

"Lucy Armstrong, what in the world is wrong with you?" she whispered to herself as she patted her face dry with a hand towel. She reached for a Kleenex and blew her nose, a hearty effort that caused her to chuckle and blow again.

After regaining her composure, she checked herself in the mirror one more time and smiled back at her aging face. *Silly girl,* she thought as she turned to return to bed.

Rather than going back to sleep, she reached for her iPad to go through her morning routine. Fully awake, and with her normal five a.m. inner alarm clock ticking closer, she started with emails and text messages.

This time, it wasn't just a cursory glance at anything that might have come to her overnight. No, she went directly to the email account designed for contact with Duncan when he was abroad. He'd warned her not to use her personal email accounts when communicating with him in case he became compromised. She never asked what that entailed, precisely, but the concept of operational security had been explained to her many times by Duncan and Dallas. Maintaining separation from family, especially when there was a possibility of them being captured, was for their safety as well as hers.

She opened the account, searching for a message from Duncan. Nothing. There were no messages via iPad Messages—*the green one,* as she called it, in order to differentiate from the *blue* Facebook Messenger icon. As the so-called IT guru of the Armstrong household, at least when it came to their iPads, Lucy was operating at a second-grade level.

She bypassed the weather app and went directly to check the news. *Has something happened?* Lucy couldn't overcome this sense of foreboding and apprehension. She had worried about Duncan in the past, but never like this.

International news dealt with the planned ICBM missile launch of North Korea, which had apparently been cancelled yesterday. The usual pundits and experts, all of whom had their own political agenda, pontificated on the reasons for the cancellation.

In national news, the American Automobile Association, AAA, issued a press release claiming a record number of travelers would hit the road for next week's Thanksgiving holiday. Nearly sixty million travelers were expected to fly or drive to visit family or take a long weekend vacation.

This reminded her of the rodeo kids' planned travels to the

Calgary Stampede in Canada next week. She knew how important it was for Cooper to compete, but his prior head injury was still cause for a mother's concern.

Is that it? Am I worried about Cooper?

Lucy rolled her head and neck on her shoulders to release the tension that was still built up inside her. Her crying spell was over and had now been replaced with a determination to find out what caused it.

While it was true that she was concerned for Cooper and the prospects of aggravating his concussion, she trusted her son's judgment. He had a lot of years of bull riding ahead of him if that was the path he chose. Lucy knew he wouldn't risk further injury, or even his life, after what he'd just been through.

She moved on to the local news. Just after dawn, NASA was launching its mysterious X-37B space plane from the newly expanded Johnson Space Center south of Houston. At the behest of Defense Secretary Gregg, the Johnson Space Center had added a rocket launch site specifically for the X-37B.

The space plane, which was a smaller version of the now retired space shuttles, was used for experimentation and risk reduction, according to the article. The robotic spacecraft was controlled by the Johnson Space Center, which had announced the mission two days ago. The impromptu press conference and the rushed schedule was unprecedented for the X-37B program.

Lucy continued reading the article. *Mission's purpose unclear—length of time in space, unspecified—experimental nature.*

The article on the KHOU website in Houston showed a graphic of the projected flight path after launch. Because of the early morning hour, clear skies, and the sun rising in the east to illuminate the rocket, the X-37B would be visible to the naked eye from Amarillo to Lubbock.

Suddenly, Lucy got excited about the prospect of a rocket flying overhead and decided to wake her husband up early so they could watch together. Her eagerness overcame her sense of dread.

Nothing is happening to us right now. It's gonna be all right.

CHAPTER 54

November 16
The Roosevelt Room
The White House
Washington, DC

President Harman and Chief of Staff Acton were several minutes late to the special briefing on the cancelled missile launch in North Korea. When they arrived, Secretary Gregg was reviewing a CIA report on tensions escalating between India and Pakistan. He intended to bring this up today, although it was most likely unrelated to the North Korean threat. It was, however, a reminder to the president that the threat of a global nuclear war should be taken seriously.

President Harman entered the room, and everyone respectfully stood and greeted her. She seemed to be in a jovial mood as she passed around two boxes of Krispy Kreme donuts purchased for the occasion.

"You know, once upon a time, all of us had jobs that didn't required this level of stress. Some of us might discuss the upcoming Thanksgiving holiday preparations. Perhaps the guys might debate who the number one college football team was. These donuts are a reminder that we were all ordinary Americans at one time, at least to a certain degree. The weighty decisions made in this room were once made by others on our behalf.

"However, all of us have agreed to take on this tremendous amount of responsibility. Our duties require more than political posturing or tweaking of economic policies. Sometimes, we make life-or-death decisions on behalf of the American people. From health-care coverage to sending troops into battle, what comes out of the room has a profound effect on everyday Americans whom we'll never meet."

You have no idea, Secretary Gregg thought to himself.

President Harman continued. "A week ago, I threw down the gauntlet to Beijing. I let them know our patience had run out and so had time for the regime in Pyongyang. I demanded they contact Kim Jong-un to cancel the scheduled ICBM test for yesterday, or in the alternative, have him reprogram the trajectory to travel over mainland China into the South China Sea. If our demands weren't met, then diplomacy would end, and all options would be on the table."

President Harman paused to allow the forcefulness of her resolve to sink in. Secretary Gregg managed a smirk as he passed on the offering of donuts. He'd never been *ordinary*, and of all people, he knew what it meant to send his troops into battle. Unlike others in this room, he'd seen death firsthand. He'd also expressed condolences to the families of the fallen, something this president couldn't find time in her busy schedule to do.

He regained his composure and resisted the urge to put the president in her place. Make no mistake, Kim Jong-un, *may the devil welcome him with open arms*, was the reason the launch was cancelled. It was because *he'd been cancelled.*

"As you know, the missile launch yesterday was in fact halted," said President Harman. "While we've not been in touch with the Chinese embassy as of yet, I will be expressing my thanks to Beijing for their role in forcing the DPRK to stand down with this escalation in their nuclear program."

Secretary Gregg continued to thumb through the CIA report on India and Pakistan, choosing to avoid the president's grandiosity. He detected a long pause in her self-congratulations and looked up. Acton had received a text message and was showing it to the president.

Well, Madame President, you are probably now learning what stopped the launch, and it wasn't your superior diplomatic skills.

"Please turn on the television monitors," instructed Acton. Two staff members scrambled for the remotes, and the screens came to life. MSNBC and CNN cable news feeds revealed a special news alert.

Each network displayed a similar chyron, the electronically generated caption superimposed at the bottom of the screen on most cable news outlets. They read *Kim Jong-un to make rare public appearance & remarks.*

Secretary Gregg frowned and shook his head. He sat up in his chair as sweat began to form on his forehead.

Calm down, Monty. This is probably a prerecorded ruse. A disinformation campaign to keep their people in line.

Everyone in the room was silent as the volume was turned up on the CNN feed. Alisyn Camerota, formerly with Fox News, had on her serious Diane Sawyer look.

"In a rare public appearance, North Korean dictator Kim Jong-un will be making live remarks at the annual Mother's Day Parade in Pyongyang in just a few minutes. In 2015, the regime declared November 16 to be a national day of remembrance in his mother's honor. A parade and associated festivities are customary for this event; however live public remarks by Kim Jong-un are unprecedented."

Secretary Gregg was now visibly shaken as the state-run media in North Korea began to provide video footage of the parade. The weather conditions in North Korea were obviously deteriorating as the rain appeared to blow sideways, but that didn't dampen the spirits of the cheering, adoring North Koreans, who dared not sit this one out.

The sweat was now pouring out of his forehead, and he tried to nonchalantly wipe it away. His hands were cold and clammy.

Come on, General, get it together. This is going to be a body double.

The cameras eventually zoomed in on the staging area where Kim Jong-un emerged wearing his father's signature fur hat pulled over his head, handcrafted with earflaps, which protected Kim's face from the blowing snow as he waved to the crowd. Protected by plastic curtains on either side of the enclosure, he stood in his signature wool coat buttoned up around his sizable frame.

"Who is the man standing to Kim's right?" asked the president.

"It's hard to be sure because of the feed's grainy, poor quality, but that appears to be his new state security chief, Jong Won-sek," replied the deputy director of the CIA, who was in attendance.

"He's a relatively young man," remarked the president.

"Certainly not cut from the same mold of past military leaders for the regime," added the CIA attendee. "He is rumored to be a brutal proponent of the totalitarian regime's military policies. His greatest achievement, which probably earned him the top spot and the right to stand next to Dear Leader, was his success in expanding their Lightning Death Squad. This commando unit can rival many nations'."

As the camera panned the observation tent, Kim Jong-un flashed his signature grin. To Secretary Gregg, it somehow seemed different this time—much bigger and toothier. It reeked of arrogance. Secretary Gregg had seen the look before—after he'd cheated death himself.

Kim began his remarks, and the English interpreter was able to expertly relay the dictator's defiant tone.

"Where is his sister, I wonder?" asked the president. "She's almost always by his side. You'd think for an event like Mother's Day, she be in his presence rather than his newest thug."

Nobody in the room answered as the interpreter continued to translate Kim's opening remarks. Reality began to set in for Secretary Gregg. The assassination attempt had failed. Kim's sister had been implicated and was likely under house arrest, or imprisoned, or dead.

The team he'd sent in to kill America's biggest nemesis was unsuccessful, which made him feel less guilty about calling off the extraction team. The risk of entering North Korean waters was too great. The two-man team had no outward connections to the United States whatsoever. Hopefully, they weren't taken alive.

The translator continued, but Secretary Gregg had lost his focus. The repercussions of failure hadn't necessarily dawned on him. His eyes darted around the room, and they met the president's. She had been studying him.

He felt cold, clammy. He imagined that his face was pale, and the sweat wouldn't stop.

"Mr. Secretary, are you all right?" asked President Harman.

"Um, no, yes. Yes, of course I'm all right. I, um, didn't take time for breakfast. It must be a blood sugar thing."

The President of the United States leaned across the table and pushed a Krispy Kreme box in his direction.

"Perhaps you should have a donut. That might make you feel better."

No, it won't.

CHAPTER 55

November 16
Sinmi-do, North Korea

Duncan floated for an eternity. He didn't know if he was alive or dead. His body was cold, so he assumed he was dead. He knew this time would come, his dad had told him so.

Son, eventually every soldier runs out of bullets. Although his armor wears thin with time, it weighs heavier on his tired body. He simply must rest, remove his helmet, and lay down his head. It is then that his duties are over.

In Duncan's semiconscious state, he replayed the words over and over through his mind. As the cold overtook him, he found himself unable to remember his father's words exactly. He struggled to gain full consciousness, sometimes becoming angry as his memory failed him.

Floating, his body limp, he gave up control of his life. This was not his way of living, but he decided it was the way to die. Giving up control to God when it was his time to be taken to Heaven.

Duncan abandoned his mental struggle to remember his father's words of advice. He looked into his mother's eyes and visualized the sadness on her face when she learned of Dallas being killed in action.

He was home on that day when the dark green sedan pulled down the driveway. Duncan didn't have to wait for its arrival before he knew what it meant. The chaplain emerged from the car first, followed by the notifying officer, and then finally a medic, who stood respectfully to the side.

His mother came running out of the house, wailing in grief, which brought Duncan and his father racing out of the barn. The chaplain did his best to comfort Miss Lucy, but it wasn't until she joined him in prayer did her grief subside.

To you, oh Lord, I lift up my soul.

Duncan could only remember the first sentence. He tuned out the rest as he began to question what kind of God would take his little brother. He'd made the mistake in confiding to Cooper days later that he was questioning his faith. He couldn't have this conversation with his parents, as their emotions were still too raw.

The comfort he'd hoped to receive from Cooper didn't happen. Instead, Cooper blistered him with hurtful, stinging words—*what kind of big brother would send Dallas off to war? You knew better! You knew better!*

Duncan had lived with the guilt of Dallas's death ever since. He had seen battle and death. He'd seen men and women maimed by powerful weapons, later struggling to make a life for themselves. Sometimes they were shunned by friends and family, which made the wounded warriors feel a pain far greater than the loss of a limb.

He'd tried to reconcile with his brother, but Cooper couldn't find it in his heart to forgive, or forget. Now, karma was taking his life as he continued floating for an eternity.

To you, oh Lord, I lift up my soul!

Floating.

Then Duncan felt himself being lifted out of the water, the icy cold moisture falling from his body. He could hear the gentle voice of a woman, yet he couldn't discern what she was saying. A man provided words of support, but they made no sense.

Duncan relaxed his body and allowed it to be taken higher, ready to meet God.

CHAPTER 56

November 17
Home of Secretary of Defense Montgomery Gregg
Georgetown
Washington, DC

Secretary Gregg was not a drinker, but tonight might have to be the exception. There would be no celebratory cigars or pats on the back for a job well done. They'd failed, and the repercussions could be more than any of them imagined. He waited in the dimly lit room for Director Carl Braun and Billy Yancey to arrive.

"Gentlemen, sit," said Secretary Gregg with a gruff. He was in no mood for small talk on this evening. He was already irritated that Yancey was out of the country when all of this went down. It had been a long thirty-six hours waiting for this conversation to take place.

Yancey attempted to speak first. "Now, Monty, I understand you're upset, as am I and, of course, Carl. All of us are disappointed that we didn't take him out. But we all knew the possibility was there."

Secretary Gregg raised his hand, directing Yancey to stop. "I thought you had confidence in these men."

"We did. They're two of our best operatives. They'd performed admirably in the—"

"Failed this time, didn't they?"

"Hold on, Monty," interrupted Yancey. "We all knew of the possibilities."

Braun added, "Monty, what happens next is only conjecture. If the men were captured, then I'm sure Kim Jong-un will tell the world what the plot was. You know, that Western powers led by the evil United States were planning to assassinate Dear Leader. We've already started a disinformation campaign to point fingers at the South Koreans, or even within his own ranks."

Secretary Gregg shook his head. "Oh, sure, the fellow from Texas was there, too, remember? How do you explain him?"

"His cover had him traveling under German documents," replied Braun. "There are no ties to us whatsoever."

"Yeah? Is he gonna start *sprechen Deutsch* when they're ripping his fingernails off or, when that doesn't work, they begin to chop them off altogether."

"They're trained," interjected Yancey.

"Nobody can be trained to withstand that!" yelled Secretary Gregg. "This ain't Hollywood."

"Let them learn the truth," Yancey countered. "It'll just be treated as spin that every government will denounce. Besides, what's Kim gonna do about it? He's huffed and puffed for years and he's yet to blow our door down."

Secretary Gregg stood and walked to his desk. He picked up a letter opener and rolled it through his fingers. "Here is one such possibility. World war three. Nukes flying all over the place. Fried women and children from Los Angeles to right here where we sit. Here's the problem. The president thinks she's a diplomatic genius. She can already envision her chapter being written in common core history books for the rest of eternity."

"I don't think—" interrupted Braun before Secretary Gregg shut him down.

"I have zero leverage over her when it comes to a first-strike option. She thinks she's won. No doubt she's already planning a state dinner to host that fat kid. The whole idea was to dissolve the Kim dynasty or set us up to fight a war in Asia, not here on American soil."

Braun continued his attempts to placate Secretary Gregg. "Monty, we've all reviewed and analyzed Kim's words yesterday. Nothing would indicate that he has any intentions of attacking us. The only thing out of sorts was the fact his sister was absent from the festivities and his new goon stood by his side."

Secretary Gregg slammed the letter opener down, sticking it into his antique desk. For a moment, the vibration of the brass knife shook like a metronome.

"I saw it in his eyes, gentlemen! I know the look and the feeling. He thinks he's invincible. He's dodged the proverbial bullet."

Yancey stood and raised his hands to calm Secretary Gregg. "Monty, all is not lost. We can still make this work to our advantage. There are other ways to accomplish—"

Secretary Gregg placed both hands on his desk and growled at his accomplices.

"Let me explain something to you both. Kim Jong-un now thinks he's invincible. He's Teflon! His sister is probably dead, and the presence of his new state security chief was a very clear message to this old soldier. If we weren't at war before, we are now. Make no mistake, gentlemen. He'll make his move. We won't know from where or how, but we'll certainly know when!"

CHAPTER 57

November 21
Armstrong Ranch
Borden County, Texas

The aroma of hot apple pie found its way into Cooper's nostrils as he came bounding down the stairs. The family planned on having Thanksgiving dinner together before the rodeo kids pulled out for Calgary. As he hit the landing, he glanced through the front windows. The sun was up, revealing a blanket of frost that had formed on the ground overnight. He hoped an approaching weather system wouldn't slow their trip to Canada.

Palmer was walking her horses with one of the stable hands. Undoubtedly, she'd have their hooves cleaned and well fed before they were loaded into the trailer. Major offered up the use of his Ford F-450 pickup for the trip. It had greater towing capability than Cooper's truck, which was necessary to pull the larger horse trailer filled with hay and three quarter horses.

Cooper agreed to be Riley's hazer during the steer-wrestling competition. The cowboys were very territorial at Calgary when it came to sharing the local hazers. Riley acknowledged that he'd be at a slight disadvantage with the less-experienced Cooper as his hazer, but he said he'd rather lose with his brother than share money with strangers.

"Momma, I've got to have a taste of somethin'," said Cooper as he entered the kitchen. He reached his hand out to snap off a piece of the apple pie's crust. It never got closer than twelve inches before Miss Lucy smacked it with a wooden spoon.

"Hey, that hurt!"

"It should," she said with a laugh. "Consider it a warning shot. If you dig into anything else in my kitchen, the next one will be on the top of your head!"

"Jeez Louise, Momma. You're awful awnry this morning."

Cooper found his way to the coffee pot and poured the morning brew into an insulated travel mug. Lucy glanced over at his choice of mug.

"Do you want me to brew another pot and fill a thermos for the road?"

"Heck yeah! The caffeine will help me drive late into the night," he replied with a grin.

Lucy slipped the pie and the cooling rack out of the way and walked over to the sink. She began to rinse her hands off and then stopped. She dabbed her wet eyes with a towel.

"Momma, I'm sorry," said Cooper apologetically. He quickly moved to her side and put his arm around her shoulder. She sniffled again and wiped her eyes dry.

"No, honey, I know you're kiddin'. It's just, I don't know, this time I'm worryin' more than usual."

"Momma, is it my head? You talked to the doctor yourself on the phone. I'm good to go."

"No, Coop, it's not that. Well, it is partly, but I just worry about you three when you have to travel so far from home. It's a long way to Calgary. You're towin' that big trailer through the Rockies, with a storm comin'."

Cooper turned his mother toward him and smiled. "We've allowed ourselves plenty of time to get there. This storm is way out in the Pacific. It probably won't hit until Friday anyway. Worst case is we have to stay another day until it clears out. I promise we'll be safe."

Lucy nodded and sniffled again. She wiped her tears for the last time that morning and began to laugh at herself. "Coop, I don't know what's wrong with me. I've had a weird feeling for days."

"About our trip to Calgary?"

"No," she replied as she patted him on the chest. She went back to readying their dinner. "At first, I thought it might have been Duncan, but I'm not sure."

She opened the oven door and began to pull out the turkey. Cooper stepped in to help.

"Let me, Momma," he said as he donned the oven mitts. She readily stood to the side. "Have you heard from him? I kinda miss him."

Lucy looked at her son after he made this statement and smiled. "No, but that's not that unusual. When he gets an assignment, he goes *dark*, as he calls it, for weeks at a time."

"Is Daddy okay?"

Lucy smiled and nodded as she slid two trays of rolls into the oven. "Yes, fit as a fiddle. Your daddy gets anxious about what's going on in the world, and it's not paranoia."

"He does focus on the news a lot. It seems to me politicians are always at each other's throats, and evil countries are always tryin' to rattle our cages. It's been that way for as long as I can remember paying attention to the news. Nothing changes in Washington, and world war three hasn't started. I don't see any sense in gettin' worked up about it."

Lucy touched Cooper's cheek and took the oven mitts off his hands. "I've noticed the happier your father is with his life, especially since retirement, the more concerned he's become about catastrophic events that are beyond our control. The way he's explained it to me is *he'll be danged if some solar flare or nuclear war or plague is gonna bring harm upon this family.*"

Cooper laughed. "He's said the same thing to me in not so many words. I appreciate that, you know. I've always felt like the Armstrong Ranch could take care of its own, no matter what's hurled in our direction. It's kinda the Texas way, you know."

Lucy began removing the fine silver and cloth napkins from a hutch at the end of the spacious kitchen. She retrieved the carving utensils from a drawer and set them on the kitchen island.

"We don't admit this to others, but we do agree somewhat with Governor Burnett on these things. For decades, the politicians in

Austin have adopted a Texas-first policy. They believe in what's best for Texans. I agree. Let other states take care of their people; we'll take care of ours."

"It's worked so far," said Cooper.

"What's worked so far?" asked Major as he entered the kitchen with another pie in his hands.

"Nothin', dear," said Lucy as she greeted him with a peck on the cheek. "What do we have here?"

"Preacher baked the kids one of his signature chocolate pecan pies for the road," replied Major. Then he laughed as he presented it to Cooper. "He didn't want them to go hungry."

Cooper laughed and then asked, "Speakin' of which, Daddy, you reckon we could get a little food and gas money for the road. You know, there's a storm comin' and you don't want us to eat the horses if there's a problem, right?"

"Cooper Armstrong!" protested Lucy as she went looking for her wooden spoon. Cooper ran around the back side of the kitchen island for protection, where he earned a playful slap to the back of his head from his father.

"Son, I oughta hold you down while your momma gives you a proper whoopin'."

"I was just kiddin'," said Cooper with a sense of relief as his dad loosened his grip. "But y'all know how Riley eats. He'll blow our budget with us on the road for nearly a week."

A still half-asleep Riley entered the fray and wandered toward the coffee maker. "Don't talk about me, Coop. You eat plenty yourself, and then you get gas, which practically runs me and Palmer out of the truck.

"Don't you kids stink up my truck," Major demanded. "And don't track a bunch of manure into it either."

Palmer could be heard kicking the frost and dirt off her boots as she entered the family room. "Whoa, this house smells better than Cracker Barrel!" she exclaimed from the other room.

"Don't you insult my cookin', young lady," said Lucy. "Come in here and help your brothers set the dining table. It's time to eat."

"It's not even eight o'clock," said Riley, who was gradually coming to life after his first cup of coffee.

"It was my idea," said Cooper. "I wanna get us on the road so we can be in Montana by Wednesday. Thanksgiving traffic will be the worst on Wednesday, except near the border where nobody would be goin' anywhere 'cause it's too far to get there."

"Doesn't matter to me. I'm starvin'," said Riley.

*****

The Armstrong family had gathered at the table and held hands as Major said the blessing.

"Our Father in Heaven, we thank you for your blessings, for our family, and our friends here at Armstrong Ranch. We ask that you watch over and protect Duncan as he does his duty in a faraway land. May you please protect him and deliver him home to his family safely.

"We ask that you consider wrapping your angel's wings around Dallas as he serves you in Heaven, God rest his soul.

"We give thanks for the bountiful food you've provided us on this Thanksgiving, and the loving hands that have prepared it.

"We give thanks for our lives, our freedoms, and our country in these times of turmoil. Today, as we partake of this food, we pray for health and strength to carry on our lives as You would have us.

"This we ask in the name of Christ and our Heavenly Father. Amen."

"Amen."

After a brief moment of silence, the table erupted in praise for Miss Lucy's cooking. She'd prepared all of the Armstrong family favorites—turkey and stuffing, mashed potatoes, sweet potatoes, cornbread dressing, gravy, green beans, sliced cranberry, and apple pie.

Plates were loaded, serving utensils made contact with serving bowls, requests to pass dishes were exchanged, and the chatter of the Armstrong family filled the dining room. It was a scene that would be repeated in millions of households on Thanksgiving Day as people celebrated a uniquely American holiday.

For some, it was the start of the holiday season culminating with the celebration of a New Year. It was a time to reflect on years past and to make plans for the future. Emotions ran high. Memories, both good and bad, were recalled. But in the Armstrong family, it was about giving thanks for the blessings God had bestowed upon them.

Without saying it, this Thanksgiving moment was about strengthening their resolve to support one another as a family. To focus on protecting the ones they love. To mend and heal old wounds. And to be ready for the dark clouds that might come their way.

Families were like the branches of a mighty oak tree. They might grow in different directions. They might bend, but they didn't break. No matter what, the Armstrong family, like the roots of that oak tree, remained as one.

CHAPTER 58

Thanksgiving Day
Armstrong Ranch
Borden County, Texas

Lucy disconnected the call and settled back under the blanket with her husband. The fire was warming the room, and they had a rare day of doing nothing together. The ranch hands were given the day off to spend with their families. Palmer had called to let them know they'd arrived safely after staying an extra night on the road in Great Falls, Montana. Major pledged to avoid finding unnecessary menial tasks to do around the ranch.

The Macy's Day parade had just ended, and Major flipped the channel on their DirecTV system to Fox News. Despite the Thanksgiving holiday, the news never stops.

Fox had talking heads debating whether the United States should attack North Korea with a preemptive strike. A member of the British Parliament argued against the action, stating U.S. allies would frown upon the escalation of hostilities without exhausting all diplomatic options. He also said European allies might not necessarily get involved on the United States' behalf if Washington initiated a first strike.

On the other side of the political spectrum, a former Marine colonel argued a fully nuclear-capable North Korea was a threat to everyone, including London. He urged the president to act now, and decisively, before North Korea caught us off guard. He felt the U.S. military was strong enough to go it alone if necessary.

"They have this same debate every day," said Lucy.

"It's a no-win situation for us," added Major. "I can't fault the president. She's had this dumped in her lap, just like all the other presidents before her. I suspect she'll try to find a way to maintain the status quo and pass Kim Jong-un along to the next occupant of the White House."

Lucy pointed at the television. "How about that British guy? He said they may not help us if we go to war with North Korea. You don't pick and choose when you stand by your friends, in my opinion. We'd help them if the roles were reversed."

Major sighed as he turned the volume down. "It raises an interesting point, which has been a part of our political conversation for years. We began to adopt a nationalistic approach to things, which I'm all for. As a Texan, I really don't know any other way. But would we turn our backs on a friend in need if they asked for help?"

"Who do you mean by we?" asked Lucy. "Are you referring to the United States, Texas, or the Armstrong Ranch?"

"Well," said Major with a pause, "I guess you could apply the concept to all three. If France attacked Russia and asked for our help, should the president send in our troops, putting them at risk?"

"I don't like the French, so I say no," replied Lucy defiantly.

"Okay, Miss Lucy, bad example. What about the British?"

Lucy again pointed to the television. "Not after what that fellow just said."

Major's chin dropped to his chest and he chuckled. "Miss Lucy, you're messin' with me, right?"

She laughed and snuggled closer to him under the blanket. "Yes, in a way, I guess I am. I see your point. We've pledged to stand by our allies in Europe, as well as Israel, Japan, and South Korea. If we've got their backs, then they should have ours."

"Fair enough," replied Major as he mindlessly played in her long hair. "Now, if it was a country we don't deal with very much, like Romania, and they attacked Russia, whadya think?"

"Not our problem. You're on your own."

Major sat up higher on the couch. He was enjoying this back-and-forth. "Let's think about Texas for a minute. You know how Marion feels about the whole *Texas strong, Texas free* thing, right?"

"Yes, and I agree with her."

"Okay, what if New Mexico didn't stockpile salt to melt the snow on its roads in the mountains. Should Texas share its salt if it meant a lot of Texas roads couldn't get cleared?"

"No," replied Lucy. "They should have planned ahead. You know, like the ant and the grasshopper. The ant spent his time during the summer gathering food for winter when there wouldn't be any. The grasshopper bounced around and played music with his legs all day. When winter arrived and the grasshopper came to the ant begging for food, the ant just shrugged his shoulders in disgust and sent him away."

"So the moral of the story is there's a time for work and a time for play, but no matter what, you have to plan for another day."

Lucy laughed. "Quite poetic, Mr. Armstrong. I'm impressed."

"Thank you." He grinned as he reached for his eggnog from the coffee table. "All right, last question, then we'll talk about what we're gonna do today."

"Fire away."

Major took a deep breath because the conversation they were about to have had weighed on his mind for a while. "Let's suppose a catastrophe were to hit us, directly impacting the Armstrong Ranch and the surrounding areas."

"Or Texas or the whole country for that matter," interjected Lucy, who was also enjoying the talk.

"Okay, a major collapse event—economic collapse, cyber attack, pandemic, EMP. We've considered and studied them all."

"Any of the above, and the citizens of this country fall apart in a matter of days, if not hours," added Lucy.

"Right. We've prepared as best we can to protect our kids and our employees on the ranch. But what happens when a neighbor and his wife, totin' three young 'uns, say they're hungry and need food. What do we do?"

Lucy pondered for a moment and then replied, "I guess the Bible tells us to share. Blessed is the one who is kind to the needy."

"Okay, what if the food they ask for is what we might need to keep our kids alive for another day? Do we give away what we've stored, or do we make sure we take care of our kids first?"

Lucy came out from under the blanket and lifted her legs onto the couch to sit cross-legged facing Major. "The Book of Timothy says anyone who does not provide for his own household has denied his faith and is worse than the unbeliever."

"Exactly," said Major. "I believe God would have us take care of our own first before we give away to others who haven't planned ahead. It's the same as the ant and the grasshopper."

"Major, how in the world do you turn away those begging eyes and hungry stomachs?"

"Lucy, you just have to. My duty is to you and the kids first, followed by Preacher and the ranch hands. Others should have planned ahead like we did."

Lucy and Major sat quietly for several minutes as his words sank in. The news began to show scenes from the first NFL football game of the day in Philadelphia. The stands remained half-filled five years after the kneeling protests had begun.

Lucy broke the silence. "I've never thought about it like this before, but you're right. As selfish as it may seem, we have to take care of our own. We've done it for years and we've sacrificed in order to protect our kids in the event of a collapse of some kind."

Major added, "You know what? I'm good with that."

"Me too," said Lucy. She picked up the remote and pushed the guide button. "The Cowboys are playing the Eagles. Do you wanna watch some football? That would be different."

"Nah, not really. I've had a problem with this NFL protest thing for years. They should have nipped it in the bud to begin with, but they were afraid they might offend somebody. Well, look at those stands. I hope the owners and that commissioner are happy with their decision."

Lucy turned off the television, but Major added one more comment.

"Besides, I've always believed a man wearing a helmet while

defending his country should make more money than a man who wears a helmet while defending a football."

CHAPTER 59

November 25
Black Friday
The Calgary Stampede
Calgary, Alberta, Canada

The Calgary Stampede was an annual event held in a Canadian city located in the province of Alberta. Just north of Montana and to the east of the coastal province of British Columbia, Alberta was known for both its mountainous terrain in the north and the desert badlands to the east.

Billed as *The Greatest Outdoor Show on Earth*, the Calgary Stampede's ten-day event attracted hundreds of thousands of visitors to the midway carnival-style rides, live country music performances and, of course, the rodeo events, including bull riding, steer wrestling, and barrel racing.

Once held in July, the rodeo was moved to coincide with America's Thanksgiving week to gain more television coverage on U.S. networks and to be the final rodeo event of the season for qualifiers to earn the right to participate at the Pro Rodeo World Finals in Las Vegas in December.

Neither Palmer nor Riley had a chance to qualify for Vegas, but the experience gained at the Calgary Stampede was invaluable. This was, however, critical to Cooper's chances to move on to the big show in two weeks. He had to have a successful eight-second ride, even if he wasn't top in points awarded by the judges, to qualify for the PBR World Finals.

Palmer went into the lobby of the Deerfoot Inn & Casino to

check into their rooms. One of the aggravations associated with participating in the Calgary Stampede was a lack of hotel rooms in the vicinity of Stampede Park. The Deerfoot Inn was located on the south side of the city and had become a favorite of the rodeo participants, especially at the discounted rate of a hundred dollars per night.

Riley and Cooper rolled back the tarp covering the pickup bed of Major's truck to retrieve their luggage. They set the bags on the pavement next to a similar rig to theirs. The rear parking lot of the Deerfoot Inn resembled overnight parking at an interstate truck stop. Instead of tractor trailer rigs lined up side by side with sleeping drivers inside, the hotel's parking lot was lined with dual-axle pickups, called *duallies*, and horse trailers.

"Should we even unpack the sponsor gear?" asked Riley. "We'll just have to load it up again in the morning for the meet-and-greet booths."

"No, I agree," replied Cooper. "If we were in the States, we'd at least take in the Remington rifles. But these Canadians are practically communists with their zero-tolerance policy. I mean, how many times did that Canadian Mountie ask us if we had any weapons in our possession."

"Yeah, I call that profiling, don't you? Just 'cause we're dressed like cowboys and are pulling a horse trailer doesn't mean we're totin' six-shooters and old-school lever rifles."

Cooper pointed toward a duffle bag. "Can you reach that?"

Riley stretched and grabbed the handles. "Got it."

The guys began to close up the back of the pickup, and the conversation continued. Cooper recalled an event that took place in the province of Alberta several years back.

"They all overreacted to that shooting in Edmonton years ago. They started outlawing all kinds of guns except what was considered a hunting weapon, like what we push for Remington. Maybe they should have focused on the Somalia dude who shot up that football stadium. He was the guy pullin' the trigger."

"Folks don't look at it that way," added Riley. "Say, do you think they'll let us each keep a rifle tomorrow? I want one of those new R-25s. In camo. Whadya think?"

"Not gonna happen, brother. Canadians see those as assault weapons. They've got a new pump-action in .308. It's the model seventy-eight-hundred, I think. Get one of those. Our rep has always been generous."

"Do we need a permit?" asked Riley.

"Nope, not for hunting weapons. Only handguns."

The guys tied down the tarp and loaded up their gear and started toward the hotel's entrance. Palmer came jogging toward them, her ponytail swishing back and forth from under her Realtree cap.

"Y'all will never guess who I saw in the lobby," she said, slightly out of breath.

"Who?" asked Riley.

"Those two jerks from the bar in Fort Worth," she replied. "They were sitting at the lobby bar, drinkin' and checkin' out girls. You know, what they think they do best."

"Did they recognize you?" asked Cooper.

"No. You know how it is. When you see someone in a different setting, it doesn't register that you know them. Now, if Riley were to go in there and pounce on the one guy, I'm pretty sure it will all come back to them."

Riley started laughing, handed Palmer her duffle bag, and began walking briskly toward the entrance of the hotel.

"Hold up! Nobody's gonna pounce on anybody," Cooper shouted to his brother. Riley frowned but slowed his pace. Cooper turned to his sister. "Did you get us rooms on the side of the hotel overlooking the parking lot?"

"Yeah," she replied, showing two electronic room cards for the second floor.

"Good," said Cooper as he directed them toward the casino entrance. "Come on, Riley, we'll hit the casino elevators to our room. You don't need to be startin' up with those guys. This weekend is strictly business."

"Can we play a little before we go up?" asked Riley.

Cooper shook his head and laughed. He grabbed his brother and pinched the back of his neck, leading him toward the door.

"You want to drive me nuts, don't you?"

"It's my job and duty as a little brother."

"Great."

CHAPTER 60

November 25
Black Friday
The Calgary Stampede
Calgary, Alberta, Canada

Cooper, Riley, and Palmer made the rounds to their sponsors' booths before they arrived at the final stop of the fan meet-and-greets at the Pro Rodeo Magazine interview stage. At Cabela's they met the muckety-mucks from Bass Pro Shops, which had acquired the outdoor retailer years before. They were very impressed with the Armstrong trio and promised to include them in future rodeo promotions.

At the Realtree booth, they signed autographs and stood for numerous pictures with fans. Palmer ribbed both guys afterwards for the attention they received from the buckle bunnies, a term bestowed upon cute, single girls who try to attract the attention of the rodeo competitors.

Finally, all three enjoyed their time at the Remington booth especially when they were rewarded with their rifle of choice. Naturally, they'd have to participate in additional meet-and-greet events over the weekend, in which they'd be required to pose with their gun of choice, but it was worth the effort for the media exposure and three brand-new rifles.

Along the way, they caught up with their friends from the bar brawl, Adriano Morales and Eduardo Pacheco. They had just been interviewed by *Pro Rodeo* magazine and now it was Cooper's turn. Morales and Pacheco waited with Riley and Palmer while Cooper took a few questions.

He climbed on stage and got settled on a bar stool in front of a microphone to address a gathering crowd. After the chants of *Coop, Coop, Coop* died down, the journalist and Cooper made some small talk and then got into the meat of the interview.

"Coop, you seem to be fully recovered from your injury a month ago. How are you feelin'?"

"I gotta tell y'all, that bull kicks hard!" replied Cooper with a laugh and to the delight of his fans. "My brother tells me there ain't nothin' to a kick between my ears, but you know, he's one to talk." Everyone laughed as Cooper pointed toward Riley, who was getting a razzing from Palmer.

"I take it, obviously, that you're gonna be good to go this evening."

"You betcha," said Cooper to the delight of the crowd.

Cooper noticed a couple of cute girls inching their way close to the stage. One in particular caught his eye. She was different from the others. This girl was less buckle bunny and more girl-next-door. He'd make a point to find her after the interview.

"Coop, you've really made a name for yourself, and with a good ride tonight, you'll qualify for the PBR finals in Vegas. Is this a dream come true for you?"

Cooper laughed and winked at the cute girl, who'd pushed her way near Palmer and the boys. "After all these years competing, I still haven't figured out why any bull rider, including myself, gets on a bull. You never really figure it out. We aren't insane, I don't reckon. We just kinda grew up with that desire to conquer that massive animal for eight seconds."

"So you're born with it?"

"I guess you could say that. It's in your blood, almost like the worst drug in the world. Very addictive."

The journalist nodded, checked his notes, and continued. "I've asked several of your fellow competitors this question, and most have answered the question the same way. But I'd like your take on it. Which sport is the most dangerous?"

"Heck, it's not even close. A one-hundred-eighty-pound guy

against an eighteen-hundred-pound bull. You do the math."

"Coop, do you think money drives bull riding?"

"No, sir. Absolutely not. It's like I said before. It's in your blood. There ain't enough money in it."

Cooper paused for a moment, and then he looked down at Pacheco and Morales. He gestured in their direction. "These fellows know what I'm talkin' about. It's that feeling of being unbreakable. You wanna be one of the toughest cowboys in the world against the toughest bulls. That's why we're all here."

"All right, Coop. Final question. You just mentioned riding the toughest bulls. Last go around, you drew One Night Stand. He's in Calgary, too. In fact, I understand he's been asking about you."

Cooper and the rest of the crowd began to laugh. "Yeah, I'm sure he has been. Well, let him know I'm gonna pull his name out of the hat on purpose. Tonight, it's gonna be lights out on this *One Night Stand.*"

CHAPTER 61

November 25
Black Friday
The Calgary Stampede
Calgary, Alberta, Canada

Cooper couldn't have written the script any better. He shook his brother's hand and high-fived Palmer. He glanced into the stands over Riley's shoulder and winked again to his new friend, whose name and cell phone number was written on the back of a Canadian five-dollar bill, then tucked into his jeans pocket.

He nodded at the cowboys, and they readied his nemesis—One Night Stand. As Cooper approached the rails to climb over, the massive bull turned his head in Cooper's direction. His nostrils flared, and then he let out a snort. Cooper stared his ride back in the eyes, unafraid and almost challenging the massive beast.

Bulls, like cows, were not known to have any type of intellect. They were animals that reacted on instinct, which was why a bull stops attempting to buck the rider once he's been thrown. Or at least most of the time, as Cooper and One Night Stand both knew from personal experience.

One Night Stand snorted again, nodded upward, and then faced forward. The high-spirited animal was ready, and so was Cooper. He adjusted his hat, gave one final nod to the cowboys manning the gate, and climbed over the rails.

"I know you now," whispered Coop as he threw his leg over One Night Stand and grabbed the rope. He worked to get his hand set, nice and snug. The routine was one he'd followed hundreds of times before.

For his part, One Night Stand followed his routine as well. Just like their last ride together, the bull slowly dropped down to his belly. Cooper tensed his body and got ready. One Night Stand began to rise from the dirt, his muscles contracting, coiling up with power.

"Here we go, boys! Here we go!" Cooper shouted as the fans roared their approval.

One Night Stand barely waited for the gate to open, crashing forward and jumping into the air. Cooper had replayed the previous failed ride through his head a million times. *Not this time, buddy.*

The bull twisted his body in midair before landing on his front legs. Cooper pushed against his rope this time, avoiding the costly mistake of moving too far forward on the bull's neck.

Like before, One Night Stand turned to the left, and Cooper handled the twist. He never lost his balance as One Night Stand gave it all he had.

I know you!

The bull was furious—just as angry at himself as he was at the cowboy who dared tame him.

Jumping, spinning, twisting, and bucking, One Night Stand was on a tear, but Cooper remained undeterred. This was his turn to be in the limelight as the first bull rider to master this two-thousand-pound beast for eight seconds.

The fans in the arena were screaming his name. The cheers were overwhelming. One Night Stand was mad as the devil. Then the buzzer sounded.

Eight seconds! I did it!

And then the lights went out.

THANK YOU FOR READING AXIS OF EVIL!

If you enjoyed it, I'd be grateful if you'd take a moment to write a short review (just a few words are needed) and post it on Amazon. Amazon uses complicated algorithms to determine what books are recommended to readers. Sales are, of course, a factor, but so are the quantities of reviews my books get. By taking a few seconds to leave a review, you help me out, and also help new readers learn about my work.

And before you go…

SIGN UP to Bobby Akart's mailing list to receive special offers, bonus content, and you'll be the first to receive news about new releases in The Lone Star Series, The Pandemic series, The Blackout series, The Boston Brahmin series and The Prepping for Tomorrow series—which includes sixteen Amazon #1 Bestsellers in thirty-nine fiction and non-fiction genres. Visit Bobby Akart's website for informative blog entries on preparedness, writing, and his latest contribution to the American Preppers Network.

www.BobbyAkart.com

Made in the USA
Lexington, KY
02 February 2019